On The Run

Shane Beaver

Published in 2014 by FeedARead.com Publishing

Copyright © The author as named on the book cover.

First Edition

The author has asserted their moral right under the
Copyright, Designs and Patents Act, 1988, to be identified
as the author of this work.

All Rights reserved. No part of this publication may be reproduced, copied, stored in a retrieval system, or transmitted, in any form or by any means, without the prior written consent of the copyright holder, nor be otherwise circulated in any form of binding or cover other than that in which it is published and without a similar condition being imposed on the subsequent purchaser.

A CIP catalogue record for this title is available from the British Library.

Chapter 1

Tuesday, 24 October, 2017 (a.m.)

She woke with a start as the back door was slammed shut. Slowly and awkwardly rolling over onto her side, she blinked a couple of times until she was just able to make out the time with the clock on the bedside table. Ten minutes past seven on the button. But then it was the same most mornings this time of the year. A new day was dawning and so he was off on his morning run. He tried not to wake her when he got up, so why the hell did he always have to slam that bloody back door when he left? And yet that wasn't the only thing that rankled with Linda Rigione about her husband of five years.

She rolled onto her back once more and for several minutes she lay there ruminating over what she suspected was his latest little peccadillo. What is it about men and their inability to keep their bloody hands to themselves, she asked herself? It hadn't always been like this, of course. They had shared some memorable times together during the ten years that they had known each other, and he had introduced her to a life of luxury and prosperity that she could have only dreamed about as a child.

Born just outside Chesterfield in 1971, Linda was the youngest of five daughters of a local steelworker. She was seven years old when the family moved to Leverton, and her father found employment at the nearby Welham steelworks. After attending a local girl's secondary school, she found employment as a seamstress at one of the town's hosiery firms. Marriage to Bob Woolley at the age of twenty-four failed to produce any offspring, and it ended in divorce in 2005. Two years later she met local businessman, Luciano Rigione, and within twelve months he had left his wife to move in with her. What satisfied her most about this was that *she* had done all the pursuing. But then she was an extraordinarily attractive woman – and she knew it!

At five feet and eight inches tall she wasn't quite what one would describe as statuesque, but she was undeniably slim and leggy for her height, and this was largely down to regular workouts at the gym. She had long blonde hair (parted down the middle) and small boobs, but what really caught everyone's attention were the high cheekbones and thin, piercing blue eyes. Add to that the small nose, thick lips and toothy smile, and it was no wonder that she was often likened to supermodel Kate Moss.

Of course it helped that she had such an enthusiastic appetite for life too, and there was no doubt in her mind that Luciano picked up on that. What's more, she had developed her persona and charm on the premise that men are always looking for a variety of experiences, and she undoubtedly presented those experiences to him. But *her* charm lay in a sensually pleasing visual experience, which she had created through elaborate attire and an air of seduction all around her. She literally oozed sex appeal, and that was all down to her truly dazzling appearance. She had an almost dangerous quality about her, and Luciano was hooked from the outset.

To begin with they found a nice house on the outskirts of Leverton, not far from the Fullerton Industrial Estate, which was the location of Luciano's business, Azzurri Furnishings. It was the biggest and most successful upholstery firm in the area, and in 2009 Luciano offered to make her his secretary. Linda had always found her reward in helping others, with a tendency for being unable to say no, and so true to form she accepted his offer without a second thought. It never even entered her head that one day she would come to regret making that decision. Nevertheless, his divorce came through in 2011, and a year later they were married at the Register Office in Leverton. The reception was held at the Armisfield Golf Club, and what a grand affair that was!

However, it soon became apparent to Linda that Luciano had a tendency towards infidelity in their marriage. There was even that time when he tried it on with that woman at work, right in front of her eyes, but she had given him the brush-off; much to his surprise and chagrin. But she was far from being the only one.

Linda had hoped that the move to their present abode at the village of Tapley in 2016 might herald a new chapter in their marriage. It was a large, detached property complete with swimming pool, and everything in the garden seemed rosy at first. There were the parties and the barbecues, and how Linda thrived on entertaining. Motivated by the desire to intrigue and seduce, she simply loved being the centre of attention, and curiously Luciano seemed to get a kick out it too. Indeed, there was every reason to believe that he had at long last curbed his enthusiasm for unfaithfulness.

She should have known better, of course. At one of their parties he was all over one of the female guests like a rash. Then there was a brief fling with the village hairdresser; and now she was pretty damn sure that he was seeing someone else, but who could that be? 'Well, anything you can do,' she had told herself.

At that moment she decided it was time to get up. Rising slowly from the bed, she still felt somewhat groggy, but she made her way over to the window without incident and opened the curtains. It was overcast outside and there was the likelihood of rain at any moment. She stood for several seconds looking across the fields at the rear of the house. It was a view that usually lifted her spirits, but not today. She turned away ruefully and began to prepare herself for work, and in the knowledge that her husband would soon be back from his morning run.

As Luciano Rigione set off on his run up Tapley Lane to the main road, the curtain's twitched in the house across the road. *Trespass Cottage* it was called; although it was nothing like a cottage. Built in 1982, it was a fairly modern detached dwelling, but the word "cottage" was appended by the occupants, who felt that it was more in keeping with their rural surroundings. It might also be said that it gave them an overwhelming sense of self-importance too.

The idea behind *Trespass Cottage* came from the lady of the house, Sharon Bacon, who came to Tapley with her husband, Nigel, in 2014. They had first met whilst working for Derby City Council, and although Nigel later moved to the Derby Jobcentre, it transpired that they shared an interest in environmental and animal welfare issues.

Cause-driven, Sharon had always set out to prove her worth through what she believed were courageous acts, and she delighted in telling Nigel – and anyone who was interested – that she had once thrown eggs at the Environment Secretary when he came to the Peak District some years previously. Needless to say, she soon persuaded Nigel to join her on a protest rally in London, and the relationship took off from there.

Neither of them had been married before, so it came as a huge surprise when they finally got hitched in 2001 when both were in their late forties. The couple initially lived in the city of Derby, but Nigel retired in 2013, and when Sharon did likewise a year later they took it upon themselves to look for a change of surroundings, and moved to Tapley along with their English springer spaniel, "Tony". There were no children of course, but then sex had never been at the top of Sharon's list of priorities. Indeed, she would be the first to acknowledge that she wasn't exactly a catch when it came to love and romance.

Skinny and flat-chested, Sharon was just over five feet and six inches tall, with grey, collar-length curly hair that appeared to be scrunched and had once been dark brown. Her brown eyes were hidden behind a pair of spectacles, which she had been forced to wear since childhood. That and the fact that her face was covered in freckles were never going to endear her to the opposite sex as far as she was concerned, but Nigel evidently saw something that deterred others. She seldom wore any make-up, and she was always attired in long skirts and dresses, both at home or at work. The only time that she wore trousers of any kind was when she and Nigel were out rambling or hiking.

Nigel, on the other hand, was slightly taller than Sharon by two or three inches, and he had short, grey receding hair that had once been light brown. He wore spectacles too, and when removed they revealed what can only be described as brown, melancholy eyes. Slightly built for his height, he was always formally attired, with a penchant for wearing a tie at all times, not only at work, but around the house, when shopping or even when rambling with Sharon. In many respects he was the archetypal bureaucrat – and he behaved like one too. One could say that the couple were made for each other, but although appearances can be deceptive, there can be no doubt who wore the trousers in the Bacon household!

In addition to their passion for environmental causes, both Sharon and Nigel were members of The Green Party and PETA, or People for the Ethical Treatment of Animals. Posters and flyers from both organisations were strewn around the house, and in particular they adorned the walls of their kitchen and living room, along with numerous photographs. They were also vegetarians, but the one thing that gave them enormous satisfaction was rambling. Indeed, the removal van had barely been gone a couple of hours before Sharon was referring to their new residence as *Trespass Cottage*, in honour of the mass trespass of Kinder Scout on 24 April 1932, and Nigel was duly despatched to have the plaque engraved that very same day.

Two years later the Rigione's moved into the house opposite, and that's when the trouble started. At least it was in Sharon's mind. For one thing their new neighbours never even bothered to come across and introduce themselves, but from the outset there were those damned parties, most of which went on into the early hours of the morning. She dreaded to think of the goings-on at the house opposite, but it was the interminable noise that irked Sharon most of all. Time and again she had nagged at Nigel to go across the road and complain, but if a thing needs doing…!

Pouring two cups of herbal tea, she was about to remonstrate with Nigel once more when he suddenly broke into conversation.

'There he goes,' he muttered over his shoulder. 'Bang on time as usual.'

'Well, we wouldn't be where we are now if you had acted sooner as I told you to,' she retorted sharply.

He turned to face her with a perplexed look on his face. 'What have I done now?' he replied.

'That's just it – you never do anything!'

'We're back on that again, are we?'

'Well…' she replied angrily, but without adding to her statement.

'Don't tell me? "If a thing needs doing…"'

'My point exactly!' she snapped.

'And look where that got you,' he said with some vehemence. 'You saw for yourself what the man is like.'

'Yes, and he's going to pay for what he's done.'

Nigel knew that there was absolutely no point in trying to stop her once she had got the bit between her teeth, and he realised that something was afoot. He narrowed his eyes.

'You've got something planned, haven't you?' he asked quizzically.

Sharon made no attempt to reply to his question, but she merely looked straight past him. After all, if a thing needs doing…!

Chapter 2

Tuesday, 24 October 2017 (a.m.)

It was 7.15 a.m. and the Croxley Moor Estate was slowly coming to life, as residents – to some extent – prepared themselves for work and mothers undertook the frequently arduous chore of getting their children up and ready for school.

Built in the late 1970's and on land that had once belonged to the National Coal Board, the estate lay on the northern outskirts of Leverton, as one headed out of the town on the left-hand side of the busy main road to Grimley. On the other side of the road was the older and predominantly working-class Gartland area of Leverton, with its myriad of two-up and two-down terraced houses, dating back to the late nineteenth century, although many had been re-developed in recent years. A former coal mining community, Gartland is still looked upon as the rough area of the town.

In stark contrast, the Croxley Moor Estate is a substantial modern residential development, with views of the surrounding countryside to the rear, including Croxley Lake and the surrounding woods. The Croxley Country Park can be seen in the distance and the Leverton Golf Course lies to the southwest. There are a number of paths and tracks through the woods and fields behind the estate, the most prominent of which is the traffic-free Peacock Pathway, used by cyclists and pedestrians alike.

To the north of the estate is the relatively modern, state-of-the-art Leverton General Hospital, and beyond that one can still see the headstocks of the former Croxley Colliery, which have been preserved as a testament to what was undeniably the major source of employment and industry in the region. To the south and heading towards the town centre stands the Leverton Police Station; this is set back off the road, and is also a recent development.

The main thoroughfare on the estate is Woodcock Drive, which can be accessed from the main road at two points roughly a quarter of a mile from each other. At the westernmost end of Woodcock Drive, some of the houses back onto the Peacock Pathway, and one such house is number seventy-eight, where the occupants were still abed.

Wendy Price had been awake for some considerable time – most of the night actually. A down-to-earth realist with a lack of pretence, she would be the first to admit that she had a natural resilience, but recently she had become a very troubled woman, and the reason for her present anxiety was the man lying beside her. She had been committed to her relationship with Brendan Molloy from the moment they had met five years previously, but now she was beginning to wonder if this was going to go the same way as her previous relationships with the opposite sex.

She came into the world in 1972, as Wendy Jarvis. Her father was a local binman. Leverton through and through, she was no different to most other local girls of her generation and background, in that she failed to achieve much at school. Indeed, she had very little time or trust for those in authority from a very early age, but if there was one thing that motivated her throughout her formative years then it was the desire to be the centre of attention.

She certainly wasn't an unattractive girl – far from it; but she was undeniably charismatic, friendly and seductive, and at her happiest when in a group and connecting with others; which probably explains why she became leader of a small clique of girls at her secondary school. She did have one or two of boyfriends from time to time and there were unfounded rumours that she had been forced to have an abortion, but it was all hearsay and nobody dared to broach the subject in her presence.

However, having found employment at one of the local supermarkets after leaving school, it came as little surprise to anyone when she did fall pregnant for the first time at the age of seventeen. It all came about after a night of revelry on the town with a group of other under-age girls one weekend, and it is doubtful if she could remember much about that evening or the name of the young man who impregnated her. Whilst her father initially looked upon the whole affair with some disdain, her mother was more supportive from the outset, and when Wendy subsequently gave birth to a boy it seemed to bring everyone in the Jarvis household together.

The boy took her surname and she doted on him. Meeting Nick Price three years later did nothing to change that, and when the happy couple tied the knot in 1993, Nick took it upon himself to adopt the boy and give him *his* name. Another boy came along a year after the marriage, followed by a girl three years later, but by 2001 Wendy and Nick had gone their separate ways, and they were eventually divorced in 2008.

It was only when the youngest child started attending secondary school that Wendy found part-time employment in one of the town's flower shops, and she enjoyed the work so much that she began attending a night school course at a local college studying floristry. Driven by the desire to be her own boss, she passed the course with distinction, eventually setting up her own floristry business in 2014.

Two years earlier she had met Brendan Molloy, and at a time when he was obviously down on his luck. Nevertheless, he provided the intimacy that she craved, and within months they and her three children had moved into a small terraced house near Leverton town centre. A year later his fortune's seemed to take a turn for the better when he got the job at Azzurri Furnishing's, working for his old mate from school, Luciano Rigione, and in 2015 they moved into their present abode.

All seemed well at first, but when the children left home his demeanour changed, especially towards her. She would be the first to admit that she had a habit of turning to the wrong people for answers, but he had always been forthcoming whenever she had sought his advice, and yet for some reason he now seemed so cold and cruel. It was the same when he started to come home late from work – and the gym. She would ask where he had been, but his response was to treat her with what she could only describe as downright contempt.

And then of course there was the sex – or the lack of it. From the very beginning he had always had an enormous sex drive, but now it was practically non-existent! Again, whenever her desire for sex was strong, he merely made the excuse that he was too tired or unwell. There was only one answer to this sudden change of behaviour; there had to be another woman.

The thought of being rejected and unloved was unbearable for Wendy, but she couldn't bring herself to confront him, and so she hit upon the idea of making herself look more attractive, in an attempt to win back his affections and lure him away from his quest.

A trip to the hairdresser's was called for, and her long, wavy, slightly greying hair was replaced by a dark brown, chin-length and somewhat bouffant style that met with her immediate approval. This went well with her dark brown eyes, but at the same time she took to wearing more make-up around them, with the addition of false eye-lashes. She had a round face with a straight nose, wide mouth and thick lips, and these were henceforth embellished with a diamond shine, universal jewel finish lip gloss.

She could do nothing about the large mole on her left cheek, but she could take to wearing nail varnish for a change, and so she also paid a visit to a nail salon, where she underwent a gel manicure and emerged with deep red-coloured nails.

She had started to put on weight too, especially around the waist and the buttocks, and so she decided upon a low-calorie diet to meet her needs. Within a few weeks she was able to slip into a pair of tight-fitting jeans, and took to wearing high heels to accompany them, even around the house. At five feet and six inches in height, she was slightly smaller than Molloy, but with the high heels she felt that she was able to look him straight in the eyes.

Alas, all was in vain, for he continued to shun her. Something had to be done and something drastic; which is why she had lain there for hours, pontificating as to her next course of action. She had almost made up her mind on this matter when the body beside her began to stir. Before he even had the chance to turn over onto his back, she had removed the covers and was out of the door wrapped in her dressing gown. Yes, she had almost made up her mind!

Shirley Finch had been up since just after 6.00 a.m. It had been like that for as long as she could remember, and now at eighty-one it had become routine. A widow for many years, she seemed to have a permanent smile, almost as if she were hiding am abundance of melancholy and pain, and her sad, grey eyes merely added to that impression.

She had always been a quiet and demure woman, which is why it came as a huge shock and surprise to family and friends alike when it transpired that she was pregnant at the age of eighteen. Tom Finch did the decent thing and proposed, and the pair tied the knot two months before the child was born, just after her nineteenth birthday.

And then tragedy struck two weeks before the child's birth when Tom was killed in an accident at the pit, and a distraught Shirley faced calls from her parents to have the baby adopted. She refused, but she withdrew more and more into herself and turned to The Bible. More importantly, there was to be no more boyfriends after that.

She had wanted to be a teacher after leaving school, but when it was discovered that her son had a neurodevelopmental disorder or what would now be termed "learning difficulties," she found part-time work in a local grocery store whilst he attended a special school. She later undertook part-time local cleaning duties at Tapley Church until her retirement at the age of sixty-eight in 2004.

She had lived on Pit Lane in one of the three terraced houses that stood opposite what was once the site of the Tapley Colliery ever since her son was born. The colliery was long gone and the site was now overgrown with a veritable plethora of untidy, neglected flora and fauna. As for her son, she was finding it more and more difficult to look after him as she got older. She was deeply religious, however, and every Sunday morning the two of them would make their way on foot to the nearby village of Tapley to attend the village church.

In recent weeks her son, Billy, had taken it upon himself to perform the daily ritual of running up and down this narrow lane that ran alongside the three terraced houses and led up to the busy main road. Donning an old string vest and a pair of blue shorts that had seen better days, he told his mother that he was "training for the Olympics", and in spite of her protestations he had set off about 7.20 a.m. that particular morning. The weatherman on the television had forecast rain for the day ahead, and as she briefly averted her eyes from the screen she noticed a few splashes on the window to her left. He'd be back soon, she thought to herself.

Sure enough, at around 8.30 a.m. the door was thrown open and in came Billy, out of puff and yet in an excited state.

'Look at the state of you,' said his mother as she slowly eased herself out of the easy chair and made her way gingerly over to him. 'It's a wonder that you don't catch your death of cold.'

Billy merely stood there, his gaunt features matched by his thin, slender body and that almost permanent grin that spread across his face all the time. He was now sixty-two years of age, but he had the mind of a ten-year-old. Needless to say, some of his contemporaries had a tendency to taunt him because of his disability, but for the most part other children always referred to him as "Silly Billy" or even "Moonstruck."

His mother grabbed at the nearest towel. 'Come on, let's have that vest off then,' she said disarmingly and motioning to Billy with her head.

'You'll never guess what I've seen?' he replied in a high-pitched, excitable and childlike voice.

'What's that then,' she asked almost absent-mindedly.

'Training for the Olympics,' was his curt but solitary reply

She wasn't really listening, but believing him to be referring to his own escapades that particular morning, she spun him around and using the towel to dry his back she made an equally brief reply. 'So I understand.'

Billy gave her a puzzled look and merely repeated himself. 'Training for the Olympics,' he said more forcefully.

'I dare say,' was all that *she* would say.

And yet if she had cared to look up she would have seen the puzzled look on his face turn to one of outright umbrage, almost as if she had just snubbed him. To his mind it was as if she wasn't interested in what he had to say or simply didn't believe him, and he flatly refused to say another word about the events of that morning; events that were to cause such anguish and distress to Detective Chief Inspector Allan Clarke of the Leverton CID!

Chapter 3

Tuesday 24 October 2017 (a.m.)

At 78, Woodcock Drive, Wendy Price was making herself a cup of tea. Her partner, Brendan Molloy, had heard her leave the bedroom and make her way downstairs, and several minutes later he heard the kettle boil. He didn't get much sleep the night before either. He eventually did drop off, and now as he woke from his brief reverie he began to recall the day that his old schoolmate, Luciano Rigione, had appeared on the scene once more several years previously.

Molloy had been working for a local B & Q outlet for two years when in walked the burly – albeit athletic – figure of Luciano Rigione one day. The short, dark brown slicked-back hair may have been receding, but Molloy recognised his old chum immediately. For several minutes the pair reminisced about old times, and each gave a short – and in Molloy's case incomplete – account of their lives since leaving school. More importantly, Luciano took pity on Molloy and offered him the job as foreman at Azzurri Furnishings.

It would mean playing second fiddle to his old friend again, just like he had to when they were at school together. That always rankled with him, because he wanted to be top dog and the one in control now and again. However, he was in a rut and he wasn't one to look a gift horse in the mouth, and so he accepted the offer. Looking back, he had no reason to regret the decision.

For one thing the job did have its little perks and sidelines, amongst other things, and he very swiftly recognised that there were opportunities to improve his circumstances substantially if he played his cards right. There was of course one other reason why he was glad that he had made the move to Azzurri Furnishings, and in many respects he had a lot to thank Luciano for, but now things had changed. Indeed, the plain fact of the matter was that Luciano stood in his way, and something had to be done.

Molloy's thoughts were suddenly disturbed by the familiar footsteps of his partner coming up the stairs. He heard her enter the bathroom and decided it was time that he was up and about too. Pulling on a pair of underpants, he then rummaged around for a pair of socks before selecting a cream-coloured open-neck shirt. He was just about to step into his light brown, camel cord trousers when the door was flung open and Wendy hurriedly entered the room.

'What time will you be back tonight?' she asked tentatively.

'How the bloody hell do I know!' he snapped without even glancing at her.

'Wish I'd never bothered asking now!'

Nothing else was said. She grabbed a pair of jeans and a light blue patterned blouse, and then headed out of the room and down the stairs. Minutes later it was as if one tectonic plate had subducted beneath another and triggered a seismic reaction directly under the building, as the outside door was slammed shut vigorously and the house seemed to shake violently as a result. Molloy then heard the car engine start, followed by a screech of tyres as Wendy swiftly pulled out of the drive and set off for work in her silver Volkswagen Polo.

He was in no mood to smile or feel a sense of smug satisfaction that his partner had gone off to work in a huff, but before heading for the bathroom and a quick wash and shave he opened the bedroom curtains, and as he looked down on the Peacock Pathway that ran along the rear of the house his thoughts turned once more to his old schoolmate, Luciano Rigione. Yes, something had to be done alright, and it was at that precise moment that an idea suddenly came into his mind.

Anyone old enough to remember would no doubt be able to recollect and recite the names of most of the collieries that had once stood in and around the Leverton area, and the Fullerton Colliery would probably be among one of the first that sprung to mind. Situated on the southwestern outskirts of Leverton, it was one of the major employers in the region until its closure in 1950. The site lay derelict for a number of years, but in the 1980's a reclamation scheme was initiated whereby the site was to be turned into a sixteen hectare industrial estate. Since then businesses have come and gone, but there are currently forty-six companies on what is now the Fullerton Industrial Estate, ranging from precision engineering works to several vehicle service and repair centres. However, Unit 1, Turnberry Court, is home to Azzurri Furnishings, one of the largest and most successful upholstery firms in the area.

Azzurri Furnishings was established at its present site by Luciano Rigione in 2005. A former upholsterer himself, he later became a senior regional trade union representative before deciding to set up his own business. With motorhomes and caravans a speciality, the company produces quality beds and divans direct from the factory. Each of the fifteen bed styles are handmade in solid beech, and the pocket-sprung mattresses contain 100% natural fillings.

In 2013 Rigione invested in a new, on-site warehouse facility to store the products, and this enabled the company to offer express home delivery. This was followed a year later by the addition of a small showroom alongside the main factory building. In order to offer a greater number of designs and a very quick turnaround, further investments in track systems and cutting machinery were made in 2016. Apart from Rigione, his wife as secretary and Brendan Molloy as foreman, there are a total of thirty-five employees, including delivery drivers.

At just after 8.30 a.m. that morning, a silver Aston Martin Vantage pulled up outside the gates of Azzurri Furnishings. Brendan Molloy had arrived for work. Somewhat over-the-top for a factory foreman perhaps, but he had always liked outward evidence of status, and the car was just one of the lavish trappings of success and prestige as far as he was concerned. He was always the first to arrive for work and open up, and then once the workforce had arrived he would brief them on their duties for the day ahead. A 'cushy little number,' was how most of the workforce regarded his job.

His initial tasks completed, Molloy made his way through the reception area and down the corridor to his little office on the right. It was a trifle cramped, but he made do for the time being. Slumping into the chair behind his desk, he glanced up at the clock. It was now 9.20 a.m. and the Rigione's had yet to arrive. The pair were often late, and frankly speaking he didn't give the matter a further thought.

At that precise moment the silence was disturbed by the whirring noise of his mobile phone. It was a text message from Linda Rigione and she wanted to know if Luciano was there. Molloy replied in the negative, and seconds later Linda was on the line, her voice trembling with anxiety.

'He hasn't come back from his run,' she blubbered.

Molloy was conscious of the fact that Luciano always made a point of going for a run before work every morning.

'You've tried calling him?' he asked in that barely audible, subdued voice of his.

'Of course I have!' she snapped.

'And...?'

'The phone was dead.' She paused briefly before continuing. 'Something must have happened to him.'

'But it can't have?'

'What do you mean?' she asked, somewhat puzzled by his last response.

Molloy appeared to be flustered. 'Well...he was due to drive down to London tomorrow...for that exhibition.'

'I know all about that!' she shouted angrily before lowering her voice. 'Well he changed his mind last night and decided to go by train, didn't he?'

'He did what!' replied Molloy with increasing exasperation.

'You should know what he's like about travelling – especially down that motorway,' she said in a matter-of-fact way.

'Yeah...I guess so,' was all that he could muster.

Molloy's mind seemed to be elsewhere and his manner was beginning to trouble Linda. She suddenly turned to the route that Luciano would have taken for his run, and she was aware that Molloy's house backed onto the Peacock Pathway.

'You didn't see him go by your place earlier, did you?' she asked quizzically.

Molloy seemed to hesitate before replying. 'No, not at all.'

It was only a slight hesitation, but she picked up on it. However, rather than press the matter she swiftly gathered her composure.

'I'm going to the police,' she said confidently.

Molloy suddenly snapped out of his seemingly pensive state as his voice increased in pitch and intensity.

'Surely now is not the time to...'

She cut him short. 'My mind is made up. After all, he *is* my husband,' she shouted before switching off her phone.

'Was,' he said out loud before promptly kicking the litter bin violently across the room!

Chapter 4

Tuesday 24 October 2017 (a.m.)

There was a surprising lack of activity at Leverton Police Station that morning as it turned 10.00 a.m. This was in stark contrast to the day before, when just about everyone had something to say about the trial and conviction of Rupert Frankland-Moore the previous week; that is everyone except the Desk Sergeant, Bob Scattergood.

Bob's mind had been elsewhere the day before – and for good reason. It would have been his late wife's fifty-third birthday. Five years had passed since she had succumbed to cancer, but time was not a great healer in Bob's case. Everyone was aware of this and even Superintendent Annable had told him that he could have the day off, but touched as he was by this rare (one might say uncharacteristic) act of kind-heartedness, he brushed it aside and insisted on coming in to work. Not that there was much work for him to do throughout the day.

It was pretty much the same on this dark and typically wet autumnal Tuesday morning, and so he decided that he would nip outside for a quick fag before returning to his reception desk. Standing in the shelter of the doorway, he inhaled deeply on only his second cigarette of the day whilst mentally cursing the weather. He was hoping that it wasn't going to be like this the following Tuesday on Halloween night, for he had promised to accompany the grandkids as they prowled the local streets trick or treating. And then the weekend after that they were all going to a fireworks display and bonfire at one of the local pubs. At least he would have the chance of a pint or two – with any luck.

As he hurriedly stubbed out his cigarette on the wall-mounted ashtray just outside the main door, the sound of a vehicle splashing through one of the puddles at the entrance to the Station car park forced him to quickly glance to his right, and he instantly recognised the familiar outline of the silver Ford Focus as it pulled into one of the few empty spaces available. Brushing the ash from his shirt and tie, he fumbled his way through the door and back to the reception desk.

Less than a minute later the door opened and in strode Detective Chief Inspector Clarke of the Leverton CID. He had taken the previous day off, but now he was back. What's more, he was wearing a dark grey two-piece suit and green tie, much to Scattergood's utter astonishment.

'What are you gawping at, Scattergood?' was Clarke's immediate reaction. 'Never seen a bloke in a suit and tie before?'

Not you thought Scattergood, as he contemplated his response. 'Erm...'

'The natural thing to do, Scattergood,' interjected Clarke before pausing. 'Actually no, the *courteous* thing to do would be to say good morning.'

'Yes, Sir...I mean...good morning, Sir.'

'There, that wasn't difficult, was it?' He could see that Scattergood was still somewhat lost for words. 'If you must know, I'm turning over a new leaf.'

Scattergood was barely able to conceal his amusement. 'Has Superintendent Annable been on at you about the importance of image again, Sir?'

'Not at all,' replied Clarke coyly.

No, thought Scattergood. More than likely his bit on the side down at The Navigation was behind this wholly uncharacteristic change of appearance. Sensing Clarke's discomfort, he realised that *he* now had the upper hand. 'All your idea then, is it, Sir?'

Clarke cleared his throat and tried to change the subject. 'Erm...is there anything of interest today, Scattergood?'

'Nothing, I'm afraid, Sir.' replied Scattergood with a smirk.

At that moment the outside door opened and the two policemen's conversation was interrupted by an attractive, anxious-looking, middle-aged woman with long blonde hair and blue eyes. Scattergood straightened up and tried to appear relaxed, whilst Clarke was conscious of the fact that the woman bore a remarkable likeness to the supermodel, Kate Moss.

'Well, I'd better be off and let you deal with this lady, Scattergood,' said Clarke with a half-hearted smile, before turning and making his way up the corridor to the right and then on to his office.

At first he could still hear quite clearly the conversation between the Desk Sergeant and the woman who had just entered the building. It was something about a missing person, and then Scattergood saying something about taking down some details. The further he ventured up the corridor, the more their voices seemed to fade, and yet they were still audible. Scattergood will no doubt get all the...

And then he suddenly froze and felt the hairs on the back of his neck stand up. Did he hear right just now? Surely he was mistaken? Yes, that's right. He'd got it all wrong. They must have been talking about someone else. For a moment he shuddered, and then pulling himself together he started to head towards his office once more.

He'd barely gone a few paces when he heard the name again, and this time it was unmistakeable. It was a name that he'd all but forgotten – and wanted to forget – but now it was as if it was back to haunt him again. The hairs on the back of his neck stood up once more and his hands felt clammy. Against his better judgement he closed his eyes briefly and the memories came flooding back – all of them bad; but then he shook his head as if to snap out of his dream-like state. Turning around, he made his way back towards the reception desk, and for some reason everything seemed to be in slow-motion. Emerging from the corridor, he ignored the startled Scattergood, and turned to face the woman.

'Please forgive me for interrupting,' he began. 'But I couldn't help but overhear your conversation with the Desk Sergeant here.'

'Who are you?' asked the woman rather brusquely.

'My name is Detective Chief Inspector Allan Clarke,' he replied calmly. 'I'm sorry, but did I hear you mention the name Luciano Rigione by any chance?'

'Yes, he's my husband, and I've come to report him as missing!'

Chapter 5

Tuesday, 24 October 2017 (a.m.)

So he had heard right after all. At the mention of the name Luciano Rigione, Clarke's first instinct was to turn and walk away, but in this instance he allowed curiosity to get the better of him. And now he had a decision to make.

Was he going to look into this matter himself – as was his duty – or would he cravenly pass the buck and let someone else establish if this was indeed a missing person's case? There was no contest really, he told himself. He was a model professional and he wasn't the kind to shy away from a challenge, even if it was likely to revive the most painful, traumatic memories for him.

He turned to the Desk Sergeant. 'It's quite okay, Scattergood – you can finish taking all the details from Mrs. Rigione later. I'll handle this for now.'

Scattergood frowned, but went along with Clarke's suggestion. 'Right you are, Sir.'

Clarke turned to the woman and gave yet another half-hearted smile. 'Would you care to join me in one of the interview rooms?' he said in a kindly, respectful manner. 'We can discuss your husband's disappearance there.'

'Okay,' she replied tersely.

'Would you like a cup of tea or a coffee, by the way?'

'Coffee, please – and could I have milk and one sugar?'

Clarke gave the instructions to Scattergood and then she dutifully followed him along the corridor to the left until they came to Interview Room 3. Clarke flicked the light switch on the outside wall and turned the nearby thermostat up slightly. The door lock on the outside was controlled by a proximity card reader, and as Clarke opened the door outwardly he chivalrously allowed her to enter the room first.

Upon entering the small room they were faced with a table and three chairs, one of which was bolted to the floor. There was a high quality audio system on the table with push button recording. There were no windows, but the walls were high and naturally soundproofed. The ceiling was solid gypsum, whilst the flooring was a seamless poured epoxy on concrete, and there was a drain in one corner. There were two cameras for the interview process, both of which were high up, and there was a pressure zone microphone on the wall.

The woman took her seat at the table first and then Clarke sat opposite. Although his close-cropped beard left a little to be desired in her view, she decided that he had a kindly face when all was said and done. He was a tad overweight, however, and certainly not as muscular as her husband. That aside, he was softly-spoken and yet his voice was undeniably authoritative, commanding both attention and respect. What's more, his voice also seemed to suggest that he was trustworthy and gentle, but also down-to-earth. Yes, she thought to herself, he would make a good friend, but what's the betting he'd make an implacable foe.

Before sitting down, Clarke removed his jacket and placed it around the chair. He then loosened his tie and took his seat. Seldom brimming with confidence in the company of women, he struggled to hide the fact that the woman who sat opposite was – in his view – enormously attractive.

It was those high cheekbones and thin, piercing eyes that undoubtedly grabbed his attention first and foremost. Even without make-up she looked absolutely stunning, and he correctly surmised that she had either recently been on holiday or – more likely – spent time at a nearby tanning salon. And judging by her figure she was probably accustomed to regular work-outs at the gym if he wasn't mistaken.

Unlike Clarke, she chose not to remove her black longline blazer, under which she wore a beige polo-neck sweater and tight-fitting jeans. She had also shunned high heels on this occasion, and wore a pair of black lightweight leather slip-on shoes. She crossed her legs and watched as Clarke made a few brief notes before commencing the interview.

'Right,' he began somewhat nervously. 'Perhaps you'd better start by telling me a little about your husband, Mrs. Rigione.'

'Please call me Linda.'

It was only four words, but it was sufficient for Clarke to discern that there were faint traces of a local accent. More to the point, as she proceeded to provide a brief description of her husband he was struck by the fact that her voice was quite deep and sensual, and this only added to her allure in his eyes.

She began by informing Clarke that her husband was a successful local businessman and owner of Azzurri Furnishings. She described the business and its location on the Fullerton Industrial Estate, before adding that she was her husband's secretary and had been since 2009. It was when she went on to briefly describe his background that she noticed that Clarke had stopped taking notes.

'Am I boring you, Inspector?' she asked with a hint of sarcasm.

'I'm sorry?' he replied as if taken aback.

'You're not writing anything down.'

'Oh I see.' Where was Scattergood with that coffee, he asked himself before shifting uncomfortably and clearing his throat again. 'Erm...I shouldn't worry. Everything will be...erm... taken into account.'

It was a pathetic response and he knew it, but he had no intention of revealing that he already had some knowledge of her husband's background, so he asked her if she had a recent, up-to-date photograph of him. She began to rifle through her handbag and after several seconds she produced a small, full-length portrait photograph of the man.

'Will this do?' she said brusquely as she handed it over.

Clarke took the photograph and thanked her. It showed a man of about five feet and nine inches in height, standing over a barbecue and wearing a Hawaiian-style short-sleeved shirt with palm trees, and a pair of beige-coloured shorts and sandals. He had short, dark brown, slicked back receding hair, olive skin and narrow brown eyes, but it was the Roman nose that caught Clarke's attention, and Linda could have sworn that she saw him shudder at this point.

'He's powerfully built as you can see,' she said as if she was reading his train of thought.

Clarke said nothing in reply, but just as he was taking in the high cheekbones, the small mouth with thick lips and the slightly irregular teeth, there was a knock on the door and after a couple of seconds in stepped Scattergood with Linda's coffee. He had been in a world of his own as he looked at the photograph, and this brief intervention had the effect of bringing him back down to earth again. As Linda took the first sips of her coffee he thanked the Desk Sergeant, who then promptly left the room.

'May I keep the photograph?' he said as he placed it to one side.

'By all means,' she replied with a shrug of her shoulders.

Clarke then resumed the interview by asking where she and her husband lived, and so she described the house on Tapley Lane and how long they had lived there, amongst other things. Then to her relief he turned to the events that led her to believe that her husband was missing.

'So, what were your husband's movements this morning?'

'He got up just after seven o'clock and went for a run,' she said reflectively. 'It was the same most mornings before work – come rain or shine.'

'And do you know precisely what route he would have taken?'

'He always went up to the crossroads, down the main road towards town and then at Sibley Pond he went up the Peacock Pathway. He particularly enjoyed running around Croxley Lake and the nearby woods, but once on the Pathway he could have used any one of several routes thereafter, all of which would have led him back to Tapley Lane.'

'And what time were you expecting him back?'

'He was usually back within an hour and twenty minutes or so.'

'So that would be about half past eight?'

'That's right. And when he hadn't returned by nine o'clock I tried calling him on his mobile,'

'But I take it there was no response?'

She shook her head. 'I sent him a text message asking him to call me back, but there's been nothing.'

'Have you told anyone else that your husband may be missing?'

Linda paused briefly before replying. 'Yes, the works foreman.'

'And his name is…?'

'Molloy…Brendan Molloy.'

At the name of Molloy, Clarke suddenly sat bolt upright, and not for the first time that morning the hairs stood out on the back of his neck. He was clearly lost for words again, and this did not go unnoticed by Linda.

'Is there a problem, Inspector?' she asked with a puzzled look on her face.

For a second or two he continued to stare blankly ahead, but once again her question seemed to make him snap out of his trance-like state.

'No, no…not at all,' he replied unconvincingly. 'It's just that…'

She interrupted him. 'Mr. Molloy is more like a Deputy Manager – and of course both he and my husband were friends at school.'

Before he even realised what he had said, Clarke blurted out his response almost absent-mindedly. 'Yes, I know.'

'How could you possibly know that?' she said with a look of astonishment on her face.

'I...erm...attended the same school,' he replied reluctantly with yet another weak smile.

'Were you in the same year?'

'No, I believe that they were a year above me,' he lied, before quickly returning to his line of questioning. 'Did your husband leave a note by any chance?'

'Not that I know of,' she replied with yet another shrug of the shoulders.

'Are there any messages on your mobile?'

'No.'

'How about your PC or laptop – any messages there?'

'No.'

'So nothing to suggest that he might have been the victim of a kidnapping attempt?'

'Nothing like that whatsoever,' she said assuredly.

He was now beginning to feel that he was back in control once more. 'Did your husband ever hint at what he intended to do?'

'No, he did not.'

'Do you know where his passport might be?'

'I've checked, and it's where he always keeps it – together with mine.'

At this point it crossed Clarke's mind that her husband could have ordered another passport under a different name, but he chose not to say as much and moved on to another question.

'Have you checked the loft, the garage or any outbuildings?'

Linda was getting tired of the questions and it showed. 'He's not there!' she snapped.

'Have you conducted a search of his route at all?'

'For God's sake!'

'Please bear with me, Linda. I have to ask these questions. Have you been down to the Pond or the Pathway?'

'Again, I haven't had the chance,' she replied through gritted teeth.

'Do you know if any clothes are missing or if your husband had packed any bags?'

'No he didn't *and* none of his clothes are missing!'

Clarke looked up and gave another weak smile before continuing. 'Has your husband been married before?'

'Yes, I believe that they were at school together.'

'Yvonne Newton,' he murmured under his breath whilst continuing to scribble away..

'I'm sorry – I didn't catch that?' she said leaning forward slightly.

'I...erm...I just wondered if you knew her name?' he shrugged, somewhat thankful that she hadn't heard him.

'Yvonne or something like that – moved back to Leverton recently with her son, I believe.'

'They had a son?' he asked with great interest.

'His name is Marco – him and his dad have only recently started seeing each other again.'

Clarke bit his lip. 'I see,' he replied almost lost in thought again.

'Is that it?' she asked making to rise from her seat.

'Just one more question, Linda, and then we're through.' he replied as she sat back down again. 'Did your husband have any enemies?'

She sighed heavily once more. 'Not that I can think of – unless you count them up at the farm.'

'And who might they be?'

'The Meakin's – they've got a farm up in the village.'

'In Tapley, you mean?'

'Yes, in Tapley.' The sarcasm was palpable.

'And what farm is that then?'

'It's Upper Grange Farm – on the left, just up the road from *The Cross Key's*.'

'And why would your husband and the Meakin's be enemies, Linda?'

And so she told him how Luciano used to go for a run across the fields at the rear of their house, and he would take their dog with him. The dog – a Shar Pei – was always off the lead, and one morning in April of that year he was out running when the dog attacked and savaged a couple of Richard Meakin's sheep. The long and short of it was that the dog had to be put down, much to Luciano's chagrin, but there was bad blood between the two men after that. It led to Luciano changing his route, but there was also a confrontation between the two men in *The Cross Key's* one evening.

'You mean there was a fight,' asked Clarke.

'It was nothing really – a few words were said, that's all,' she replied unconvincingly.

Clarke was now satisfied that he'd asked her all the relevant questions, so as he rose from his chair Linda did likewise and followed him out of the door. They then made their way back up the corridor and on reaching the reception area he now proceeded to tell her what he intended to do.

'We shall be launching an investigation into your husband's disappearance. Naturally this will include a visit to Azzurri Furnishings.'

'Will you be interviewing Mr. Molloy – the foreman, I mean?' she asked somewhat cagily in Clarke's opinion.

'We will have to question him, yes.'

'I see,' she replied nodding her head whilst looking down at the floor.

Clarke thought that she was going to add to her reply, but when nothing came he continued with his briefing.

'I must ask you to leave your house and everything in it alone. Don't clean anything until it has been searched and any evidence collected. In the meantime, if you can remember anything then give me a call me on this number,' he said proffering her a card.

She took the card without saying a word, and then Clarke made an unconvincing attempt to reassure her that most missing people are found or return in the first few days. However, he had a gut feeling that this was going to be a long, drawn-out investigation, but he wasn't going to tell her that was he? So he asked her if there was anyone who could stay with her in the meantime.

'Not that I can think of,' she replied succinctly.

'In that case we'll provide you with a Family Liaison Officer.'

She turned to face him. 'But I don't need a Family Liaison Officer,' she snapped.

'I'm sorry, but I must insist.'

She turned away petulantly and stared out of the door. Clarke wasn't impressed, but he'd made his point and that was that. He told Scattergood to get hold of DC Preston, who would act as FLO, and then asked her to finish giving her details to the Desk Sergeant. Bidding her farewell for the time being, he headed for his office before making his way upstairs to see Superintendent Annable.

For several minutes Clarke sat in his office pondering the ramifications of the tale he had just been told. A man had been reported as missing and he knew *who* that man was; a man he had known from his childhood – a man he thought would never enter his life again. From the information he had been given he also knew roughly *when* that man went missing. However, in spite of his trepidation, his reluctance and his fundamental antipathy towards this man, it was now his job to establish *what* had exactly happened to him, *where* it had happened and *why* it had happened.

Leaving his office, he made his way back down the corridor and towards the staircase that led to Superintendent Annable's office. Scattergood was now sitting alone at his desk in the reception area and he nodded to Clarke as the latter made his way up the stairs. Annable's office just *had* to be on the upper floor, didn't it? It meant that he could look down on everyone else, thought Clarke. As he turned to make the last few steps up to the floor above, he shot a quick glance out of the window that looked down on to the car park below and there stood Linda Rigione on her mobile phone. Again, curiosity got the better of him as he began to wonder who she could be talking to if not her husband.

Chapter 6

Tuesday, 24 October 2017 (a.m.)

Superintendent Annable was in an unusually upbeat mood that particular Tuesday morning. What with the successful conclusion of the Frankland-Moore case, he had taken part in a round of golf with some friends at the weekend, and just for once he had played one of the best eighteen holes of his life. Nothing could have dampened his spirits today. Or could it?

He had taken to using *Men Only, H-45 Dark Brown* hair shampoo now and again before coming into work. All he had to do was lather in, wait five minutes and then shampoo out. He was convinced that it did what it said on the bottle – eliminating grey hair in five minutes and lasting up to eight weeks. It saved him having to hide a bottle of hair colouring in his desk drawer at work and touching his hair up in the office. Even his secretary was impressed – although she refrained from passing comment that particular morning. As she briefed him as to his schedule there was a knock on the door to his office.

'Entaaah,' he shouted as if drawing out the word.

The door opened and in stepped Clarke. Reporting to his boss was not one of the most favourite aspects of the job, but it had to be done. 'Morning, Sir,' he said in that softly spoken and yet authoritative voice of his. 'Am I disturbing you?'

'Not at all, Clarke,' he replied before turning to his secretary. 'That will be all for now, Prentiss. We'll come back to this later.' As she rose and left the room, Annable turned once more to Clarke. 'And what brings you in here on this fine Tuesday morning, Inspector?'

Clarke looked over Annable's shoulders and out through the rain-dashed window. Bloody hell – he's in one of those moods, he thought to himself before replying. 'It looks like we've got a missing person, Sir.'

'And no doubt you want to launch an investigation?'

'That's right, Sir.'

'Do we know who this missing person is?'

'The man's name is Luciano Rigione.'

A stunned look appeared on Annable's face as he suddenly sat bolt upright. 'Luciano Rigione? But…'

'You know the man, Sir?'

'Well…we are members…' He suddenly stopped and seemed to correct himself. 'We sometimes played a round of golf together – we were both members of the Armisfield Golf Club.'

Clarke could have sworn that he was going to say that they were members of the local Freemason's lodge at first, but he thought it wise not to suggest as much. 'Were you really, Sir?'

Annable glowered at Clarke through narrowed eyes for several seconds. 'What are you proposing?'

'It's clear to me that specialist searches will need to be conducted using helicopters, dogs and of course the Underwater Search Team.'

'Oh my God,' replied a stupefied Annable.

'Surely you…'

'Yes, yes, yes,' he snapped once more. 'But think of the costs, Clarke – think of the costs!'

'I am perfectly aware of the costs, Sir.'

Annable shot another anguished glance at Clarke. 'Very well, but this matter needs to be resolved *ASAP* – understand? Christ knows what the ACC will say.'

Clarke didn't answer at first and appeared lost in thought for the moment. He then looked down at the ground and shifted uncomfortably in his chair before continuing.

'I was wondering…' he began unconvincingly. 'Perhaps it might be better if…what I'm trying to say is…'

'Forgive me for saying so, Clarke, but I get the distinct impression that your heart isn't in this already. Is there something that you're not telling me?'

Clarke looked up and directly into Annable's eyes. 'I knew the missing man from school, Sir. And I think that it might be better if someone else takes on the case.'

Annable was having none of it. 'Out of the question, man,' he snorted. 'If you knew the man during your time at school, then I can't think of anyone better to lead the investigation at the end of the day?'

And this particular day had started off so well!

Detective Sergeant Jacqui Fletcher was feeling pleased as punch at being given the post of Deputy SIO with Leverton CID on a permanent basis. True, Clarke did like to keep one step ahead of her or hold something back, both of which she found exceedingly irritating, and at times he could be a misogynistic bugger too, but all in all he was a damn good copper and most important of all he looked after his troops.

He was back today, having had the Monday off, and she was looking forward to his first briefing. As she gazed across the major incident room, there seemed to be a buzz amongst her colleagues as they too awaited the arrival of their boss. Her thoughts were suddenly disrupted by a tap on her shoulder. It was Detective Constable Webster.

'Care for a coffee, Sergeant?' he asked her with noticeable apprehension.

'Why, thank you, Webster,' she replied, taking the mug from him. 'That's very good of you.'

'Good to have you with us again.'

'From what I've been told, that wasn't what you said when I turned up at Brockley Hall on that eventful Saturday morning!'

Webster blushed and attempted to change the subject. 'Wonder what's in store for us today?'

'We'll soon find out, no doubt.'

As she took a sip of her coffee the doors suddenly burst open and in came Clarke, and to everyone's amazement he was wearing a suit and tie. Strangely enough, for someone who wasn't usually slow at coming forward, Webster was uncharacteristically reticent, and stood opened mouthed at the vision before him; even Fletcher looked on in astonishment. Elsewhere there were one or two sniggers and casual asides from male colleagues, whilst the female members of staff were reduced to fits of giggles.

'Okay, okay.' began Clarke, aware of the effect his appearance was having on those present. 'You've had your bit of fun, now can we get on with the matter in hand?'

'Yes, Sir,' came the combined and yet muffled response from the crowd before him.

And so Clarke proceeded by pinning a photograph on one of the boards and telling them that they had a missing person on their hands – a very important missing person in the eyes of Superintendent Annable, who had sanctioned a search. The man in the photograph – everyone would be supplied with a copy – was a local businessman by the name of Luciano Rigione, which was sufficient to prompt Webster to make an audible wisecrack, much to the annoyance of Sergeant Fletcher and to the irritation of Clarke.

'Care to share your joke with everyone, Webster?'

'Pardon, Sir?'

'You clearly find something amusing, do you not? Why not let us all in on the joke?'

'I was just...erm...saying that...erm...Well, I hope this hasn't got anything to do with...erm...you know…the erm...the Mafia, Sir.'

'You think you're kidding, Webster?'

'No, Sir. But…'

Clarke interrupted him and turned to the audience. 'The missing man's father was from Naples, and there was a rumour that he had fled the Camorra – the Neapolitan criminal society, which is very much like the Mafia.'

Those gathered turned to each other and there were mumblings amongst them before Clarke brought them back under control and continued with the profile of the missing man and his family. He told them of his interview with Mrs. Rigione, who had reported her husband as missing, having not returned from his morning run – here he touched on the likely route that the missing man would have taken. He then went on to give them a brief summary of Azzurri Furnishings, including the services it provided, its location and its workforce – here he mentioned the works foreman, Mr. Molloy. Finally he told them of the "bad blood" that apparently existed between the missing man and the Meakin's of Upper Grange Farm at Tapley.

'Any questions so far?' he asked peering around the room.

Fletcher chimed in. 'Presumably Superintendent Annable has given the go-ahead for specialist searches of Mr. Rigione's route and the surrounding area?'

'He has indeed, and this will include helicopters, dogs and the underwater search team.'

'Don't let Webster near any dogs – they always end up biting him!' shouted a female voice from the back of the room.

'Ha bloody ha,' replied a suitably chastened and embarrassed Webster as everyone else was reduced to laughter.

Having restored order once more, Clarke then began to issue his own orders and reveal what his first steps would be. Fletcher was given the task of allocating investigations to team members, including door-to-door enquiries throughout the area. She also had to organise SOCO's at the missing man's home and at his place of work, get someone to check his PC's, establish if there were any CCTV camera's on the route and check local hospitals, including those at Leverton, Derby and

Nottingham. Webster was to contact Joel Bishop at The Leverton Gazette in order to issue a press release, and then he was to join Fletcher in following-up on the searches and assessing them. He then proceeded to disperse the team.

'What will you be doing, Sir?' asked Fletcher politely as they stepped to one side.

'I shall be going to Azzurri Furnishings first,' he replied rubbing his chin. 'I must interview the foreman.'

'And then?'

'And then I shall be paying a visit to the Meakin's at Upper Grange Farm.'

Unbeknown to both Clarke and Fletcher, their brief conversation was overheard by a male uniformed member of the team, who broke away from his colleagues and made his way past them to the toilets. Satisfied that he was alone, he then closed one of the two cubicle doors behind him and proceeded to withdraw his mobile phone. Searching under the "Contacts" menu, he came to the name he was looking for and tapped the button. He didn't have to wait long before the call was answered.

'Hi, it's me,' he whispered. 'There's something you need to know.'

Chapter 7

Tuesday, 24 October 2017 (a.m.)

Within an hour of Superintendent Annable sanctioning the search for Luciano Rigione, there was a heavy police presence in the Leverton area, including the nearby communities of Great Sibley, Tapley and Croxley. In the grey, rain-filled skies above, two police helicopters hovered over the area for the rest of the morning and into the afternoon, causing tongues to wag and rumours to abound. However, the area of greatest police activity was along the Peacock Pathway.

Lying to the north and northwest of Leverton, the Peacock Pathway winds its way through land that had once belonged to the National Coal Board. A traffic-free path, it runs from Sibley Pond in the south to Riley's Pond in the north, and covers a distance of roughly five and a half miles. Popular with both cyclists and pedestrians alike, it was named after the nearby Peacock Colliery which closed in 1895.

Much of the land is wild scrubland, but the Leverton Golf Course in the south was part of the 1980's reclamation scheme that included the Fullerton Industrial Estate. From there one passes the Croxley Moor Estate on the right, before proceeding on to Croxley Lake and the woodland that surrounds it. On reaching Riley's Pond, one comes upon a narrow lane that leads to Croxley Country Park on the left or the main road from Leverton to Grimley on the right. There are a number of footpaths leading off from the Pathway, most of which are maintained by local voluntary groups.

The scrubland is dominated by blackthorn and hawthorn, whilst many of the plants are pioneer species, including bramble, dog rose and gorse. Reedmace proliferates around the lakes or ponds, as does the alder. The woodland around Croxley Lake and nearby is a mixture of ash, rowan (or mountain ash), silver birch and sycamore, although here and there elder has been added.

Birds such as the yellowhammer, willow warbler, blackbird and dunnock use the scrubland too, whilst occasionally migratory birds like the waxwing can sometimes be seen. Although butterfly populations are said to have fallen sharply in recent years, the orange-tip, the peacock and the large tortoiseshell are still prominent. Among the most endearing sights during the summer months is that of the Emerald dragonfly, even though the Large Red damselfly is more common.

However, this was a typical autumnal day and the rain was now coming down heavier, reducing visibility and suggesting that the search for Luciano Rigione was not going to be the most pleasant of tasks.

The police sealed off all entrances and exit points to the Pathway, and the public were denied access until further notice. The Underwater Search Team pulled into the car park opposite Long Lane at Croxley, and then made their way down the narrow lane to Croxley Lake; Riley's Pond would be searched later. Furthermore, depending on the results of CCTV cameras, Sibley Pond might have to be searched too.

Sniffer dogs were put to work from the outset, with one group setting off from Sibley Pond and another group commencing at Riley's Pond, but there was a third group that began combing through Croxley Wood. Door-to-door enquiries were initiated at Great Sibley, along the road to Leverton and in Tapley village.

And still it poured.

Joel Bishop was feeling very pleased with himself. Five years earlier he had set himself the goal of realising a vision, when he had seen a chance to start a new weekly rag to rival and then take over from the failing Leverton Weekly News. He had a passion for seeing new ideas take shape, so he came up with the Leverton Gazette. Now the only paper for the Leverton and Grimley areas, it operates six days per week and he is the sole editor.

The trial of Rupert Frankland-Moore at Nottingham Crown Court had been front page news in the Gazette the previous week, and Bishop was hard pressed to recall a more sensational story during his time as editor. There was nothing quite like that for today's edition, with the car crash near Grimley the previous evening in which two people were trapped inside their vehicle likely to emerge as the probable leader. However, the decision would be his and his alone, and that wasn't bad for someone who had started off his working life as a postman.

Born in Nottingham during the summer of 1967, he was the youngest son of Barbadian parents who came over to the UK in 1958.

After attending school in Nottingham, he got the job as a postman with Royal Mail, but he had every intention of progressing to managerial status. However, after a few months of pounding the streets of his home town he realised that this was not what he wanted after all, so he turned to the Open University and began studying for a BSc in English Language in his spare time. Three years later and he got his degree, much to the delight of his parents.

He then took a year out and went to Miami to gain work experience, before returning to undertake a four-month course in journalism accredited by the National Council for the Training of Journalists. Soon afterwards he was taken up by the Nottingham Evening Post as a journalist. Rational and investigative by nature, he later became a senior reporter and then Sports Editor. His finest hour at that post came when he interviewed Sir Garfield Sobers, chiefly about his career with Nottinghamshire County Cricket Club.

Needless to say, however, cricket was not going to figure prominently in the Gazette until next year now that the season was over, and football would be dominating the back pages for the foreseeable future. Not that he was an avid football fan. Journalism, cricket and family were the key interests in his life, and probably in that order if truth were known. Married to Syrena since 1996, they still live in the Nottingham area with their two children, Marlon (19) and Alicia (17). Indeed, he had just finished talking to his wife on his mobile – she had rang to inquire as to his preference for their evening meal – when it suddenly went off again. It was Detective Constable Webster of Leverton CID.

'Ah, Matthew,' he began with a hint of apprehension. 'Should I be pleased to hear from you or are you after something?'

Webster was used to Bishop being reticent at the best of times, in the sense that knowledge known will only be shared with others bit by bit until they have proved themselves worthy of the information that they seek. 'I would have thought that you'd always be pleased to hear from me or my colleagues, Joel, old boy.'

'Less of the "old", if you don't mind, Detective Constable,' replied Bishop with a touch of umbrage. 'How can I help you today?'

It hadn't escaped Webster's notice that Bishop rarely dropped his aitches, but he decided against making one of his amusing quips on this occasion. 'We've got a missing person, Joel.'

'So, it's a press release then?'

'That's right.'

'And do we know the name of this missing person?'

'He goes by the name of Luciano Rigione.'

At the mention of the name Rigione, Bishop's reaction was immediate. 'That name rings a bell,' he retorted sharply. 'Isn't he some sort of businessman – something to do with caravans and the like?'

'That's the man.'

'Well I never…' He paused briefly as if in contemplation, and then continued. 'I assume that you have a photograph?'

'We do indeed *and* much more besides.'

And so Webster filled him in with everything the police had on Luciano Rigione. When he had finished Bishop was in a decidedly more co-operative mood.

'I'll make sure this gets front page in tonight's edition,' he said enthusiastically.

'Thanks, Joel. That'll keep my boss happy.'

'And how is Detective Chief Inspector Clarke of Leverton CID?'

'You won't believe this, but he's turned up for work today in a suit and tie.'

'Bloody 'ell!' replied Bishop, *sans* the aitch.

Thirty minutes or so later and Webster had joined Fletcher on the Peacock Pathway. She had set about the tasks that Clarke had allocated to her, including initiating the door-to-door enquiries, amongst other things, and was now standing alone beside Croxley Lake beneath her umbrella and watching the Underwater Search Team at work. She didn't hear Webster approach and appeared to be in a world of her own as the rain continued to pour down.

'Thought I'd catch you here, Sarge,' said Webster with his collar up but minus an umbrella.

Fletcher jumped a mile. 'Jesus Christ, Webster,' she cried out alarmingly. 'Must you always creep up on people like that?'

'Sorry, Sarge. Didn't mean to frighten you.'

'Somehow I find that hard to believe,' she replied as she struggled to catch her breath. 'I assume you've contacted the Gazette about a press release?'

'Yes, Sarge,'

'Any problems?'

'None at all, Sarge.' There was a brief pause before he continued. 'How are things down here?'

Fletcher turned to face the lake once more. 'It's going to be like looking for a needle in a haystack.'

'My sentiments exactly, Sarge,'

'Come on, let's get back to the office,' she said before turning to head back to her car. 'There's little we can do here.'

'Yes, Sarge,' replied Webster, somewhat aggrieved that Fletcher never offered him the opportunity to stand under her umbrella!

Chapter 8

Tuesday, 24 October 2017 (p.m.)

Clarke wasn't looking forward to going to Azzurri Furnishings one bit. It wasn't that he considered the task of interviewing the foreman of an upholstery works as being beneath him; far from it. It was the prospect of coming face to face with someone he hadn't seen for over thirty years, and someone he had once loathed and despised intensely. Indeed, the very thought repulsed him and made him feel physically sick, but he knew that he had to go through with it. As he turned into the yard of Azzurri Furnishings, he couldn't help thinking that this was one of those occasions when he would have traded places with a steeplejack rather than be a policeman; and him a self-confessed acrophobic!

Climbing out of the silver Ford Focus, he noticed one or two people in white coveralls entering and leaving the building; SOCO's had evidently arrived to commence their work. He made for the same door and entered what was obviously a small reception area. Proffering his card to the young woman behind the desk, he asked to speak to the works foreman, Mr. Molloy. The woman picked up the phone and announced to the person on the other end that a policeman was here to see him.

Minutes later and a man wearing a dark brown tweed jacket, cream-coloured open-necked shirt, light brown camel cord trousers and brown shoes entered the reception area. He was about five feet and nine inches in height with short, curly greying hair that had once been ginger, and blue eyes. More importantly, he obviously hadn't foreseen that the policeman who was here to see him would be known to him, and yet he recognised him immediately.

'Well, well, well. Look who's here,' Molloy began with a sneer. It's "Sniffer" Clarke – I should have known that you'd end up working for the pigs.'

The crudeness of Molloy's greeting came as no surprise to Clarke, as he looked his old adversary up and down. The man was always a bit of a slouch, in spite of his athletic appearance. He also came across as being stern and shifty too, but there was that familiar Grecian nose dropping straight down from the forehead, and those so-called beestung lips – narrow and very full. Furthermore, Clarke noticed that he still had a tendency to hold his head to one side (to the right in this instance). 'I see that you haven't changed much either, Brendan,' he replied calmly and yet with undisguised disdain.

'You'd better come this way,' said Molloy as the sneer disappeared and he beckoned Clarke to follow him.

And so the two men made their way through a door and down a corridor, until they came to an office on the right. Molloy opened the door and Clarke entered first. It was a small office in the latter's view and rather cramped for his liking, but as he watched Molloy slump into the chair behind his desk, he took his seat opposite and looked down at an empty desk.

'Yes, your men have taken away my laptop,' said Molloy caustically. 'And they've taken away those in the other offices. Is there any need for this?'

Clarke leaned forward. 'We have a missing person, as you well know,' he replied authoritatively. 'And there may be clues as to his whereabouts or what may have become of him on those laptops.'

Molloy brushed aside Clarke's response. 'I don't know what all the fuss is about – he's probably with one of his bits on the side.'

That was somewhat scornful, thought Clarke, especially since Molloy and Rigione had been so close at school. 'So your old friend has a tendency to be unfaithful then?'

Clarke's little dig caused Molloy to glare at him for several seconds, but then he looked out of the window. 'I don't know how she puts up with it.'

'I assume that you're talking about Mrs. Rigione?'

He glared at Clarke once more. 'She has the patience of a saint with regard to Luciano's...' He paused briefly before continuing, 'with regard to her husband's infidelities.'

Interesting, thought Clarke; scornful towards his employer and one-time friend, and yet defensive and protective of the man's wife. He changed the line of questioning slightly. 'Are *you* married by any chance?'

'I live with my partner, Wendy' replied Molloy with a frown.

'Have you been together long?'

'What's that got to do with the disappearance of...?'

Clarke cut him short. 'Just answer the question.'

'We've been together five years if you must know.'

'Indeed I must. We may need to speak to her at some stage of the investigation.'

'What in God's name for?' shouted Molloy angrily, but Clarke ignored him. 'You're beginning to get my back up.'

'Well I must be doing something right then,' replied Clarke with increasing confidence.

'I'd call it harassment.'

Clarke ignored him once more and proceeded with the questioning. 'And how long have you been working for Rigione?'

'Four years.'

'How did you get the job?'

'Look, am I a suspect or something?' snapped Molloy rising from his chair. 'In which case I'd like my lawyer to be present.'

'Sit down now!' bawled Clarke with substantial vehemence.

Molloy did as he was told before answering Clarke's previous question. 'He took pity on me and offered me the job.'

'Took pity on you?'

'I was working for B & Q when he came into our store one day. He offered me the job as foreman there and then, and I accepted.'

'And what about your movements today?'

'No different to any other day – got up, got dressed and came straight to work.'

'Did Rigione hint that something might have been wrong?'

'He never said anything to me.'

'Did he have any enemies to your knowledge?'

Molloy threw his head back and laughed. 'You know what he was like – I suspect that he had enemies all over the place.'

Clarke nodded his head and then stood up. 'Well, that's about it – for now.'

'You mean there could be more of this shit?' shouted Molloy glaring once more at Clarke from his chair.

'It pays to be thorough in my experience,' replied Clarke a trifle sardonically. 'Oh, please don't get up – I'll see myself out.'

And with that Clarke left Molloy staring open-mouthed as he headed out of his office and then the building. Climbing into his car, he sat for several minutes collecting his thoughts and going over the conversation that he'd just had with Molloy. One thing was for sure, he hadn't changed his opinion of the man – he was still a loathsome bastard. For that reason and that reason alone, he already had him down as his prime suspect, and Diana Marshall's previous advice about being more objective wasn't going to enter the equation – not by a long chalk!

'Guilty as sin,' he heard himself say as he placed the key in the ignition and started up the engine.

Linda Rigione had returned to her house on Tapley Lane and she wasn't a happy bunny at all. SOCO's had already arrived to look for any evidence that might lead the police to discover what had become of her husband. They'd also taken away his laptop too – and hers!

To add to her vexation, the Family Liaison Officer – DC Preston – had arrived. A tall and slender woman with her dark brown hair taken up in a slicked-back bun, Laura Preston was aged thirty-seven and she was the perfect choice as FLO. She had excellent interpersonal skills and an inquisitive mind, but her primary purpose was that of an investigator, gathering evidence and information from families or individuals that contributed to the case. What's more, she had been a FLO for eight years now, and her experience in the role was second to none.

Indeed, within minutes of her arrival at chez Rigione, she was conscious of the fact that her presence wasn't entirely welcome by the lady of the house. She seemed nice enough at first glance, but the reception she gave Preston was somewhat frosty, and she had barely spoken to her since her arrival. She decided that it was time to break the ice.

'They'll soon be gone,' said Preston as she stood in the doorway to the living room with a mug of coffee.

Linda was looking out of the window at the rear garden when she turned suddenly and frowned at Preston. 'You what?' she snapped.

'The SOCO's – they won't be long before they've finished their work.'

'Oh,' replied Linda, before turning to look out of the window once more.

Preston shook her head and blew out her cheeks in frustration. Getting a conversation going sure as hell wasn't going to be easy with this woman. She was racking her brains to think of what else to say when Linda's mobile suddenly sprang to life on the table in the middle of the room, notifying her that she had received a message. She dashed over to the table and picked up the phone.

'News of your husband?' asked Preston anxiously.

'No, no...Nothing like that,' replied Linda and a little too cagily for Preston's liking. 'Just the...erm...just the hairdresser wanting to know if I'll be keeping my appointment this week.'

It was a lie of course and Preston guessed as much. 'So you'll be going then?' she asked.

'Sorry?' replied Linda as if in a trance.

'You'll be going to the hairdresser's?'

'Oh...erm...I haven't made my mind up yet.' She then made to leave the room. 'Hope you don't mind, but I need to use the loo.'

With that she made her way briskly up the stairs with her mobile and closed the bathroom door behind her.

Preston was more convinced than ever that Linda was trying to keep something from her, but just as she was about to follow her up the stairs and earwig her conversation one of the SOCO's came in from the outside.

'Well, that's us finished,' he said before glancing up the stairs. 'Would I be right in thinking that the lady of the house is using the toilet?'

'I'm afraid so,' replied Preston.

In spite of his apparent distress he was going to have to wait a little longer – but then so was Preston!

Chapter 9

Tuesday, 24 October 2017 (p.m.)

Clarke didn't have to travel far to his next port of call. Upper Grange Farm was situated on the Main Street of the village of Tapley, about a couple of minutes walk from *The Cross Key's Inn*, and he was there in just under ten minutes.

The farm had been in the same family for at least four generations, and the Meakin's were well known throughout Tapley and the surrounding area. Covering roughly 200 acres (80 hectares), it is a pastoral farm for the most part, consisting chiefly of Holstein Friesian dairy cattle and Hampshire sheep, which are rotated from paddock to paddock and bred for their meat. There are also a number of free range hens, with access to the outdoors for a period of the day.

Always marked out to succeed his father at Upper Grange Farm, Richard Meakin took to farming like a duck to water from the outset – it's been his life. His father died in 1988, shortly after he met Kath Saxton, who was the daughter of a farmer from neighbouring Croxley. Although there were two other brothers (a sister, Rosemary, died in infancy), he naturally took over the running of the farm, and when he and Kath married in 1990 she moved in. They had two children, Ricky (born 1993) and Rachel (born 1998), and then Richard's mother died in 2004.

On this rather wet and miserable October afternoon, Richard and his son were out in the fields carrying out hedgelaying work – removing some of the old fencing and wire, cutting and pulling out scrambling plants such as bramble, and preventing the re-growth of stumps. However, it would soon be time to milk the cows again, so they were preparing to call it a day on their particular stretch of hedge.

With daughter Rachel working down at the Golf Club, Kath Meakin was busy feeding the free range hens when the silver Ford Focus pulled into the yard. Attired in a cream coloured Aran pullover with warm winter down vest-cum-waistcoat and Wellington boots, she looked up briefly to see a man wearing a suit and tie get out of the car.

What's more, he had a close-cropped beard, and as he started to make his way towards her, she continued feeding the hens.

'Afternoon,' said the man politely, although he didn't look particularly happy at having a conversation with the rain teeming down.

'Afternoon,' replied Kath Meakin without looking up.

'Would you be Mrs. Meakin by any chance?'

'I would,' was her rather curt response.

'I was hoping to speak to your husband.'

'Was you now.' Her voice was certainly deep and loud.

'Yes, I was,' said the man with a sense of increasing irritation in his voice.

Kath looked up. 'And who might you be?'

The man produced his card at last. 'I'm Detective Chief Inspector Clarke of Leverton CID.'

She leaned forward and squinted whilst attempting to read what was on the card, and then emptied the bucket she was carrying before turning and making her way towards the house. 'My 'usband's out in t'fields,' she boomed. Her local accent was unmistakeable. 'You'd better come in t'ouse.'

'At last,' muttered Clarke under his breath.

Kath stopped suddenly and turned to face him. 'Did you say summat?'

Clarke was forced to stop and he backed away slightly. 'No, I didn't say a word.'

Kath glared at him before turning and heading for the house once more. As they entered the kitchen through the outside door, Clarke was able to form a clearer impression of the woman. She was about five feet and six inches in height, he surmised, with short, strawberry blonde hair and blue eyes. Her face was worn, weather-beaten and wrinkled, and he put that down to her being accustomed to the outdoor life. There was no make-up whatsoever, and other than a couple of small earrings and her wedding ring there were no other decorations. Without doubt she was a very well-built woman, and she had a rather large bust too.

'Mug o' tea or coffee?' she asked deeply and loudly.

'No, thanks,' replied Clarke. 'I'll be fine,'

Kath merely shrugged. 'Please thissen.'

'As I said, I was hoping…'

She interrupted him. 'Owt you've got to say you can say it to me,' she barked.

Realising that there was little point in standing his ground and demanding to speak to her husband, Clarke began his line of questioning.

'One of your neighbours has been reported as missing, Mrs. Meakin, and I'm leading the investigation into his disappearance.'

'The name's Kath,' she retorted brusquely whilst folding her arms.

'I'm sorry?'

'My name's Kath – you can call me Kath.'

'Okay – Kath it is.'

'I've 'eard all about it.'

'Heard about what?'

'That flashy bugger down t'lane 'as gone missing, or so I'm told.'

'If you mean Mr. Rigione, then yes he's gone missing.' Clarke paused briefly and then continued. 'I understand that he and your husband were involved in some kind of feud?'

'Who told you that?'

'Well, I questioned Mrs. Rigione and…'

She cut him short again. 'That bloody tart!' she scoffed as she briefly glanced out of the window.

Clarke ignored her and continued. 'Mrs. Rigione told me that there was an incident, whereby her husband's dog attacked some of your sheep.'

'That's right – dog wer' allus off t'lead,' she snarled. 'Knew summat like that wer' gonna 'appen sooner or later.'

'The dog was put down, but then there was a confrontation between your husband and Mr. Rigione in the pub down the road here. Is that right?'

'It wer' nowt – a few words wer' said, but that wer' all.'

Clarke wasn't entirely sure that she was telling the truth, but he had one more question for her. 'Tell me, Kath, where was your husband between the hours of seven and nine o'clock this morning?'

She sighed heavily. 'Well, 'im and t'lad wer' up at five to milk t'cows. They came in and 'ad some breakfast before 'eading out into t'fields, and they've bin there all day.'

'Okay, well thank you for your time,' said Clarke with some relief.

'Is that it then?'

Clarke was just about to reply when through the window he observed a tractor pulling into the yard complete with a trailer full of wood, clippings, old furniture and a host of other sundry items.

Kath followed his gaze. 'Ah, looks like Derek's 'ere with some stuff for t'bonfire,' she shouted as she made for the door. 'It's my brother-in-law from t'farm down t'road.'

Clarke watched as Kath went out and conversed with the man on the tractor. He couldn't hear what they were saying because of the noise, but after a couple of minutes she started heading back towards the house. The tractor then continued on its way past the building and through an open gate to the fields beyond.

'So, you're having a bonfire then?' asked Clarke with a degree of interest.

'We 'ave one every year,' she replied cheerfully. 'It's a week on Sat'day and folks come from miles around. There's gonna be plenty of booze and food too. Why don't you come along?'

'We shall have to see,' replied Clarke with a half-hearted smile. 'It's to be hoped the weather has improved a lot by then.'

With that he thanked Kath for her time and then made his way back to his car. As he was about to pull out of the yard, he looked through the rear mirror and was just able to make out the tractor and trailer disappearing down the hill behind him.

He tried to recollect the joke about the copper arresting two people on Bonfire Night, and it came to him as he pulled up in the car park of *The Cross Key's Inn*. 'Of course,' he said out loud. 'He arrested one for drinking battery acid and the other for eating fireworks, so he charged one and let the other one off!'

Chapter 10

Tuesday, 24 October 2017 (p.m.)

Thirty minutes or so after Clarke had left Upper Grange Farm, Derek Meakin pulled up outside his brother's farmhouse on his tractor and switched off the engine. The trailer was empty and he had finished offloading its contents onto the bonfire in the field down the hill. As he dismounted the tractor his face betrayed very little, but then it was always very difficult to interpret his moods as his facial expression appeared to be permanently set all of the time. Today was no different.

Although he was very much like his older brother, Richard, in that he was a six-footer with collar-length, tousled grey-brown hair, wide blue eyes and gnarled, weather-beaten features together with a bulbous nose, Derek was very thin-lipped and rarely smiled or laughed. He was mocked about this at school, but his detractors were few and far between, for the simple reason that he could look after himself and from a very early age.

Born at Upper Grange Farm, he attended the local primary school and then a comprehensive in Leverton, but he had very little time for school life. He did excel at woodwork, however, but the fact remains that he left school with no qualifications, and this was because he never turned up for his exams. He just loved farming and farm life so much that he preferred to help his dad out rather than take part in something that he considered to be utterly pointless. He had few friends to speak of either, other than those in the village of Tapley.

So he worked on the Upper Grange Farm with his father and then his older brother, but when Lower Grange Farm became available a mile or so to the east, he moved in and began renovating it. There was of course the accident with the power-saw, when he lost part of the little finger of his left hand, but at least he now had his own farm at last. He too decided upon a small herd of Friesian milkers, but his pride and joy has always been his herd of Aberdeen Angus beef cattle. He is aware of the fact that calves are usually born smaller than is acceptable for the market, so he cross-breeds these with his dairy cattle for veal production.

To begin with he had two assistants help out on the farm from nearby communities, but he loved to get away to the Peak District as and when he could. For this reason he stored a caravan at the Collymore Lake Caravan and Motorhome Club Site in the Peak District between March and November every year, and he considered nephew Ricky capable of looking after the farm whilst he was away, in spite of his young age.

One day in 2012 he was attending a barbecue at *The Bulls Head* pub in the nearby village of Great Sibley when he met Nicola Flewitt. Thirteen years his junior, Nicola had been through two failed marriages, neither of which had produced any children. However, to everyone's amazement they hit it off and following a whirlwind courtship they married in 2013.

At just under five feet and seven inches in height, Nicola's bleached blonde pixie – or golden crop – hairstyle had the effect of enabling her to stand out in a crowd. An attractive woman, but she had a long face with sad looking blue-grey eyes, and her make-up did little to alter that impression. Her mouth was small and her teeth were straight and white, but she gave up painting her nails after she married Derek Meakin. After all, she was going to be a farmer's wife and she was expected to get her hands dirty.

Unfortunately, however, it has to be said that Nicola never really took to farming life, much to Derek's disappointment, although she did persuade him to open the Lower Grange Farm Shop in 2014, and this has been a moderate success. In fact it was Nicola that was on his mind as he entered the kitchen of the farmhouse at Upper Grange Farm.

'Anyone there?' he shouted.

Kath Meakin appeared from the pantry and she seemed surprised to see him. 'Ey up, Derek,' she shouted back. 'I thought you'd gone 'ome.'

'No, I thought I'd pop in and say 'ello.'

'Is everythin' alright me duck – you look like you've seen a ghost?'

'Nicola's left me,' he whispered quietly whilst looking down at the floor.

'Not again?' she replied with considerable exasperation.

'Am afraid so.'

'When wer' this then?'

'Last night – we 'ad another row.'

'I don't know,' she said shaking her head and moving over to the sink. 'I dare say she'll be back, just like last time and the time before that.'

Before Derek could answer, the door opened and in stepped his brother, Richard. 'Ey up, Derek,' he bawled. 'Thought that wer' your tractor outside – you brought some stuff for t'bonfire?'

'Aye, but there's more to come.' replied Derek, still looking at the ground.

Kath butted in. 'That's not why 'e's 'ere,' she said shaking her head once more.

'Oh, I see. Is summat wrong?' inquired Richard with a puzzled look on his face.

'Nicola's gone and left 'im again.' she said somewhat derisively.

'Bloody 'ell, not again!' shouted Richard with equal derision.

Derek attempted to change the subject. 'Look, I've come to ask if you could lend us Ricky in t'meantime whilst I look after t'farm shop this comin' Sat'day.'

'I reckon I can manage without 'im for a while.'

'It won't be for long – just until I can get somebody else in to 'elp out.'

'Or until she comes back,' scoffed Kath once more.

'Aye, or until she comes back.' repeated Derek.

'I'll let Ricky know when 'e comes in,' said Richard reassuringly.

'Thanks,' replied Derek with discernable gratitude. 'Well, if you'll excuse me I'll be off now then.'

And so he disappeared out of the door, climbed onto his tractor and off he went. Richard and Kath Meakin looked at each other and shook their heads.

'I allus said that woman wasn't cut out for farmin',' said Kath with a wry grin.

'My sentiments exactly,' he replied nodding his head.

'Tit short of an udder if you ask me.'

'Aye, you're not wrong there lass.'

He was about to head up the stairs to the loo when Kath shouted after him. 'Forgot to tell you – we 'ad a visitor this afternoon.'

'Who was that then, luv?'

'The police paid us a visit.'

'And what did they want?'

'Wanted to know what you wer' doin' between seven and nine this mornin'.'

'And what did you tell 'em?'

'Told 'em you wer' out in t'fields.'

'Did they believe you?'

'Reckon so.'

'Good,' he replied with a smile. 'Now if you don't mind am bostin' to go to t'lav!'

As Richard emptied his bladder in the upstairs loo, Kath's mobile went off to the tune of *I've Got a Brand New Combine Harvester* by The Wurzels. She recognised the number and greeted the caller with a barely audible 'Ey up.'

'Did you receive a visit this afternoon?' asked the caller.

'Yes,' whispered Kath. 'About three o'clock.'

'Who did the talkin'?'

'I did.'

'Did you give them any reason to believe that the family were involved in any way?'

'Course I didn't. Just said I'd 'eard Rigione was missin', and that Richard and Ricky 'ad been out in t'fields all day.'

'Good, I'll keep you informed as to any developments.'

'Okay, bye for now.'

'Bye.'

Kath put the phone down on the kitchen table, and then stood for a while mulling over the events of the day and her reaction to them.

Focused and determined since childhood, she had always fought to overcome adversities and prove herself in a man's world. For the most part she succeeded in spite of the odds, and she put that down chiefly to stamina and confidence – but a bit of courage helped here and there. And yes, she had to bring all these things into play today, she told herself.

But from the beginning of her marriage she set out to create a prosperous, successful family, for she was always driven by the desire to be in control, and yet she is equally determined to achieve her goal of becoming respected for how *she* has orchestrated the complexities of family life by being systematic, organised, level-headed and perceptive. Nothing must be allowed to happen to undermine *her* family in any way, and that goes for *her* aspirations too.

She suddenly found herself shaking and noticed that her fists were clenched. At that moment her thoughts were interrupted as into the kitchen stepped her son Ricky, looking windswept and sodden in his anorak, jeans and boots.

'Everythin' alright mum?' he asked with some concern.

'Fine,' she replied as if she had just come out of a spell. 'Everythin' is fine.'

'Is dad 'avin' a shower?'

'Yeah, I reckon so.' She paused briefly before continuing. 'Police wer' 'ere earlier.'

'Oh yeah,' he replied with a frown. 'What wer' all that about then?'

'About 'im down t'lane.'

Ricky's face lit up. 'They're lookin' for 'im then are they?'

'Don't you go sayin' or doin' owt you shouldn't,' she said pointing a finger at him.

'As if I would,' he replied with a smirk.

'Your Uncle Derek wer' 'ere too.'

The smirk disappeared abruptly. 'Summat 'appened?' he asked tentatively.

'Your Aunt Nicola 'as done a runner again and 'e wants you to 'elp 'im out on Sat'day,' she said assertively. 'We said you'd be 'appy to oblige.'

Judging by her son's facial expression he wasn't "appy" at all, but that probably wasn't because he would have to help his Uncle Derek out!

Chapter 11

Tuesday, 24 October 2017 (p.m.)

Just down the Main Street from Upper Grange Farm is *The Cross Key's Inn*, which prides itself on being a traditional country pub. It is now the only pub in the village of Tapley since *The Blacksmith's Arms* was forced to close several years previously. Food is served six days a week, and this includes the highly commendable Sunday carvery. It is a Free House, which means that it is independent and not tied to any brewery. The pub boasts a good selection of drinks, including local real ales, and it is popular with walkers, ramblers and cyclists who enjoy the sights and sounds of Croxley Wood as well as the nearby Croxley Country Park.

Mine hosts at *The Cross Key's* for the last twelve months or so have been Dennis Foster and his partner, Susan Addison. Although they have had some experience in the hospitality trade, having ran two pubs in Newark and one in Nottingham, this is their first attempt at running a Free House.

Now aged fifty-three, Grantham-born Dennis spent most of his life after school selling insurance. His marriage ended in divorce, but it did produce two children who both see their father regularly. He met Susan Addison (formerly Armstrong) on an internet dating agency site in 2008, and she moved in eighteen months later. Fed up with selling insurance, he persuaded Susan to go into the hospitality trade and she agreed quite readily. After the three pubs in Newark and Nottingham, they jumped at the chance to take on *The Cross Key's* at Tapley. A fanatical supporter of Nottingham Forest Football Club, he was at Hillsborough on 15 April 1989, but he couldn't bring himself to go to the restaged match at Old Trafford on 7 May.

Three years his junior, Susan was born in Newark. She got bitten by an adder as a child when on holiday with her family in the New Forest. Rushed to hospital, she suffered sickness and diarrhoea amongst other things. It was this experience that prompted her to become a nurse after leaving school. Her marriage ended in divorce too, and although there are two boys she doesn't see as much of them as she'd like, what with one at university and the other back-packing in Australia. She went into the care industry after the boys started secondary school, but she wanted a change, and when she moved in with Dennis she was only too happy to accept the challenge of running a pub with him.

On this wet and miserable Tuesday afternoon, Susan was behind the bar with one of the young girls who had just started her shift. It hadn't been a very busy day under the circumstances, but one or two regulars were starting to arrive, much to Susan's relief. At five feet and six inches in height, with a light brown pixie bob hairstyle and blue eyes, she was a quite slim and attractive middle-aged woman, but her most distinguishing features were her "chipmunk cheeks" – which is how one of the regulars described them. With little evidence of make-up, she wore a black tee-shirt, jeans and a pair of black slip-on sneakers. She had just finished serving one of the regulars when Clarke walked through the door and approached the bar.

'What can I get you, luv?' asked Susan in a low, softly-spoken voice.

Clarke was impressed by her amiable manner. 'I'm tempted to have a double whisky,' he quipped. 'But I think I'll try a pint of your *Chatsworth Gold*, please.'

He hadn't intended to call in at the pub initially, but he was glad that he had. It was a long time since he had been in the place, but little had changed. It still seemed a very cosy, likeable hostelry, he thought as he glanced around him, and yet there did appear to be quite a lot of Nottingham Forest football regalia on the walls around the bar. His thoughts were interrupted by Susan.

'That'll be £3.30 please, luv,' she said with a winning smile.

Clarke handed over a five pound note and then stood at the corner of the bar waiting for his change. He took a quick sip of his beer and was delighted to discover that it was of a very high standard.

'Cracking pint,' he said as she returned with his change.

'That's very good of you to say so.'

He took another sip of beer before continuing. 'Someone a Nottingham Forest fan?' he asked whilst nodding in the direction of some of the regalia.

'That'll be my partner,' she replied with raised eyebrows.

'So you're the...erm...you're the landlady then?' he asked somewhat gingerly.

'That's right?'

He decided that it was time to produce his card. 'I'm Detective Chief Inspector Clarke of Leverton CID,' he said quietly and yet authoritatively. 'I'm investigating the disappearance of a gentleman from down the lane here...'

'Mr. Rigione,' she said cutting him short.

'You've heard about him then?'

'I should think that the entire village knows by now.'

'Well, I was wondering if you...'

Clarke's conversation was interrupted by the sound of a door opening and shutting behind him, and he turned to see a rather portly, muscular man with very close-cropped receding hair and wearing a red Nottingham Forest football shirt tucked into a pair of jeans heading towards him.

'Have you got a minute, Dennis?' asked Susan in a low voice as she beckoned her partner over to the bar. 'This gentleman is from the police.'

'Better be on my best behaviour then,' he joked as he lumbered his way slowly behind the bar. 'Would this be about him from down the lane?'

'Yes, it would,' replied Clarke.

'Never liked him,' said Foster shaking his head. 'Bloody troublemaker – you can tell his sort a mile off.'

'He comes in here then?'

'He used to – liked to throw his money around.'

'And he tried it on with some of the bar staff,' added Susan.

'Barred him eventually,' continued Foster.

'Why was that?'

'Picked a fight with one of the regulars.'

'Would that be the farmer up the road – Richard Meakin?'

'So you've heard about it then?'

'I've been told that there was a confrontation of sorts.'

'It was more than just a confrontation I can tell you.'

There's no stopping this guy, thought Clarke. 'Go on,' he said with growing interest.

So Foster confirmed that Rigione's dog had attacked Meakin's sheep, and that the pair had never seen eye to eye since the incident. But there was more to come.

'Well, Rigione came in one night with his wife and started taunting Meakin,' continued Foster. 'There was a lot of finger pointing, and then the next thing you know the pair of 'em were throwing punches and rolling about all over the floor – tables and glasses were flying everywhere.'

'A proper fight then?'

'Too bloody right it was. A few of us stepped in to pull 'em apart, and that's when I barred him.'

'You didn't bar Meakin?' asked Clarke with a surprised look on his face.

'I told his wife and his brother to take him home.'

'But they were still mouthing at each other outside, weren't they, Dennis?' interrupted Susan once more.

'That's right,' replied an increasingly excited Foster. 'I remember Meakin pointing his finger at Rigione and threatening him.'

'Can you remember what was said?'

'You're gonna get what's coming to you, you dago bastard.' said Foster after pausing momentarily. 'Or something like that.'

'I see,' said Clarke thinking that Foster had finished.

'And then his brother dragged him away,' Foster continued.

'That would be Derek Meakin I take it?'

'No, it was Pete Meakin,' said Foster with a degree of irritation. 'I'm surprised you don't know him.'

'Why is that?' replied a puzzled-looking Clarke.

'He's one of your lot – a copper!'

After finishing his pint and his conversation with Dennis Foster and Susan Addison, Clarke made his way back to his car feeling slightly befuddled. Although he had yet to find any proof, he'd already marked out Brendan Molloy as the prime suspect for the disappearance of Luciano Rigione, and that was largely because he didn't like the man. But he had to admit that Richard Meakin had a damn good reason for wanting to do away with him.

He was about to open the car door when he heard someone calling his name, and he turned around to see Susan Addison running towards him with something in her hand.

'Inspector Clarke,' she shouted. 'I'm so glad I caught you. I forgot to mention this and I thought that you should see it.'

Clarke gave a half-hearted smile. 'And what's that you've got there, Ms. Addison?'

'This was shoved through our letterbox some weeks ago.'

She handed him what appeared to be an A4-sized sheet of printing paper that had been folded in half. There was nothing on one side, but on the other side there was a photograph of a dog – clearly a breed of Spaniel – and underneath this someone had printed the words:

DOG KILLERS!

THE RIGIONE'S KILLED OUR BELOVED "TONY" – AND THEY WILL KILL YOUR DOG TOO!

'Do you know who is responsible for this?' asked Clarke as he continued to look down at the paper.

'The Bacon's,' replied Susan firmly. 'They live in the house opposite the Rigione's.'

'And you're certain of this?'

'They're a pair of fruitcakes if you ask me, but they've been putting it about that the Rigione's poisoned their dog.'

'And what do you think?'

'It's possible I suppose.' She paused briefly. 'But the dog was always off the lead and it probably ate some rat poison put out by one of the farmers. You know what Spaniel's are like?'

'I assume that you're not the only one to have received one of these?'

'From what I can gather they went around the whole village, but we don't have a dog.'

'I'd like to keep this if I may?' he asked before placing it in the inside pocket of his jacket. Susan nodded and they then parted company.

Slumping into the driver's seat of his car, he closed his eyes and held his head back. If he was somewhat befuddled before, then this bugger had certainly put the cat among the pigeons!

Chapter 12

Tuesday, 24 October 2017 (p.m.)

Sergeant Peter Meakin was feeling wet, cold and downright fed up; he wasn't alone. He had been conducting door-to-door enquiries in and around Great Sibley with about five of his colleagues, and as part of the search for Luciano Rigione. Armed with leaflets showing a photograph of Rigione and the words "Have You Seen This Man", Meakin and his colleagues hoped to gather local information and intelligence from the community, but this dark, dank and miserable day just kept getting darker and danker still, and he decided that it was almost time to call it a day.

Roll on January 2018, he kept telling himself throughout the day. He would be turning fifty on the twenty-seventh of the month, and that was when he planned to retire. No more days like today, he thought as he closed the gate of yet another house behind him. Maybe spend more time with his daughter, tending his garden or watching Derbyshire County Cricket Club during the summer months. And then there was the fishing that he had loved since childhood.

Born at Upper Grange Farm, Tapley, he was the younger brother of farmer's Richard and Derek Meakin. Unlike his brothers he wasn't rough and tumble at school, but he would always step in if someone was being bullied. He preferred to go fishing rather than help out on the farm, which didn't exactly endear him to his brothers. More importantly he was the brightest of the three brothers and did well at school, but it still surprised everyone when he announced that he was going to join the police. He always insisted that it came from his desire to help and protect others.

In many respects one couldn't have asked for a better colleague, for he was friendly, sincere and compassionate. And there of course lay the problem. His disinclination to say no to others – or take risks on their behalf – sometimes resulted in him getting harmed himself. In fact he once took the gamble of coming to the aid of a young woman being abused by her violent, drug-taking partner and got attacked by the man wielding a knife. He suffered one or two cuts as a result, but other officers came to *his* aid on that occasion. In spite of this he never really had any close friends within the force, but there was no denying the fact that he was well-liked.

As a matter of fact he spent many years as a local police constable, attempting to build a rapport with both colleagues and members of the public. Later in his career he became a police sergeant, supervising thirty police officers and managing immediate response teams in the fight against crime, together with community policing. Always receptive and committed to new ideas, he has a reputation for being imaginative and forward-thinking, although others have suggested that he can sometimes escape from reality. Consequently he can occasionally withdraw into himself, especially if others are inclined to offer a different perspective. This tendency to be more in love with his ideas than those around him was perhaps one of the reasons for the break-up of his marriage.

Married at the age of twenty-three, he and his wife had a daughter, and she currently lives with her boyfriend in Leverton. However, he and his wife separated in 1997 and they were divorced in 2001. He has never remarried and there is nobody in his life at present. It has been suggested that he has a tendency to be emotionally detached, and that this has led to him being "married to the job", which may in fact be somewhat close to the truth.

Indeed, with retirement looming colleagues have hinted that there will be a huge void in his life after January 2018, but he has let it be known that there will be plenty of work for him to do around the house and garden. Home is in fact a semi-detached house on the outskirts of Leverton, and this affords him views over the largely rural community of Great Sibley, where he had been working for most of the day.

He had been at the briefing earlier that day, when Inspector Clarke had announced that they would be investigating the disappearance of Luciano Rigione. He recognised the name immediately *and* he was damn sure that Clarke would get to hear about the incident at *The Cross Key's*, amongst other things. Whether or not he would dig deeper and suspect his brother of involvement in Rigione's disappearance was another matter. He knew Clarke of course, but their path's had seldom crossed.

For the time being the only path that concerned him was the one leading to 112, Derby Road, Great Sibley, as this was going to be his last port of call for the day. Pulling out the last of his leaflets, he reached the door and gave it a good rap. Within seconds the door was opened by an elderly woman in her seventies, who was somewhat surprised to be confronted by a policeman in his uniform.

He was a tall man, she surmised, about six feet in height with blue eyes. She was just able to make out that he had close-cropped hair which was going grey, especially at the sides. He had a kindly face, with a few wrinkles here and there, and a rather large, bulbous nose. However, what really pleased her most of all was his smile.

Indeed, his was a broad smile, and having introduced himself he produced the leaflet and put the question to her. 'Sorry to disturb you, luv, but have you seen this man?'

Chapter 13

Tuesday, 24 October 2017 (p.m.)

Linda Rigione had spent most of the day trying to distance herself from the Family Liaison Officer, Detective Constable Laura Preston. Indeed, conversation between the pair had been limited to say the least, and Linda was determined to keep it that way, much to Preston's frustration and disappointment.

The SOCO's had finished searching the house for evidence and had left some time ago. It was now dark outside and Linda decided to go upstairs and draw the bedroom curtains. She had almost reached the top of the stairs when there was a knock on the door.

'I'll get it,' she shouted as she literally flew down the stairs. Opening the front door of the house she could smell the beer on his breath the moment he spoke.

'Hello, Linda,' said Clarke somewhat tentatively. 'May I come in?'

'Inspector Clarke,' she replied with a sense of disappointment in her voice. 'I've been expecting you.'

Stepping back from the door, she ushered Clarke into the hallway. Preston was standing in the doorway of the kitchen and Clarke nodded to her before turning to Linda. 'I just thought that I'd call and brief you on what we know so far.'

'You'd better come this way,' she said as she made her way into the lounge followed by Clarke. Pouring herself a brandy and coke, she turned to face him once more. 'Can I get you anything?' she asked.

The offer was tempting, but he declined. 'Not while I'm on duty, thanks.'

She shot him a quick glance as if she couldn't believe what she had just heard. 'Please yourself,' she said before curling up on the sofa. 'Take a seat, Inspector.'

She looked so sexy and seductive as she adopted a reclining position with her legs close to her body, but yet again he forced himself to turn down the offer. 'I'd prefer to stand.'

She shrugged her shoulders. 'Well, what have you got to tell me?'

And so Clarke began by telling her about his visit to Azzurri Furnishings and his conversation with Molloy. He neglected to mention that Molloy came across as being very protective of her; he decided to hold fire on that for the time being. However, he did say that he would probably have to speak to the man again. She remained passive, much to Clarke's surprise, and so he moved on to his visit to Upper Grange Farm.

'Mrs. Meakin confirmed that your dog attacked their sheep and she also mentioned the confrontation at *The Cross Key's*,' he said before pausing momentarily. 'However, I have it on good authority that this confrontation was a little more heated than both you and Mrs. Meakin led us to believe.'

'You've been speaking to them at the pub,' she conceded.

'As a matter of course,' he replied.

'Okay, so it got out of hand.'

'I think it was a little more than that.'

'My husband was upset because we had to have the dog put down,' she snapped suddenly. 'How would you feel under the circumstances?'

Clarke remained calm and assured. 'That's still no reason to pick a fight with someone, Linda.'

'Meakin was goading him.'

'From what I was told it was the other way around.'

'Well you heard wrong!'

Clarke decided to let it go for the time being. 'What can you tell me about your neighbour's across the road?'

'The Bacon's?' she replied looking down her nose. 'What about them?'

He showed her the leaflet given to him by Susan Addison at *The Cross* Keys. 'They've been putting it about that you or your husband poisoned their dog.'

She snatched at the leaflet. 'Load of rubbish,' she scoffed. 'We were having a barbecue one night and she came across to complain about the music.'

'Mrs. Bacon?'

She was clearly getting tired of the questioning. 'Yes, Mrs. Bacon!'

'And so what happened?'

'Nothing happened,' she snapped again. 'Luciano – my husband – told her to mind her own business and that was that!'

'So he took no further action?'

She literally flew off the sofa. 'Of course he bloody well didn't – the woman is an idiot!' She headed for the drinks cabinet again and then turned to face him once more. 'I thought that you were supposed to be looking for my husband?'

'And we are, Linda.'

'Then why do I feel that *I'm* the one being interrogated?'

Clarke sighed heavily before replying. 'We need to know *everything* if we are to find your husband,' he stated firmly. 'And you *have* been a trifle economical with the truth to some extent, haven't you?'

She glared at him for a few seconds and then slumped on the sofa once more. 'Was there anything else?' she asked somewhat sourly.

'Only if you can remember anyone else who might have wanted to see your husband come to any harm.'

She paused for several seconds before replying. 'Now I come to think of it,' she said pensively. 'There was of course the Duckmanton's.'

'And who might they be?'

This time it was Linda who gave a heavy sigh. 'My husband tried it on with one of the girls at work.' she admitted reluctantly. 'Her name was Emma Duckmanton, and she made it very clear that his advances weren't welcome.'

Clarke recalled his conversation with Molloy once more, especially with regard to Rigione's predisposition for promiscuity and unfaithfulness, but again he chose to keep that to himself for the time being, and so he continued with his line of questioning. 'So she rebuffed him?'

A smile spread across Linda's face as she gave her reply. 'Oh yes, she rebuffed him alright.'

'And what happened after that?'

'She made the mistake of telling her husband, Gary.'

'How do you mean?'

'He came storming into the office one day to confront Luciano and...' she paused and bit her bottom lip.

'And what...?' said Clarke with a sense of exasperation.

'If you must know, Luciano head-butted him in the face,' she replied before turning her head away.

Clarke shook his head. 'Is violence your husband's answer to every problem?' She failed to respond, so Clarke pressed ahead. 'What was the outcome of this affair?'

She turned to face him once more. 'The girl was forced to leave Azzurri Furnishings under something of a cloud, shall we say,' she replied with a smirk. 'She now works at a garden centre – or so I've been told.'

'I don't suppose you know which one?'

'I haven't got a clue.'

'Never mind, I'm sure we'll find out soon enough,' said Clarke. 'And what can you tell me about Gary Duckmanton?'

'I believe that he has his own business – he's a plasterer or something like that.'

Clarke could see no point in continuing. 'Okay, I think that will do for now.'

'Thank God,' replied Linda with some relief.

'Please try not to keep things from us, Linda,' he said persuasively. 'We'll always find out one way or another in the long run.'

With that he thanked her and insisted on seeing himself out, but before leaving he had a quick word with DC Preston.

'Has she said anything that might help us in our investigation?'

'Nothing at all, Sir,' replied Preston disappointedly. 'She seems very reticent.'

'Hopefully our conversation tonight will encourage her to be more forthcoming.'

'Let's hope so, Sir.'

'There's one more thing, Preston. Mrs. Rigione doesn't come across as someone who is at all anxious about her husband's disappearance?'

'That's the impression I had, Sir.'

'I'm glad we agree,' he said with a wry smile. 'Well, just keep me informed of any developments.'

'I will, Sir.'

Having said goodnight to the FLO, Clarke made his way back to his car. It did cross his mind to pay a visit to the Bacon's across the road, but he'd had enough for one day. They could wait for now, he told himself. As he pulled away from the Rigione's and headed for the main road back into Leverton, he still had Molloy down as his prime suspect, and nothing that anyone said would make him change his mind; not even the divine Diana Marshall. And what he would have given to have been with her right now!

Brendan Molloy arrived home late from work that night and he was in no mood for being interrogated by *his* partner. Luckily for him, she wasn't up to questioning him about *anything*. Or so it seemed. And yet she still remained deeply suspicious of his activities.

There was a bottle of *Jameson Irish Whiskey* at the far end of the kitchen unit, and he poured himself a large glass. Wendy noticed, but she deemed it wise not to say anything. He stood staring out of the kitchen window as she placed a plate of Spaghetti Bolognese on the kitchen table.

'Your dinner's ready,' she said somewhat frostily.

'What did you say?' he replied as if he had just come out of a trance.

'I said your dinner's ready.'

'Oh, right.'

He continued to stare out of the window for a few seconds, but then he knocked back the glass of whiskey and poured himself another one. This can't go on, thought Wendy, but just as she was about to say something Molloy opened up.

'We had the law come into work today,' he said in a low monotone voice.

'The law?' she replied with a puzzled look on her face. 'Why, what's happened?'

'You obviously haven't heard.'

'Heard what?'

He turned to face her. 'Luciano's done a runner.'

'Done a runner?'

He sighed and then finally took his seat at the table. 'Yes, he's gone missing and the cops are looking for him.'

'Gone missing?' she said incredulously. 'What are you talking about?'

He was growing tired of her questions, but he proceeded to tell her that neither Luciano nor Linda had turned up for work, and that she had gone to the police. He also went on to say that Azzurri Furnishings had been turned upside down by police and forensic officers, and that he had been questioned by a senior officer from Leverton CID.

'What would they want to see you for?' Wendy asked with some trepidation.

'I'm the bloody foreman, aren't I?' he replied somewhat tetchily.

'You're not involved, are you?'

It was a mistake.

Molloy suddenly swept the plate full of Spaghetti Bolognese from the table and sent it flying across the room, as if he were throwing a discus in the modern decathlon.

Rising from his chair, he snapped at her in a voice that was probably heard all over the estate. 'What is it with all these fucking questions?'

For several seconds Wendy stood frozen to the spot, terrified of what her partner might do next. To her immense relief he stormed out of the kitchen, and then she heard him slam the front door behind him and start up his car.

She was still breathing heavily as the tears began to flow, but for what reason she couldn't determine. Slowly seating herself at the kitchen table, she buried her head in her arms and began sobbing uncontrollably. What was she to do? That was the question that she kept asking herself over and over again. What was she to do?

Eventually the sobbing gradually came to an end and she felt herself slowly drifting off into the land of nod. Within several minutes she was fast asleep.

Then she saw herself running, but she didn't seem to be getting anywhere. And was she running away from something or someone, or towards them? Everything seemed to be in slow motion, when suddenly she saw something in the distance, and as she got nearer she realised that it was a caravan. Upon reaching the caravan she peered through the window, and she was able to make out two figures; one was a man with greying hair that had once been ginger, and the other was a woman who was force-feeding him Spaghetti. What's more, the woman bore an uncanny resemblance to the supermodel, Kate Moss!

Chapter 14

Wednesday, 25 October 2017 (a.m.)

Clarke found himself back at school and *everyone* seemed to be picking on him, but for some reason he seemed to be able to handle himself. Strangely enough, those who were picking on him weren't those he was at school with, but people he had known throughout his life; people he didn't like, including his former boss, DCI Maxine Greenhough. As he looked her in the face and fired off a salvo of expletives, he suddenly woke with a start – it had all been a dream; albeit not a very pleasant one.

God knows what time it was, so he rolled onto his side and blinked a few times; it was just gone eight o'clock and his mouth felt like the bottom of a parrot's cage! Sure enough, there was the empty glass of whisky beside the clock and the almost empty bottle of Laphroaig to the rear. What would Diana Marshall say?

Gingerly climbing out of bed, his head throbbed as he pulled on a pair of pants and wrapped his dressing-gown around him. Why did he do it, he asked himself? He then made his way through to the galley of his narrow-boat, *Emily*, without any incident. Climbing the steps, he opened the rear doors of the narrow-boat and staggered out onto the deck. Almost immediately the change in temperature as he met the fresh air produced a bout of coughing. At least it had stopped raining, although it was a cloudy morning on the Edgeley Canal. He decided that a glass of fresh orange juice would be just the ticket before taking his shower.

Returning to the galley, he went to the refrigerator and poured himself a larger glass of orange juice than was usual. He could have drank the entire contents of the bottle, but he chose to sit at the table and recollect the events of the previous day, and then contemplate the day ahead.

It seemed to him that everyone he had questioned so far was being economical with the truth, from Linda Rigione and Kath Meakin on the one hand to his old adversary, Brendan Molloy, on the other. What had they all got to hide? He was *still* convinced that Molloy knew more about Luciano Rigione's disappearance than he was letting on. He suddenly had an idea, but he decided to keep things close to his chest as always. 'I know,' he said to himself. 'I'll get Webster to do it.'

He turned his attention to what lay ahead, and the realisation that he would be coming face to face with yet another ghost from the past didn't exactly fill him with joy. However, it was something that had to be done and it was only right that he should be the one to do it. He finished off the last of his orange juice and felt better already. It was time to take a quick shower and then get himself ready for whatever the day was going to throw at him. Mustn't forget the suit and tie, must we?

Within thirty minutes Clarke was driving away from the *Emily*, suitably attired in dark-grey suit, brand new white shirt and a rather snazzy navy blue tie with a guitar pattern emblazoned upon it. Not quite to Superintendent Annable's taste maybe, but at least he was making an effort.

Arriving at Leverton police station just before nine o'clock, he had a quick word with Scattergood before shutting himself in his office to glance through the reports on his desk. Deciding that there was nothing of any importance or relevance, he stepped out into the main office just before 9.30 and called everybody together. The slim and slender figure of DS Fletcher stood waiting for him at the top of the room, with her medium-length dark brown hair tied back in a ponytail as was usual. She looked quite appealing in a white short-sleeved shirt and charcoal grey boot cut trousers, and as he stood beside her he whispered something to her before addressing those gathered before him.

'Can we have some order, please?' he shouted, and then waited for everything to fall silent. 'Right, what do we know so far about the disappearance of Luciano Rigione?'

Fletcher was the first to speak up. 'Well, the searches haven't revealed anything as yet, Sir,' she said with some disappointment. 'But then the weather didn't help yesterday.'

'No, I appreciate that it couldn't have been easy for everyone,' Clarke acknowledged. 'What about the Underwater Team – how have they been getting along?'

'They've had no success so far, Sir, but they should have completed their search of Croxley Lake later today.'

'Did you say that they would be searching Riley's Pond too?'

'Yes, Sir.'

'Okay, do we know anything from our door-to-door enquiries?'

Fletcher gave a sigh and shook her head. 'We've covered Great Sibley so far, and although one or two people know of Mr. Rigione *and* that he goes for a run every morning, nobody seems to have seen him yesterday.'

'We're continuing with our enquiries today?'

'Yes, Sir. We hope to cover Tapley and the Croxley Moor Estate.'

'Have CCTV camera's revealed anything?'

'Only that Mr. Rigione was seen passing the *Lyttelton Arms* and Sibley Lake, Sir.'

'Have you carried out a hospital check?'

'We've checked them all, Sir, and nothing doing I'm afraid.'

'I don't suppose SOCO's have come up with anything yet?'

'Not as yet, Sir.'

Clarke rubbed his chin. 'Pint or a penny we find something on his laptop's, including those from his home and his workplace,' he said pensively.

'We'll have to wait on those, Sir.'

Clarke turned to Webster. 'I assume you issued a press release?'

'It went out last night, Sir,' replied a pleased-looking Webster. 'Front page I was told.'

Clarke nodded his head. 'Good, Webster,' he replied. 'Good.'

Fletcher sensed that Clarke was holding something back. 'Did you discover anything yesterday, Sir?' she asked a trifle guardedly.

Clarke was expecting just such a question from his Deputy, but he wasn't quite ready to reveal all that he had "discovered" the previous day. 'Only that we may have to talk to some people again, Sergeant.'

'I see, Sir,' replied Fletcher as she glanced across at Webster with raised eyebrows.

Clarke then began to issue orders to those gathered. The searches were to continue as were the door-to-door enquiries. Hopefully SOCO's would come forward and provide details of any evidence found at the missing man's home and his place of work, especially information from his laptop's. He then turned to Fletcher.

'I want you to make enquiries about an Emma and Gary Duckmanton, Sergeant,' he said authoritatively. 'I think you'll find that she works in a local garden centre and he is a plasterer of sorts.'

'Yes, Sir.'

'And when you've done that, you can head off to the Peacock Pathway again and assess the searches. Okay?'

'Will do, Sir,' she acquiesced, although she was already beginning to have doubts about the direction of the investigation.

As she was about to turn away Clarke called her back. 'There is just one more thing, Sergeant.'

'What's that, Sir?'

'It's noticeable that none of the locals or members of the public have put together a team to help in the search for Rigione.'

'That's true, Sir.'

'What do you make of that?'

Fletcher paused momentarily before replying. 'Not a very popular man perhaps?' she hinted.

'You could be right,' he said nodding his head, 'you could be right.'

Clarke then turned to Webster. 'I want you to look into the Rigione's neighbours – the Bacon's.'

'Yes, Sir,' replied Webster obediently.

'We will need to question them, so go and see them ASAP. Oh, and if either of them gets stroppy, then get stroppy back. Is that clear?'

'Perfectly clear, Sir.'

Fletcher chimed in once more. 'What will you be doing, Sir?'

'Me?' he replied apprehensively. 'I shall be going to see the first Mrs. Rigione.'

With that he brought an end to the team briefing for that morning and sent everybody on their way. However, as they all began to file out of the room he asked Webster to remain.

'Was there something you wanted, Sir?' he asked with a slightly puzzled look on his face.

Clarke waited until they were out of earshot of the others before proceeding. 'When you've got a moment, Webster, I'd like you to do something for me,' he began.

'What's that, Sir?'

'I'd like you to do a PNC check on one of those I questioned yesterday.'

'Who's that, Sir?'

'The man's name is Brendan Molloy.'

'Right you are, Sir,' Webster replied and turned to go.

'Hang on, hang on,' exclaimed Clarke. 'I haven't bloody finished yet.'

'Sorry about that, Sir.'

Clarke shook his head frustratedly. 'I want you to find out if this man Molloy has got a record. Got that?'

'Yes, Sir.'

'But I want you to keep this between you and me. Understand?'

'You can rely on me, Sir.'

I wonder, thought Clarke to himself as he watched the young detective head out of the door. Indeed, he was already beginning to wish that he hadn't asked him to carry out this little task. After all, if a thing needs doing...

Chapter 15

Wednesday, 25 October 2017 (a.m.)

Detective Sergeant Fletcher was pleased that Clarke had given her something to do from the outset this time, which was more than can be said when they first worked together on the Frankland-Moore case. They hadn't got off to a good start by any stretch of the imagination, but he also had an infuriating habit of keeping things very close to his chest at times, and she was already beginning to suspect that he was behaving true to form on this case too. What's more, she had also developed her own theory has to what had happened to Luciano Rigione, but if Clarke was going to be a secretive bugger, then so was she!

He was right about Emma Duckmanton though, and it didn't take Fletcher long to track her down. There were only two or three garden centres in the Leverton area, and on the second attempt she discovered that the Tyndale Garden Centre had an employee by that name. Donning her long, double-breasted khaki-coloured trench coat, she grabbed her bag and duly set off for Tyndale.

Situated on the Nottinghamshire side of the River Edgeley, Tyndale is only a couple of miles outside of Leverton, and the garden centre is just off the main road to Nottingham. An independent family-run garden centre, it began selling plants and compost in 1979. Since then the business has expanded in both size and new products. Indeed, new glasshouses were added to the existing ones to create a larger retail area, and a small cafe opened in 1991. Retail items now include a range of home and lifestyle products, not to mention a popular Christmas display, which was already set up for this year's Yuletide extravaganza. There is a large customer car park in front of the L-shaped building, and Fletcher found plenty of room to park her cream-coloured Mini Cooper convertible with black roof.

Climbing out of her vehicle, she paused briefly to allow a heavy goods wagon to pass and head for the delivery yard over to the far left, and then she then she made her way down the steps to the automatic doors on the right that led into the main building. Showing her identity card to a middle-aged male member of staff, she gave the reason for her visit and was told to try her luck in the houseplants section.

Passing through what was clearly the home and lifestyle section, she glanced briefly at the Christmas display over to her left. Not one of life's most enthusiastic shoppers's, she seemed to shudder at the sheer multitude of festive gifts and decorations, and her pace visibly increased until she came to a large, spacious room containing Cacti and other Succulents. Tending to a series of indoor bamboos was a woman in a dark green, long-sleeved poly-cotton polo shirt, and she was wearing gloves. Fletcher was just able to make out the embroidered logo on her left breast, and she put the woman at about thirty-five years of age. She had a mass of fair hair that was taken up at the back, but there seemed to be little evidence of make-up. However, clearly visible on the left-hand side of her neck was a heart-shaped tattoo comprised of interlocking flowers.

'Emma Duckmanton?' asked Fletcher confidently.

'That's me,' replied the woman without initially looking up.

'I'm Detective Sergeant Jacqui Fletcher from Leverton CID,' she said proffering her card once more. 'I wonder if we could have a little chat.'

Emma looked up at the card and then back down again. 'What about?'

'About your time at Azzurri Furnishing's.'

Emma seemed to sigh heavily before standing up to face Fletcher. 'Look, I've tried to put that period of my life behind me.'

Fletcher was persistent. 'It will only take a few minutes.'

Reluctantly removing her gloves, Emma sighed again. 'We can talk in the cafe.'

And so Fletcher followed Emma out of the houseplants section and back towards the main part of the building. It wasn't one of the busiest days of the year admittedly, but when they entered the cafe there was barely an empty table to be seen. However, as luck would have it an elderly couple had just decided to depart, and Emma promptly sat at the table that they had just vacated.

'Care for a latte?' asked Fletcher with a weak smile.

'Suits me,' replied Emma with a shrug.

Leaving Emma to fiddle with her thumbs, Fletcher went over to the counter and ordered two lattes. A couple of minutes later the pair sat opposite each other with their steaming hot drinks, and it was Emma who chimed in first.

'What's all this about then?' she asked a trifle impatiently.

Fletcher attempted to appear relaxed as she gave her reply. 'We're investigating the disappearance of your former employer, Luciano Rigione, and...'

'You're kidding?' interjected Emma abruptly, as a look of stunned amazement spread across her face. 'Disappeared?'

'I take it you haven't seen the news?'

'Erm...no, no. We don't...' Emma suddenly seemed completely lost for words, and it was a few seconds before she eventually recovered her composure. 'I can't quite take this in. Disappeared, you say?'

'That's right. He failed to return from his early morning run yesterday.'

'Well I never...'

'Naturally his wife is upset and she is anxious to find out what has happened to him.'

'I'll bet she is...' Suddenly Emma realised the purpose of Fletcher's visit. 'And you think that I may have had something to do with her husband's disappearance?'

At this point Fletcher revealed what the police knew about the events leading up to her husband's confrontation with Rigione, and the fact that she subsequently left Azzurri Furnishing's for one reason or another. 'So it might be construed that you and your husband had some justification in wanting to exact revenge on Mr. Rigione.'

'I told you – I want to forget about that time of my life,' replied Emma vigorously.

'But perhaps your husband might see things differently?'

Emma sat back in her chair and turned away briefly. 'Not after what that bastard did to him.'

'So, what exactly did happen, Emma?'

Emma gave yet another heavy sigh before replying. 'It all started from the moment I got the job at Azzurri Furnishing's,' she began. 'It was the way he looked at you – you know, as if he was God's bloody gift.'

Fletcher knew what Emma meant alright, but she urged her to continue. 'Go on,' she replied.

'Well, one day as I was coming out of the ladies loo, he was making his way to his office and he stopped to chat. He put one hand up against the wall to stop me from returning to my work, and the next thing I know he's feeling my bum with his other.'

Fletcher could see that Emma was becoming increasingly agitated, but she pressed her to continue. 'And what did you do?'

'I warned him not to do it again and attempted to get past him, but he wouldn't take no for an answer.' She paused briefly and turned away again before continuing. 'So I just slapped him across the face – just as Mrs. Rigione was coming out of the office.'

'How did she react?' asked Fletcher with a growing sense of admiration for the woman who sat opposite.

'I didn't stop to find out, but when I got home that night I told my husband what had happened…'

Emma suddenly stopped and for the first time her eyes began to well up with tears. Fletcher leaned across and took hold of her hand. 'We can stop now if you like?' she said with some compassion.

Emma wouldn't have it. 'No, no,' she insisted, as she removed her hand from Fletcher's and used it to wipe away a few tears. 'I wish to God I hadn't told him now though.'

'What did he do?'

'I begged him not to, but he went around to Azzurri Furnishing's the first thing next morning to have it out with Rigione.'

'And what happened?'

'Rigione told Gary that I'd led him on – and his bloody wife backed him up.' Emma snapped as she leaned across the table. 'Can you imagine that? She saw what bloody happened and yet she…' Emma bit her lip rather than repeat herself.

'And how did your husband react to that?'

'He refused to believe either of them…'

Fletcher sensed that there was more to come. 'And...?'

Emma paused again before continuing. 'Gary tried to throw a punch, but the bastard head-butted him in the face – he made a right mess too.'

Fletcher literally winced at the last remarks, but she hadn't finished yet. 'And what happened to you?'

'I was told in no uncertain terms by Mrs. Rigione that I was no longer welcome at Azzurri Furnishing's,' replied Emma somewhat scornfully. 'What's more, I was given a payoff for my sins.'

'You mean they tried to bribe you?'

'But of course,' she said with a hint of sarcasm. 'Let bygones be bygones, the woman said as she handed me the package.'

'And you took it?'

There was a few seconds of silence before Emma gave a reply. 'I didn't want to,' she said guiltily. 'I wanted to throw it back at her. But when I saw how much was inside…'

'And how much was inside, Emma?'

Emma turned away again and then muttered somewhat sheepishly. 'Five grand.'

'Five grand!' repeated Fletcher.

'Yes!' she snapped.

Fletcher decided it was almost time to bring the interview to a close. 'And you can categorically assure me that neither you nor your husband had anything to do with Rigione's disappearance yesterday?'

'I've told you,' she replied as if bored with the line of questioning. 'We both want to put that episode of our lives behind us.'

Fletcher stood up. 'Okay, thanks for helping us with our enquiry, Emma,' she said with some sincerity. 'But we will still have to talk to your husband, so where can I find him?'

Emma thumped the table. 'You're not listening to me,' she cried. 'He had nothing to do with that bastard's disappearance!'

'It's part of police procedure, Emma. We have to follow every line of enquiry.'

Not for the first time, Emma gave a heavy sigh. 'He's working on a house at Welham, near the Church.'

'Thanks, Emma.'

'Can I go now?'

Fletcher nodded and watched as Emma left the cafe hurriedly and returned to her work in the houseplants section. She was sure that the young woman she had just been interviewing was telling the truth, and she would say as much in her report and at the next team briefing. Whether or not Clarke would accept her suggestions was a different matter altogether.

Chapter 16

Wednesday, 25 October 2017 (a.m.)

It was his latest acquisition, and for several minutes Nigel Bacon stood admiring his spotting scope that he had placed on the table before him in the living room of *Trespass Cottage*. His wife, Sharon, was upstairs in the "office", no doubt working on her PC and immersed in yet another cause to which she had become engrossed and absorbed.

Moving over to the bookshelf on his left, he pulled out his copy of *The Illustrated Guide to Birds and Birdwatching*, by Neil Ardley (1980). A keen birdwatcher since childhood, he had always felt more comfortable in books rather than around people, and this was his favourite.

Born in the Peartree area of Derby, he was an only child and as a result he became isolated from others at a very early age. This led to him being introverted and somewhat socially lacking, but it also acted as a catalyst for his prime motivation in life, which was the pursuit of knowledge in order to discover the truth in all areas.

By working hard and studying hard at school, he attained his GCE O-Level's and A-Levels, but in doing so he became further isolated as so few of his peers were on the same intellectual plane. This had the effect of making him critical and pompous, and this became evident when he left school and found employment with Derby City Council. Indeed, his colleagues there were prepared to insist that he came across as being opinionated and judgemental on the one hand and myopic on the other, in that he was frequently unable to concede that he could be wrong. In other words, he had an infuriating habit of always taking the superior, know-it-all stance.

Fully committed to his career, he was the archetypal bureaucrat or – as some would suggest – pen-pusher, because in saying that he always had to be seen to do things by the book. Thriving on responsibility, he had an almost morbid fear of failure in the workplace and of getting too intimate with others. This is why it came as a huge surprise to everyone at Derby City Council when he began seeing one of his colleagues, Sharon Hobson, and especially as he was known to be boring for all his naive innocence. However, unbeknown to their colleagues, both were committed environmentalists, and they were finally married in 2001.

Another surprise came in 2003 when he left Derby City Council and moved to the Derby Jobcentre Plus, where he became an adviser. In doing so he brought to his new post the very same characteristics and principles that he had maintained whilst working for the Council, so that he came to regard his new colleagues as being on a lower plane of thinking too, and in their eyes that had a tendency to make him come across as unfeeling. If proof were needed of this, then it was never better illustrated than on the day when he was attacked by a member of the public for threatening to suspend his benefits!

That was all in the past as he flicked through the pages of his book, stopping to ingest all the facts relating to the European Green Woodpecker. His brief moment of contentment and gratification was suddenly interrupted by the doorbell, and with a sense of irritation he placed the book down on the table on top of some leaflets. Straightening his tie, he then made his way to the door. On opening it he was confronted by Detective Constable Webster.

'Mr. Bacon?' asked Webster politely. 'Mr. Nigel Bacon?'

'Ye-es,' replied Bacon cautiously. 'I do hope you're not selling anything?'

Webster pulled out his card. 'I'm Detective Constable Matthew Webster of Leverton CID, and I wish to ask you and your wife some questions about your relationship with your neighbours from across the road.' he said looking over his shoulder.

'Well, this is really most...'

Webster interrupted him. 'May I come in?' And before Bacon could reply Webster took his chance and brushed past him into the hallway. 'You are aware that Mr. Rigione has been reported as missing?'

Their conversation was suddenly interrupted by a voice from the top of the stairs. 'Who is it, Nigel?' shouted Sharon Bacon.

'It's a gentleman from the police, dear.' replied Bacon nervously. 'And...erm he...erm wishes to talk to the two of us.'

As Bacon ushered Webster into the living room, there was the sound of doors opening and shutting from above, and then footsteps moving quickly down the stairs. Seconds later the two men were joined by Sharon Bacon.

Attired in a white long-sleeved blouse and long bright cobalt-coloured satin maxi skirt, she looked down her nose and over her glasses at the young policeman. 'Good morning,' she said somewhat apprehensively and slightly out of breath.

Bacon attempted to make the introductions. 'This is Detective Constable...' he began anxiously, but then paused. 'I'm sorry, but I didn't quite catch the name?'

'It's Webster,' replied the detective.

'Webster, that's it – how forgetful of me,' said Bacon as he turned to his wife. 'This is Detective Constable Webster of Leverton CID, dear.' He then turned back to Webster once more. 'This is my wife, Sharon.'

She came over and offered her hand. It felt cold and clammy, and for some reason Webster was reminded of the character Uriah Heep from the novel *David Copperfield*, by Charles Dickens. 'Good morning,' he said with a slightly embarrassed look on his face.

Bacon interjected once more. 'Would you like a cup of tea, Constable?' he asked a trifle too disarmingly. 'My wife and I only drink herbal tea I'm afraid.'

Webster put his hands up. 'Not for me, thanks,' he replied as he watched Bacon head for the kitchen.

At this point Sharon Bacon suddenly spoke up. 'Erm...I'll just go and...and help my husband with the...the tea,' she said somewhat apologetically before promptly following her husband into the kitchen.

Webster was understandably flabbergasted. 'We've got a right pair here,' he muttered under his breath. However, he suspected that they were up to something, so he moved over to the door – which had been left slightly ajar – and tried to listen in to their conversation. Unfortunately he wasn't able to pick up much of what they were saying, but he was fairly sure that he heard Sharon insist that she would do all of the talking.

Giving up on his attempt to earwig their conversation, he turned his attention to the layout of the living room. Everywhere he looked there were posters and flyers relating to one cause or another, but there were many photographs too, including several of a young dog which Webster assumed was a Spaniel of some sort, and very likely the subject of the so-called "dispute" between the Bacon's and the Rigione's.

It was then that his eyes fell upon the spotting scope, and so he moved over to the table to admire it. As he did so he noticed the book that Bacon had been reading earlier, underneath which was a poster.

He was able to make out the words "dog killers" printed in bold type, but just as he was about to lift up the book and withdraw the poster, Sharon Bacon entered the room followed by her husband.

'Do you like birdwatching, Constable?' asked Bacon upon seeing Webster looking at the book and the scope.

The only birds that Webster was interested in were those that flocked to the bars and nightclubs every weekend, but he wasn't about to admit as much. 'Erm...I'm afraid that I don't have the time.' Growing increasingly impatient with the couple who stood before him brandishing their cups of herbal tea, he decided to get to the point. 'Look, can we talk about the reason why I'm here, please?'

'By all means, Constable,' replied Sharon Bacon as she took her seat on the nearby easy chair, with her husband standing slavishly beside her and with a benign look on his face. 'Please fire away.'

'Thank you,' said Webster with some relief. 'I assume that you will have heard by now that your neighbour from across the road – Mr. Rigione – was reported as missing yesterday whilst out on his morning run?'

'We are aware, yes,' replied Sharon in what Webster thought was a rather supercilious manner. 'But we don't know the details.'

'Could I ask you what your relationship with Mr. and Mrs. Rigione was like?'

'My husband and I like to keep ourselves very much to ourselves.'

'I see,' said Webster before biting his lip and then continuing. 'Well, it has come to our attention that you and your husband have something of a fractious relationship with your neighbours.'

'What *are* you trying to suggest?' replied Sharon as if taken aback.

Webster picked up one of the photographs on the sideboard near the door. 'This was your dog I take it?'

Sharon appeared to brush away a tear. 'Yes, "Tony" was his name.'

'And what happened to him?'

'If you must know that "thing" across the road killed him!' replied Sharon vehemently.

'What do you mean by "thing", Mrs. Bacon?'

'Him!' she snapped.

'You mean Mr. Rigione?'

'Yes!'

Webster remained calm. 'Do you have any proof that Mr. Rigione killed your dog?'

For the first time Sharon appeared flustered. 'No,' she replied a trifle unconvincingly. 'But...well...it had to be him!'

'Mrs. Rigione has denied emphatically that neither she nor her husband had anything to do with the death of your dog.'

Sharon turned her head to one side. 'That slut!' she muttered under her breath.

'I beg your pardon, Mrs. Bacon?' replied Webster seemingly growing in confidence.

She turned to face him once more. 'They were forever having wild parties and orgies every weekend.'

'Wild parties and orgies?' repeated Webster.

Nigel Bacon attempted to intercede. 'I think what my wife is trying to say...'

She glared at him fiercely. 'I *can* speak for myself, thank you very much!'

Webster almost felt sorry for the man as he now stood beside his wife with his tail between his legs, and looking decidedly admonished. 'Would you care to explain, Mrs. Bacon?'

Sharon turned around and attempted to compose herself. 'It was the shouting and the screaming, and to make matters worse there was the loud music. I'm sure the whole village could hear it.'

'Did you make a complaint to the Rigione's?'

Sharon gave a look at her husband that can only be described as contemptuous. 'I asked my husband to intercede, but...'

Webster was clearly getting frustrated. 'But what, Mrs. Bacon?' he said with a slightly raised voice.

She turned to face him once more. 'I ended up going myself!'

'That I *can* imagine,' thought Webster before putting the next question to her. 'So, what happened?'

Sharon looked a trifle embarrassed. 'He swore at me.'

'Can you be more precise?'

'If you must know he used the f-word.'

'Okay, I think I get the picture.'

Again, Nigel attempted to intercede. 'It was shortly after this that our dog died.'

'And you think that the Rigione's had something to do with the dog's death?'

'Yes,' snapped Sharon. '*He* poisoned our beloved "Tony" out of spite!'

'Poisoned?' said Webster with a puzzled look on his face.

'He was constantly being sick throughout the day and into the night,' interjected Nigel as his wife wiped away a few tears.

'Did you call out a veterinary surgeon at all?'

'No, we did not,' replied an embarrassed-looking Nigel.

'Then how do you know that he had been poisoned?'

'It was the kind of thing that *he* would have done,' insisted Sharon.

'You mean Mr. Rigione?'

'Yes,' she snapped once more.

Webster shook his head in disbelief. 'Might I ask what became of the dog?'

Nigel shifted uncomfortably. 'We buried him in the back garden.'

Webster paused and appeared to be lost in thought for a few seconds, but then he continued with the questioning. 'You both drink herbal tea, but do you use other herbal products by any chance?'

'We use herbal products for most things,' replied Sharon rather haughtily.

'And did you give any of these products to your dog?'

Sharon shook her head, but Nigel decided to speak up again. 'We used tea tree oil for his eczema,' he replied as Sharon glowered at him. 'We were told to give it to him as an antidote to parasites.'

Webster asked to see the tea tree oil, and as Nigel scuttled off into the kitchen Sharon was becoming noticeably agitated. Moments later Nigel returned with the tea tree oil and handed it to Webster.

'It says here that it's harmful to pets,' the young detective pointed out incredulously. 'Did you consult a vet about this?'

'No, we did not,' was Nigel's curt reply.

Webster informed the couple that he would be taking the tea tree oil away for analysis, and that the remains of their dog would probably have to be dug up in order for an autopsy to be carried out. As Sharon glowered at her husband once more, Webster made to leave, but upon reaching the door he turned and put one final question to her.

'You referred to Mrs. Rigione earlier as a slut,' he said with a frown. 'Why was that?'

This time it was Sharon's turn to look embarrassed. 'Like I said, they were forever having wild orgies,' she replied.

'And that's it, is it?'

Sharon gave a heavy sigh. 'It's common knowledge that both of them were having affairs.'

'Both Mr. and Mrs. Rigione?' he said inquisitively.

'Yes.'

'And do you know who they were having affairs with?'

Sharon blushed. 'I'd prefer not to say.' she replied coyly.

Shaking his head, Webster stepped out of the house and headed for the gate. He had to admit that he felt sorry for Nigel. 'Poor bugger,' he thought to himself. Perhaps it would be better if *his* wife disappeared!

Opening the gate he turned to the couple who now stood watching him from the doorway of the house. 'And get rid of those bloody posters about dog killers,' he shouted angrily. 'If I see just one of them on my next visit, I'll have the pair of you arrested!'

Chapter 17

Wednesday, 25 October 2017 (a.m.)

Whilst Fletcher set about tracking down and interviewing the Duckmanton's and Webster confronted the Bacon's, Clarke had decided to undertake what he considered to be yet another onerous task, namely interviewing the missing man's first wife. However, it was only onerous because he had known *her* from his schooldays too. After all, she and Luciano Rigione had been childhood sweethearts – of a sort.

Yvonne Newton – as she then was – had been born and bred at Leverton, and she was in the same class as both Clarke and Luciano Rigione at Leverton Grammar School. Indeed, she was considered leader of a group of girls from that same class, all of whom smoked and all of whom had boyfriends. She began dating Luciano Rigione from the age of fourteen, and unbeknown to Clarke the relationship evidently continued thereafter.

He had discovered that Yvonne was employed at the University of Nottingham, where she interviewed applicants for nursing courses. However, she was apparently on annual leave as luck would have it, determined to carry out some decorating work that she had been putting off for several months. Home was a semi-detached house on the southern outskirts of Leverton, just off the Welham Road, and which she shared with her son.

She was bound to remember him, he thought as he eventually pulled up outside the house on Ladybower Close that morning. Built in the 1980's, Ladybower Close was in a quiet, residential part of the town, and the inhabitants were for the most part retired or elderly couples. There was a small brick wall at the front of number ten and behind the wrought iron gate stood a red Toyota Yaris. There was a small lawn at the front of the building, surrounded by a border; roses appeared to predominate, all of which had been pruned, tidied up and the spent blooms removed. One thing that did strike Clarke as he was about to open the gate was the almost complete lack of litter, and he felt somewhat uplifted.

Nevertheless, having made his way down the path to the front door, he seemed to compose himself before knocking, almost as if he was about to attend an interview for a job, and yet he was the one who was supposed to be doing the interviewing. He could hear the sound of music from within, and presumed this to be a radio, so he gave the door a hard and hefty knock.

The music suddenly stopped and several seconds later the door was opened by a woman of about five feet and six inches in height, with a short, light brown (slightly greying) pixie hairstyle and blue-grey eyes. There was little evidence of make-up other than the fact that her nails were painted in a dark brown colour, and yet she had thin, rounded eyebrows. She had numerous wrinkles, brought about no doubt by her smoking habit and love of the sun (or so Clarke surmised). She had a button nose and a small mouth with thin lips. Her ears were small, but she wore large circular earrings. Underneath the navy blue, paint-spattered overalls was a woman with a slim figure and a small bust. And she wasn't happy at being disturbed whilst doing the decorating.

'This had better be good,' she snapped!

'Hello, Yvonne,' replied Clarke a trifle nervously. 'Long time no see.'

Her reply was automatic. 'Sniffer Clarke,' she exclaimed in a deep and earthy voice. 'What the bloody hell are you doing here?'

He produced his card. 'Sorry to disturb you, Yvonne, but I'm here to talk to you about Luciano – you do know that he's been reported as missing?'

She threw her head back and laughed. 'I should have known it – a bloody copper!'

'May I come in?'

She was still chortling to herself as she stood back and opened the door wide to let him in. 'Go straight on through to the kitchen – but mind where you go,' she said with faint traces of the local accent. 'I'm decorating the hallway and staircase as you can see.'

Clarke gave a weak smile as he entered the house and attempted to avoid the folding step ladder that stood before him. The staircase was to the right and the living room on the left, but he managed to reach the kitchen without getting any paint on him. The kitchen unit was directly in front of him under the window, and there was a door to the right that evidently led to the rear garden. There was a three-seater dining table on the left that Clarke suspected was from IKEA, and as Yvonne closed the kitchen door behind her she told him to take a seat.

'Thank you,' he replied without looking at her.

'Fancy a cuppa?' she asked politely before remembering that Clarke was averse to both tea and coffee. 'Of course – you don't drink the stuff, do you?'

A wry grin appeared on his face. 'I'm afraid not, but thank you all the same.'

'Anything else I can get you – diet coke, orange squash or fruit juice maybe?'

'I'm okay, thanks.'

'Well I'm going to put the kettle on – I'm dying for a cuppa.'

Clarke gave yet another weak smile as she filled the electric kettle with water, plugged it in and switched it on. She had her back to him as he spoke once more. 'You haven't answered my question,' he said with what seemed like bated breath.

Turning to face him, she folded her arms before replying. 'Yes, I read about Luciano's disappearance in the Leverton Gazette,' she said after several seconds. 'I've been expecting a visit from the police, but I never expected Sniffer Clarke to turn up on my doorstep. I had you down as being a vet or something like that – you used to like animals, didn't you?'

Clarke shifted a little uncomfortably in his chair. 'You have a good memory, Yvonne – I'll give you that.' He then pulled out a notepad and continued. 'So, tell me about you and Luciano after you left school?'

Yvonne turned around again to pour herself a cup of tea, and then sitting opposite Clarke at the table she lit a cigarette and began to tell him about life with Luciano Rigione.

She had trained to be a nurse after leaving Leverton Grammar School, and subsequently settled at the local Leverton hospital, where she later became a ward sister. Luciano, on the other hand was offered a trial by Nottingham Forest Football Club, but he failed to make the grade.

'How so?' asked Clarke inquisitively.

'They said he was lazy and arrogant, disobedient and frequently absent,' she replied with a wry grin.

After some weeks on the dole, Luciano apparently found employment with a local Leverton company, Depedale Furnishings, as an upholsterer, but it seemed as though he was going to continue in the same vein. Thanks to the intervention of one of the company's longest-serving workers, he was persuaded to join the Furniture, Timber and Allied Trades Union (FTAT) at the age of twenty in 1986.

In the meantime, she and Luciano moved into a terraced house in the Gartland area of Leverton in 1989, and a year later he became FTAT representative at Depedale Furnishings. A very left-wing Union, the FTAT merged with the GMB Union (General, Municipal and Boilermaker's) in 1993, and the following year he quit his job with Depedale and began working for the GMB full-time at their area offices in Nottingham.

'Then in 1995 we finally decided to get hitched,' she said as she stubbed out her cigarette. 'We moved into a spacious detached house on the outskirts of Nottingham, and not long after that I transferred to the Queen's Medical Centre in Nottingham.'

'I see,' said Clarke as he scribbled a few notes on his notepad. 'And what about Luciano?'

It transpired that Luciano was surprisingly elected GMB regional head when the post came up in 1996, narrowly beating rival, Phil Whittaker. Apparently Luciano cockily taunted Whittaker in the immediate aftermath, expecting allies to back him, but Whittaker tore into him and they ended up brawling – it was broken up by allies on both sides.

'There was bitterness, rivalry, abuse and threats thereafter,' she added.

Clarke continued to scribble away. 'Go on,' he said without looking up.

Storm clouds were already beginning to form on the horizon, with regard to both the job with the Union and the marriage. What's more, rumours were beginning to circulate that he had been bullying staff within the GMB Union, and had bribed members to win the post as regional head. Rather than let these matters come to the surface he accepted an undisclosed sum and left the Union in 2005.

'We're talking about a golden handshake, I take it?' inferred Clarke.

'You could say that,' she replied. 'And with the money he set up his own business, Azzurri Furnishings, on the Fullerton Industrial Estate. Oddly enough, there's no Trades Union representation, but I understand that the business is a resounding success,' she said with an element of sarcasm in her voice.

Clarke gave an ironic smile at the last sentence whilst continuing to add to his notes, and then he changed the line of questioning. 'I'm told that you have a son?' he asked with growing confidence.

'Yes, Marco,' she replied with a proud look on her face. 'He was born in 1997. I had to quit my job as a ward sister, and so I initially became reliant on Luciano of course.'

Suddenly the smile disappeared and it was replaced by a pained expression that Clarke picked up on. 'Is that when things started to go wrong between you and Luciano?'

She lit another cigarette and casually blew the smoke away to one side. 'Let's just say that he had something of a roving eye from the moment Marco was born.'

'Did you confront him?'

There was a long pause before she replied. 'I received a slap for my insolence.'

'And was your son privy to this?'

She paused again before continuing. 'I tried to avoid conflict to appease Luciano – I didn't want Marco to witness the violence...'

'But he did?'

'Yes, he did.'

She went on to relate how Marco remained close to her thereafter, and that he also wanted to see his father punished for what he had done to her. Clarke let this go for the time being.

'And when did Linda – the present Mrs. Rigione – come on the scene?'

'That would be 2007, and then Luciano and I finally separated. Oh, he continued paying maintenance for Marco, but...'

Clarke looked up as her voice tailed off. 'But what?' he asked with a frown.

She sighed heavily and stubbed out her second cigarette. 'If you must know, I mounted what you might call a muck-spreading campaign against Luciano.'

'A muck-spreading campaign?' he repeated.

So she told him how her worst fears had come true and that she had fallen out of favour. She answered by retaliating – rumour-spreading, backbiting and passing along information that was exaggerated and intended to disempower her former husband.

'I wanted everyone to know what a bastard he was,' she snapped!

'I see,' he replied with a raise eyebrow.

'I dare say you do, but I shouldn't worry – it soon came to an end.'

'How so?'

'We only have one life, and I decided to get on with mine,' she stated firmly. 'After a couple of years I decided to return to Leverton, together with Marco, and so we moved into our present abode. Luciano and I were finally divorced in 2011.'

There was another brief pause before Clarke put his next question to her. 'Were you aware that Luciano had taken on Brendan Molloy?'

The question seemed to take her aback. 'No, I wasn't!' she stressed earnestly. 'But it comes as no surprise to me.'

Another wry grin came to Clarke's face, but he had the distinct impression that she was telling the truth. 'And how about you – since the divorce?' he asked almost as if it were an aside.

'There have been one or two boyfriends I suppose, but they've amounted to nothing.'

'You mentioned earlier that your son – Marco – wanted to see his father punished. Would you care to elaborate?'

'I would have thought that was obvious,' she replied with a touch of irony. 'He just didn't like seeing the way that Luciano was treating me. However, since the divorce a lot of his anger seems to have dissipated.'

'Okay.'

'I should add that Luciano and I reached something of a truce about three years ago.'

'A truce?' he repeated.

'Yes, I started nagging him to give more time to his son. They now see each other once a week, and for his birthday earlier this year he bought Marco the Kawasaki motorcycle.'

'So, they've patched things up then?'

'Well, he's also helping him out with the fees for his engineering course too.'

'I still may need to talk to him.'

'Do you have to?'

'It's all part of procedure I'm afraid,' he replied closing his notepad and rising from his chair. 'Where can I find him?'

'He works at the golf club – and go easy on him.'

She remained seated as Clarke thanked her for her time and patience. 'I'll see myself out,' he said with what appeared to be a slightly disconsolate look on his face. It didn't escape her notice.

'They gave you a hard time, didn't they?' she said somewhat apologetically.

He looked down at the floor and merely nodded before making his way out without saying another word. As she heard the door close behind him she lit yet another cigarette. There was a time when she would have stood by and watched him suffer at the hands of others – even encouraged them. But now as her eyes began to fill with tears, she was suddenly overcome by an overwhelming sense of guilt that would stay with her for a long time to come.

Chapter 18

Wednesday, 25 October 2017 (p.m.)

It was only five or ten minutes drive from Ladybower Close, but *The Plough Inn* at Welham had a good reputation locally for its fine ales and food, and Clarke was hoping that they were open for lunch; for one thing he was hungry, but he was gasping for a pint too, and as he pulled into the car park at the rear of the pub he was mightily relieved to see that they were indeed serving beer and food.

The Plough was one of two pubs in the village of Welham – the other being *The Horse and Hounds*. It was popular with golfers from the nearby Welham Golf Course, but also with the more well-to-do members of the community. As Clarke entered the pub at the rear, he opened the door on the left that led to the lounge, and was pleased to see that there were only two couples enjoying their lunchtime meals. He was even more delighted when he saw that they were serving *Sarah Hughes Dark Ruby Mild*, and he had no hesitation in opting for a pint when asked by the girl behind the bar. She also asked if he would be ordering food, and when he replied in the affirmative she handed him a card showing the pub menu.

His mouth began to salivate when he saw the first item on the list, which was slow cooked lamb shank with all the accoutrements. However he resisted the temptation to plump for this sumptuous repast and instead decided upon the beer battered fish with triple hand cut chips and mushy peas (not forgetting tartare sauce on the side). Having paid for his beer and food, he pointed to a table in the far corner of the bar, and the girl assured him that she would bring his food over when it was ready.

Seating himself at the table, he was impressed by the cosiness of the bar, but especially by the traditional olde worlde décor. There was music in the background, but to his relief it wasn't ear-splitting modern music, turned up so loud that the ground vibrated. It was just relaxing music that seemed appropriate for the pub environment.

However, as he took a large gulp of his beer, his mind turned to the interview that he'd just had with Yvonne Rigione, and there was no denying that he was still experiencing a range of emotions.

He had expected it to be a daunting task interviewing someone who he had at one time disliked intensely; after all, she was attention-driven as a teenager, but then being centre stage came naturally to her. In many respects she was as bad as the guy she later married in his view. Indeed, in addition to being surprised to see him, she came across as being a trifle scornful at first. However, when he wound up the interview he couldn't help feeling that she seemed genuinely sorry for what had happened all those years ago, and regretted her part in what had been a very traumatic time for him.

Admittedly he was somewhat surprised that she had become a nurse after leaving school, but she had clearly found her reward in helping others. However, marriage to Luciano had resulted in her losing a sense of her own path, but since her divorce she had undoubtedly found some form of autonomy. She had apparently reached something of a truce with her former husband if she was to be believed, and Clarke had the impression that she had subsequently made it her goal to keep any drama from veering into melodrama.

His thoughts were suddenly interrupted by the girl from behind the bar, who with a beaming smile upon her face placed his meal before him. He thanked her politely and then began to tuck into the beer battered fish and hand cut chips with mushy peas. He was ready for this, and for the time being all thoughts of the interview earlier were temporarily put aside. Anyone would think that he hadn't eaten for days, and now and again he sheepishly looked up and cast his eyes around the bar to see if he was being watched. Needless to say, it didn't take him long to eat every morsel on the plate before him, and with a satisfied look on his face he washed it all down with several more gulps of his ale.

Suitably replenished, he then turned his thoughts once more to the interview with Yvonne Rigione, and to what he was able to discern from it.

From what he could gather, Luciano had changed very little since leaving school. He was clearly still an arrogant and cocky bugger, with a predilection for bullying others, but it was the violence that repulsed Clarke. Brawling with a Union rival was one thing, but he was obviously not averse to using violence against the women in his life too. Talking of which, thought Clarke, the man had a propensity for promiscuity, and it was just possible of course that another woman had entered his life recently. 'May need to talk to Linda again,' he muttered under his breath before taking another swig of his ale.

Yvonne had taken to shit-stirring in order to get back at that "bastard", Luciano, but she was adamant that they had reached something of a truce, and that she had persuaded her former husband to do more for his son. Could she have been involved in his disappearance? Not a cat in hell's chance, thought Clarke; unless she and her son were in it together? The boy did dislike his father intensely initially, but time and a peace offering in the shape of a Kawasaki motorcycle seemed to have brought the pair closer together. Nevertheless, he would have to be interviewed too.

Clarke was disappointed that Yvonne knew nothing of Luciano's decision to take on Brendan Molloy, and could therefore shed no light on what part he might have played in her former husband's disappearance. Knocking back the last dreg's of his ale, he took his empty glass and plate back to the bar, thanked the girl profusely and then headed back to his car.

As he sat behind the wheel, he left the door open whilst he made a call to the station. He didn't have to wait long before it was answered.

'Ah, Scattergood,' he barked. 'Anyone free at the moment?'

'I believe that DC Webster is knocking about – somewhere?' replied Scattergood with a discernable lack of confidence.

'Well get him to call me back – pronto. I've got a nice little job for him.'

'Will do, Sir.'

And as Bob Scattergood put down the phone, he was mightily glad that he was a mere Desk Sergeant and not a detective!

Detective Constable Webster had good reason to believe that he was flavour of the month with DCI Clarke – for now. On top of his interview with the Bacon's, he had been tasked with doing a PNC check on a possible suspect. What's more, he had been told to keep *that* between himself and the boss. He was feeling rather pleased with himself indeed.

He was feeling hungry too that particular lunchtime, but unlike his boss Webster had opted for a couple of sandwiches from the station canteen. On his way there he decided to pay a call of nature, and as he entered the toilets he could see that one of the cubicles was occupied.

What's more, the occupant was engaged in conversation with someone – presumably via a mobile phone.

As Webster approached the urinal, he was reasonably sure that he recognised the voice behind the cubicle. The conversation was somewhat muffled, but he could have sworn that whoever was behind the cubicle was telling the person on the other end of the phone how the case was going, and that he was about to set off to conduct more door-to-door enquiries.

Webster washed and dried his hands before leaving the toilets, but he had a puzzled expression on his face when he emerged. If he was right about the individual behind the cubicle, then that person wasn't married, and if that was the case then who was he talking to? His deliberations were suddenly interrupted by Sergeant Scattergood.

'Webster,' shouted Scattergood from behind the reception desk.

Webster turned sharply on his heels and put his hands up before him. 'Okay, it's a fair cop,' he replied with what can only be described as a silly smirk on his face.

'Less of the bloody jokes, Webster,' snapped Scattergood. 'The boss wants you to give him a call.'

'But I haven't had anything to eat yet?'

'Now, Webster,' bellowed Scattergood. 'Now!'

There was no use arguing the point!

Clarke was still sitting behind the wheel of his car at *The Plough* when his phone rang. He answered it immediately.

'Ah, Webster...'

'I've done that PNC check for you, Sir, and I've interviewed the Bacon's,' interrupted Webster ebulliently. 'And...'

'Not now, Webster!'

'There's something else you should know, Sir...'

'Webster, for God's sake calm down!'

'But, Sir...'

'Webster!'

'Yes, Sir?'

'That's better,' said Clarke with some relief. 'There's another job I want you to do for me.'

'What's that, Sir,' replied the young Detective Constable with slight trepidation.

'I want you to track down and interview a Phil Whittaker – you should be able to find him through the GMB Union.'

'And what do you want me to ask him, Sir?'

'I want you to ask him what he knows of Luciano Rigione and why they were such great rivals within the Union...'

'Okay, Sir.'

'Wait a minute, Webster – I haven't finished yet!'

'Sorry, Sir.'

'Above all, I want you to find out where he was and what he was doing at the time of Rigione's disappearance. Got that?'

'Yes, Sir. But...'

Clarke sighed heavily. 'What is it, Webster?'

'Do you want me to keep *this* just between you and me too, Sir?'

'Put the report of your findings on my desk in the morning, and we'll discuss it at the team briefing. Now get cracking.'

Webster blew heavily as he switched off his phone. Strangely enough he no longer felt hungry, and as he swaggered back to his desk he was feeling mightily pleased with himself once more. Flavour of the month indeed!

Chapter 19

Wednesday, 25 October 2017 (p.m.)

Fletcher had been completely unaware that her boss had called at *The Plough Inn* when she entered the village of Welham to speak to Gary Duckmanton. Whilst he tucked into his fish, chips and mushy peas (not forgetting the tartare sauce) just a few yards up the road, she came away from her interview with Gary learning little more than what his wife had already told her.

Gary had been very much as Fletcher had expected – tall and muscular with thick, dark brown curtain hair parted down the middle, and thick pouting lips. He also wore an earring in his left ear. He had a deep baritone voice, but what did surprise her was that there was very little evidence of the local dialect.

He certainly wasn't happy at having someone interrupt him whilst he was at work, and especially not when it transpired that the woman standing before him was from the police. However, he too was as gobsmacked as his wife when told that the visit was in relation to the disappearance of Luciano Rigione. Naturally Fletcher also told him that she had spoken to his wife earlier, and his reaction was little different to that of hers.

'So you think that I might have had something to do with that bastard's disappearance?' he said whilst kneeling and rummaging through his toolbox.

'We have to look at every possibility,' replied Fletcher.

'Well you can forget it. After what he did to me, I wanted nothing more to do with him or his bloody family.'

'So, what was your immediate reaction when Emma told you that Rigione had tried it on with her at work?'

Gary gave a heavy sigh. 'What do you think?' he replied with an element of sarcasm. 'I wanted to sort the bastard out there and then, but Emma pleaded with me not to.'

'And yet you ignored her and went to see Rigione the following morning?'

'Like I said, I wanted to teach the bastard a lesson.'

'So what happened, Gary?'

He stood up straight and gave his reply. 'He blamed Emma.' he said angrily. 'Can you believe that? He had the audacity to blame her, and his bloody wife backed him up.'

'Then what happened?'

He paused before continuing. 'I just saw red and lashed out at the bastard.'

'But he retaliated?'

The question clearly caused him considerable embarrassment. 'Yeah, he head-butted me in the face.' he muttered whilst looking down at the floor.

'And what was Emma's reaction to this?'

'We rowed,' was his curt reply.

'And what was your reaction when Emma was forced to leave Azzurri Furnishings?'

He looked up a trifle knowingly. 'You mean the money?'

'Yes, I mean the money.'

'I told her that we didn't need it,' he replied forcefully. 'But she insisted on keeping it.'

'And that was the end of your involvement with the Rigione's?'

He bent down to go through his toolbox once more. 'I just want to get on with my life.'

'Okay, we may need to speak to you again, but for the time being, thanks.'

Fletcher turned to go, but as she reached the door he shouted after her. 'I hope that someone has done away with the bastard and done the world a favour!'

The tall, shaven-headed figure of Phil Whittaker gazed miserably out of the kitchen window of the semi-detached house in the Beeston area of Nottingham that he shared with his wife, Denise. Their daughter had called earlier to whisk her off for an afternoon of shopping in the city centre, and just before leaving he had hinted to her that he *might* get around to giving his dark grey Hyundai i40 a wash in her absence. He glanced up at the clock; it was almost 3.30 p.m. He looked out of the window again – it had been threatening to rain all afternoon. 'Forget it,' he said to himself. The car would have to wait.

It was now a question of what do with himself for the time being, or at least until he went to pick his grandson up and take him to the match later that evening. As a keen supporter of Nottingham Forest Football Club *and* season ticket holder, he couldn't wait for kick-off, but he had a couple of hours to kill in the meantime. Retirement did have its advantages, but he missed being Regional Secretary of the GMB Union, and the power and control that this brought him.

Born in the Sneinton area of Nottingham in 1951, he bore all the hallmarks of being a tyrant and an authoritarian from his earliest years, so that the desire to be in control manifested itself at a very young age. In addition, he always had stamina, confidence and courage in abundance, and in many respects these are the factors that drove him throughout his life. Make no mistake, he had to fight to overcome numerous adversities from the very beginning, but he always rose to the occasion and beat the odds. Indeed, nobody could ever accuse him of being "chicken" – nobody dared!

In spite of the fact that he was both physically and mentally strong, he nevertheless left school with few qualifications. He eventually found employment with the Nottingham Corporation Waterworks, and then joined the National Union of Water Works Employees (NUWWE) shortly afterwards. This merged into the General and Municipal Workers Union (GMWU) in 1972, which was the year he married Denise Plowright. Two years later, the Nottingham Corporation Waterworks was superseded by the Severn Trent Water Authority, and he continued to play an active role in union affairs.

He had a reputation for being outspoken and radical in a cutting-edge way that many individuals wish they were. This revolutionary radicalism seemed to scream for a sense of social consciousness, away from materialistic designs, and he thrived on seeking to change those things that he felt needed to be changed. This would make the world a better place in his view.

In 1982 the GMWU merged with the Amalgamated Society of Boilermaker's, Shipwright's, Blacksmith's and Structural Worker's to become the General, Municipal, Boilermaker's and Allied Trade Union (GMBATU). This was often shortened to GMB Union, and that became the official name in 1987. Two years previously he became Branch Secretary of this union, based in Nottingham.

He was by now recognised as a man with strong personal ideals, seeking and earning the respect of those around him, in particular for the manner in which he exercised power. What's more, he revelled in this power, but he had a propensity for using it to dominate those around him instead of defending them. However, this kind of power was merely delusional, and maintaining it brought about a sense of insecurity. Indeed, he was at his most desolate when feeling powerless and ineffectual, to the extent that any perceived threats to his authority were met with anger and occasionally violence.

This was never better illustrated than when he was the rival for the post of Regional Secretary of the GMB Union with Luciano Rigione in 1996. It was a bitter contest from the outset, but he expected to emerge triumphant, so when Rigione was surprisingly elected to the post he took it very badly indeed. To make matters worse, Rigione taunted him afterwards and he took the bait. Reckless and aggressive at the best of times, he launched himself at his rival and a punch-up ensued. It was only thanks to the intervention of his and Rigione's supporters that nobody was seriously hurt, but the incident and the defeat rankled with him thereafter. He just wasn't going to back down or concede defeat. Brimming with arrogance, it was as if there was still a battle to fight. It became an obsession with him, and he simply had to win.

Convinced that his rival had used dirty tricks, he mounted an investigation to look into the matter right under Rigione's nose, and when it transpired that the latter had resorted to bribery in order to win the post, he was left with no option but to resign. Whittaker was cock-a-hoop, and he succeeded to the post of regional head of the union unopposed, eventually retiring in 2011.

Now the only battle that he was interested in was that which Nottingham Forest faced in the EFL Championship and that was on his mind as he turned away from the kitchen window and made his way along the hallway towards the stairs. Passing the framed photograph of the 1979 European Cup winning team, he had just started to ascend the stairs when he heard the knock on the door. 'Bugger,' he said to himself as he turned around sharply before slowly descending the few steps of the stairs to answer the door.

Webster seemed to jump back in fright as the door opened and the tall, shaven-headed figure in short-sleeved shirt and slacks loomed before him. He must have been over six feet in height, thought Webster, and he had a large bulbous nose, big ears and a double chin. However, what stood out for Webster were the man's hands – they were like shovels. And as he struggled to produce his police ID card, he hoped that he would never have to confront him in a fight.

'Mr. Whittaker?' asked Webster nervously. 'Mr. Philip Whittaker?'

'Yeah,' grunted Whittaker.

Webster finally managed to produce his ID card. 'I'm Detective Constable Webster of Leverton CID,' he said with a weak smile, 'and I've been given your address by the GMB Union.'

'What's this all about then?'

Webster relaxed slightly. 'I'm investigating the disappearance of...' He paused briefly. 'How can I put this? I'm investigating the disappearance of your predecessor at the GMB Union...'

'You mean Rigione,' interrupted Whittaker with clenched teeth and what Webster interpreted as a snarl.

'That's right,' replied Webster. 'Mr. Rigione – I take it that you were unaware of the circumstances of his disappearance?'

Whittaker still seemed to bristle at the very mention of Rigione's name. 'Yes, I was unaware,' he said with yet another snarl.

'May I come in, please?' pleaded Webster. 'There are one or two questions that I need to ask, if I may?'

Whittaker stood back and Webster duly entered the house. Passing the framed picture of the Forest team in the hallway, Whittaker led him into the living room and showed him to his seat. As he sat down on the easy chair, Webster couldn't help but notice that there were more pictures and mementoes to the club all around him. His brief musings were suddenly interrupted by Whittaker.

'Come on then,' he snapped. 'What's this all about?'

Webster composed himself before replying. 'Mr. Rigione was reported missing by his wife yesterday, and...'

Whittaker threw his head back and chuckled to himself as he interrupted Webster. 'And you think that I might have something to do with his disappearance?'

'It has come to our attention...'

Whittaker interrupted him again. 'Yes, we were rivals for the regional leadership of the GMB Union,' he growled. 'And yes, we did come to blows after the contest ended. So what?'

Webster seemed lost for words for a moment. 'Erm...you...erm...took the result badly, I understand?'

'The cocky dago bastard deliberately wound me up,' snapped Whittaker before leaning forward. 'What's more, he bloody well cheated – and I knew it all along!'

'He resorted to bribery to win the post?'

'That's right – the dirty, cheating bastard!'

'And he was forced to resign?'

'He got found out, didn't he? He had no option but to resign.'

'Quite a handsome pay off, I understand?'

'He shouldn't have got a bloody penny!'

'But that was the end of the matter as far as you were concerned?'

'Justice had been done!'

'Did you ever see him again after that?'

'No, I did not,' replied Whittaker fiercely. 'It was good riddance to bad rubbish.'

Webster paused for a moment before continuing. 'I have to ask you this question, Mr. Whittaker, but where were you between the hours of 7.00 and 9.00 a.m. yesterday morning?'

Whittaker sat back and laughed heartily. 'I was still in bed and my wife will confirm it.'

Webster seemed a trifle embarrassed. 'Yes, we may have to ask her, I'm afraid.'

'I dare say you will,' replied Whittaker before rising from the sofa and making for the hallway. Grabbing a coat from one of the hangers, he turned to Webster once more. 'Now if you don't mind, I've got a grandson waiting to be taken to the City Ground.'

'Okay, thanks for your co-operation, Mr. Whittaker.'

As they bade farewell and Webster opened the door to leave, Whittaker made one final comment. 'They're playing Sheffield Wednesday at home tonight,' he shouted. 'About time they did to Mark Warburton what we did to Rigione!'

Chapter 20

Wednesday, 25 October 2017 (p.m.)

Hardly the weather for golfing, thought Clarke as he drove down Colliery Lane, past the Fullerton Industrial Estate and on towards the Leverton Golf Club, and especially as it was looking a bit black over Bill's mothers. He'd never actually played the game himself, although he always used to watch the Open Championship on the television, and occasionally the US Masters. Perhaps it might be something that he'd consider when he eventually retired; but then again, perhaps not.

It was the cliquishness of the game that put him off, and who better to exemplify that than his boss, DCS Annable, who was a member of the Armisfield Golf Club, between Grimley and Derby, and which was considered the most superior of the clubs in the area. It was certainly the most expensive with regard to membership. In fact it was a game that his former wife, Lesley, might have taken to. Not that she would have actually played the game herself – oh no. But she would have wallowed in the snobbery and exclusivity that is associated with the game, and attempted to encourage him to join a club such as Armisfield. Come to think of it, he couldn't understand why she never did so.

Strangely enough, as he pulled into the car park there seemed to be an abundance of women coming in and out of the clubhouse to his surprise, and using the nearby Driving Range too. It had certainly become a popular venue since its creation in the 1980's.

As with the Croxley Moor Estate to the northeast, Leverton Golf Club was built on land that had once belonged to the National Coal Board, and the course itself was part of the same reclamation scheme that had included the nearby Fullerton Industrial Estate. At one time it was all wild scrubland, and this was taken into account when the course was designed. Consequently water features are few and far between, save for the small brook that runs between the first and eighteenth fairways. The Peacock Pathway runs alongside the western side of the course – or the outward nine holes – and yet it is considered out of bounds. There is an abundance of wildlife too, with rabbits, badgers and foxes predominating, although during the autumn month's birds such as the blackbird, robin and dunnock are the most prevalent.

Membership of the Club is considered reasonable at just over a grand, and there is also a joining fee of one hundred pounds. The Club is keen to encourage new golfers, so there is an induction programme for new members. There are also beginner and improvement packages, together with top quality coaching. To reserve a tee time one only has to call the Pro Shop. Needless to say, club etiquette must be adhered to, but the dress code is quite informal.

The Club boasts the elegant 100-seater Craig Harrison Function Suite and Restaurant (named after a former club professional), and prides itself on providing first class dining facilities. All in all, it is an ideal venue for any event, with hospitality facilities available for private functions, such as weddings, birthdays and parties. The Club's Meeting Room can be set aside for corporate training and business meetings, seminars and conferences. With a professional staff to cater for every whim, the Club appears to be going from strength to strength.

Climbing out of his car, he was surprised at the number of vehicles that seemed to be encamped in the car park, many of which were clearly recent or new models. But there was one vehicle that stood out from the others, and it wasn't of the four-wheeled variety either. Almost directly in front of the clubhouse entrance was a Kawasaki Ninja 650, coloured lime green and black, and closing the car door behind him he made his way over to it. He had never been interested in motorcycles throughout his life, but this one really caught his eye. It had to belong to Marco Rigione, he thought as he stood admiring it for a few moments.

His mind briefly went back to his youth and the *George and Dragon Inn* at Leverton. Now no longer standing, it was recognised as being a biker's pub at the time, although one would have been hard-pressed to have come across a Kawasaki or any other Japanese model. No, the pub was like a biker's version of the Freemason's, membership of which required that one had to be the owner of a British bike, such as a Triumph, a BSA or a Norton (although Harley-Davidson's were grudgingly accepted). On one occasion there was a trike motorcycle in the small car park and the owner clearly took great pride in it. Clarke recalled going to the outside toilet of the pub on that particular night, and as he passed three long-haired, bearded gentlemen in their leathers and Wrangler cut-offs, he inadvertently brushed past the gleaming, recently-polished trike with his jeans. The owner was *not* happy. 'Touch my trike again and I'll kill yer!' Clarke made a point of avoiding the trike *and* the three bikers on his return journey from the toilets!

Pulling himself away from the Kawasaki, he smiled to himself as he began to climb the steps to the clubhouse doors. Suddenly there was a movement off to his right as a young couple turned the corner of the building and made their way towards him, heavily engaged in conversation – and each other. The young man was quite tall, and about the same height as Clarke, or so he thought. He had thick, dark brown hair in what can only be described as a pompadour style (but no sideburns), and he was wearing a pair of navy blue overalls. The young girl was about three or four inches smaller, with long, straight, light brown hair, parted down the middle. She was wearing a black short-sleeve shirt and matching trousers. There appeared to be a name badge above her left breast, but he couldn't make out the name.

Finally entering the clubhouse, he made his way over to the reception desk, behind which sat a glamorous-looking woman of about the same age as Clarke, with dark-brown shoulder-length hair, brown eyes and a lot of make-up. She too was attired in a black short-sleeve shirt and matching trousers, and she went by the name of Sylvia; or at least that's what *her* name badge implied. What's more, as he reached the desk he found her perfume to be a trifle too overpowering.

'Good afternoon,' she said with a winsome smile. 'Welcome to Leverton Golf Club. How may I help you?'

Clarke took a step back before producing his ID card. 'Good afternoon,' he replied with what can only be described as a wince. 'I'm from Leverton CID and I'd like to speak to a member of your staff, please.'

'Oh yes, and who might that be?'

'His name is Marco Rigione.'

At that moment the young couple that he had seen outside entered the clubhouse, but then parted with a kiss. 'You're in luck, Sir.' said the receptionist before pointing in the direction of the door. 'That's Marco over there.'

Clarke turned and glanced at the young man, but as the young girl passed him and headed for the bar, he was now able to discern that the badge on her shirt bore the name Rachel. Thanking the receptionist, he strode over towards the young man and caught him just as he was about to step outside the door.

'Excuse me,' he called out. 'Are you Marco Rigione?'

'Yeah,' grunted the young man with a frown and a puzzled look on his face.

'I'm Detective Chief Inspector Clarke of Leverton CID.'

'Is this about my dad?'

'It is indeed,' replied Clarke. 'You're obviously aware that he's been reported missing by Mrs. Rigione – that is the present Mrs. Rigione?'

Marco ignored the question. 'Have you spoken to *my* mum?'

'I spoke to her this morning,' replied Clarke hurriedly. 'Look, is there somewhere we can talk – I'll try not to keep you too long?'

'This way,' said Marco with a sigh, and Clarke followed him outside.

Crikey, thought Clarke, the lad was almost a spitting image of his father in his youth, what with the olive skin, dark brown eyes and that Grecian nose. He was slow-moving too, and Clarke had the impression that he wasn't very talkative. They appeared to be making their way towards the maintenance buildings, but as they passed the Kawasaki Clarke broke the ice.

'Would that be yours by any chance?'

'Yeah,' replied Marco with a look of pride on his face.

'A present from your father I understand?'

Marco suddenly stopped and turned to face Clarke. 'What's my mum been saying?'

So Clarke told him about the interview that he'd had with his mum, and how she had pointed out that he had witnessed his dad being violent towards her. Then there were the "other women" and Linda, before it all ended in divorce.

'It must have been a difficult time for you – growing up with all that?'

'I suppose it was,' replied Marco with a shrug.

'Was he ever violent towards you?'

Marco seemed to pause briefly before replying. 'He had very little time for me as I was growing up,' he said as if avoiding the question.

Clarke made a mental note of this, but decided to move on to the next question. 'So you were always closer to your mum?'

'I guess so.'

A man of few words indeed, thought Clarke as they eventually reached the maintenance buildings. 'Your mum hinted that you wanted to see your dad punished,' he said suddenly. 'What did she mean by that?'

Marco sighed heavily. 'I just didn't like the way he was treating her,' he mumbled.

'You never thought of stepping in yourself?'

'You don't know what he can be like.'

Oh yes I can, thought Clarke. 'So he *was* violent towards you then?' he asked once more.

'Sometimes,' admitted Marco grudgingly.

'So how did you hope to see him punished?'

'I don't know.'

'Did you ever think of contacting the police?'

Again, Marco hesitated before answering. 'Dad always told me not to trust the police,' he replied with a slight sneer.

Clarke was half-expecting just such a response. One minute the lad's dad is public enemy number one, and the next he's the fount of all bloody wisdom!

'Yes, your mum did say that you and your dad are now reconciled with each other,' said Clarke somewhat wryly. 'How did that come about?'

Marco suddenly seemed to come out of his shell. 'He started seeing me regularly when I was about seventeen,' he replied in a slightly more upbeat manner. 'And he started accompanying me to Donington, Mallory Park and Oulton Park.'

'You take a keen interest in motorcycling then?'

'I've been interested in bikes since I was a kid.'

'And then your dad bought you the Kawasaki?'

'It's not as fast as the Yamaha R7, but I can still reach 100kmph in about four seconds.'

'Is that a fact?' replied Clarke disinterestedly and yet somewhat irked at the lads use of the metric system.

'The R7 picks up nicely at around 4,000 rpm, while the Ninja 650's torque curve is flatter.'

Clarke was beginning to wish that he hadn't mentioned the bloody Kawasaki. 'And your mum said that your dad is helping you out with a course,' he interjected swiftly. 'What course is that, if I may ask?'

'It's a BTEC Level 4 HNC course in Manufacturing Engineering,' replied Marco proudly. 'It's an online course – I started last month.'

'And your dad helped with the fees?'

'That's right.'

'You don't plan on staying here then?'

'I'm fed up with doing mundane jobs – working in supermarkets and now this.'

'What would you like to do?'

'I'd like to manufacture and create my own bike,' was Marco's confident response.

Clarke was visibly impressed. 'Well, I wish you every success in that venture.' he said with a nod of the head. It was almost time to bring the interview to a close, but there was one final question that he needed to ask. 'So your dad never hinted at what his future plans might have been?'

Marco shrugged. 'He never said anything to me.'

'Okay, thanks for your help.'

'Just find out what's happened to him will you?'

'We'll do our best.' And with that Clarke made as if to go, but as he was walking away he suddenly stopped and turned to Marco once more. 'Why are there so many women here today?'

Marco looked at him incredulously. 'It's the Ladies Autumn Club Competition today.'

Ask a silly question, thought Clarke!

Chapter 21

Wednesday, 25 October 2017 (p.m.)

After leaving Leverton Golf Club, Clarke returned to the station to read some of the reports on his desk and then brief DCS Annable on the day's events. As expected, Annable was in one of his tetchy moods and impatient for results, but Clarke had very little to offer on that score, so he was mightily relieved when the briefing ended and he was able to call it a day. It was already dark by the time that he climbed into his car and headed for home, and the rush hour traffic had thankfully all but evaporated. Nevertheless, as he pulled up alongside his narrow boat, *Emily*, he still felt exhausted and ready for a glass or two of *Laphroaig*.

Moored on the port side of the Edgeley Canal and facing the direction of Grimley, *Emily* had been Clarke's sole place of residence for the last three years, and he had never had cause to regret opting for life on board a narrow boat. On the contrary, it was definitely one of his better decisions – or so he told himself.

What's more, since the arrest of Rupert Frankland-Moore back in July he had finally got around to giving *Emily* a lick or two of paint – navy blue with a white roof and trimmings. He'd be the first to admit that it took some motivating, but he decided to take some leave and completed the task to the best of his ability in two weeks. It was a break from the routine of course, but as he stepped into the shower he was conscious of the fact that it hadn't allowed him much time for rest and relaxation. More importantly in his view, he wasn't able to see much of the divine Diana Marshall.

Diana had ferried him back and forth during Rupert's trial in Nottingham (and it was hoped without her husband's knowledge), but he longed to spend more time with her; even a romantic weekend getaway somewhere in the UK would suffice for the time being. Her husband was always going off to Spain on one of his bloody golfing weekends, so why couldn't she make some excuse to take a break now and again?

This was a source of immense frustration to him, but there was nothing he could do about it for the time being, so he climbed out of the shower, dried himself and then donned a black tee-shirt and a pair of khaki-coloured shorts. He wasn't particularly hungry, so he poured himself a large glass of *Laphroaig* and made his way into the saloon. Not what one would describe as a "telly addict," he rummaged around his DVD collection for a couple of minutes before settling for *The Day of the Jackal*, starring Edward Fox in the lead role. He then switched the TV on, inserted the disc into the DVD player, and then sank back into one of the pull-out armchairs to relax and watch the film.

Barely able to stay awake, he had just reached the part in the film where Fox was being interviewed for the role of a contract killer by the French Secret Army Organisation (OAS) when he finally succumbed to slumber.

He was back at school again, and he was being impaled on the wrought iron fence that stood at the front of the main building either side the main door, as he tried to retrieve his scarf; they had taken it from him and thrown it behind the fence. At first he couldn't make out which one of the gang was trying to force him down onto the spikes of the fence, but all the others were laughing. And then he was able to turn as if in slow motion, and he recognised the lad with the short, dark brown, slicked back hair, olive skin, narrow brown eyes and the Roman nose.

It was at this point that he woke with a start and found himself in a cold sweat. It had all seemed so real, and yet it was at one time – long ago.

He shuddered and then looked up at the screen in front of him. To his surprise the film was still playing and it had reached the scene where the British Special Branch discover that a man by the name of Charles Calthrop was believed to have carried out the assassination of a Central American dictator. What's more, further investigations by the Special Branch lead them to discover that one individual bearing the name Charles Calthrop had gone on holiday, leaving his passport at home in the process. This passport, together with the fact that Jackal in French is *Chacal* (the first three letters of his first name and last name respectively), caused the English to assume that this specific Charles Calthrop is the assassin.

His bad dream now seemed to be forgotten as he realised that he needed to pay a call of nature. Rising from the armchair, he pressed the pause button on the remote control and then made his way to the toilet. As he emptied his bladder he began to ponder whether to rewind the DVD or switch it off altogether. After all, he had seen the film countless times, so he wouldn't be duly put out at having missed most of it. And yet there was something about the film that began to nag away at him; something about the character Charles Calthrop and the possibility that he was the man that came to be known as the Jackal, or *Chacal*.

Flushing the toilet, he quickly washed his hands and returned to the saloon. He then rewound the DVD to the scene where the Special Branch first became involved in the search for the Jackal, and then sat forward in his armchair glued to the TV. After a few minutes he pressed the pause button on his remote again - his face was a picture of puzzlement and frustration. What was it about this part of the film that was troubling him? He rewound the tape for a second time – and then a third. But to no avail.

And then he recalled that earlier in the film the assassin (Fox) had scoured a cemetery looking at the headstones in the hope of finding one bearing the name of a child who had died in infancy, but one who had been born roughly around the same time as him. Having succeeded in his quest, he then set off for Somerset House and applied for a copy of the birth certificate of a Paul Oliver Duggan. He then forged the copy and used it to obtain a passport under that name. He also stole the passport of a Swedish tourist and took on his identity too. Now it transpired that he had also adopted the identity of this Charles Calthrop!

But what had this to do with the disappearance of Luciano Rigione? Pouring himself another large glass of whisky, he was confident that it would come to him eventually.

Before heading home to her flat in Nottingham, Detective Sergeant Fletcher had called at the Tesco supermarket at Leverton, where she purchased two bottles of her favourite Argentinian Malbec red wine, among other things. Traffic wasn't as bad as she had thought, and to her relief she was letting herself into the flat less than an hour later. She was immediately greeted by her cat, "Benji", who purred with delight and weaved his way around her legs demanding to be fed.

Having completed that particular task, she then poured herself a glass of wine and made a beeline for the bathroom. Unlike Clarke she preferred a long soak in the bath to a shower, and several minutes later she was blissfully easing herself into the hot, steaming water accompanied by the glass of Malbec.

She too was tired and somewhat exhausted after yet another frustrating day, but she just about managed to prevent herself from closing her eyes and going to sleep. 'Just chill,' she told herself; but that was easier said than done. Taking another sip of wine, her thoughts initially turned to her interviews with the Duckmanton's, and she was convinced that they played no part in the disappearance of Luciano Rigione.

Her mind went back to the team briefing earlier, and the fact that she already had doubts about the direction of the investigation. Indeed, the more she thought about the case, the more she was persuaded to believe that Rigione had actually gone and done a runner.

Perhaps he was planning to leave his wife and had arranged to meet up with a secret lover? Maybe he was in financial difficulty or he'd committed some indiscretion and was concerned that the authorities were on to him? Either way, thought Fletcher, the man had scarpered, and he'd done so using one of the many exit points from the Peacock Pathway.

However, she now faced a dilemma. If she put her case to Clarke in the morning he would no doubt scoff at her, for the simple reason that he was just as convinced that someone had done away with Rigione. But if she went over his head and gave her side of the story to Annable, then Clarke would never forgive her.

'For God's sake snap out of it,' she told herself as she climbed out of the bath, dried herself and then wrapped a bathrobe around her. 'Another glass of Malbec perhaps?' she said to herself. 'I don't see why not.' So she poured her second glass of wine and then curled up on the sofa with her cat.

Turning on the television, she was delighted to see that *Coronation Street* had just started. Unfortunately, however, she did not get to see the full episode, as she too fell asleep almost as soon as the programme had started. Minutes later she was conducting an underwater search of a lake for a missing man; and a man by the name of Clarke!

Chapter 22

Thursday, 26 October 2017 (a.m.)

As Thursday morning broke, the inhabitants of Leverton woke to a drizzling rain, and by the time that those involved in the case revolving around the disappearance of Luciano Rigione arrived for the team briefing at Leverton Police Station at 9.30 a.m. it was still a miserable, drab start to the day.

Although he wasn't feeling particularly miserable (or drab) when he arrived for work, Clarke was nevertheless frustrated at both the lack of progress on the case and his inability as yet to link Brendan Molloy to the disappearance of his boss and former sidekick; for he was still damn sure that Molloy was heavily involved.

He had turned up for the briefing in a suit and tie yet again, much to the merriment of those gathered before him, and yet he had little trouble in quelling this relatively minor disturbance.

'Alright, alright, alright,' he began with a modicum of tedium. 'Can we make a start, please?' He then turned to Fletcher who responded with an update on the searches.

'The underwater teams have finished searching Croxley Lake, Sir,' she stated in a matter-of-fact manner, 'but they have been unable to find anything, apart from several supermarket trolleys.'

'Sounds about right,' he grunted. 'Go on.'

'They'll be searching Riley's Pond today.'

'Okay.'

'Helicopter surveillance and dog searches – indeed all searches – have as yet revealed nothing.' She then continued. 'Oh, and all door-to-door enquiries should be completed today.'

'Do we have *anything* from Rigione's laptops and PC's?'

Webster chimed in. 'Not as yet, Sir.'

'Well it's about time some bugger got their act together,' growled Clarke.

'These things take time, Sir,' replied Webster, half-expecting an expletive-ridden outburst from his boss.

Instead Clarke turned to Fletcher once more. 'How did the interviews with the Duckmanton's go?'

Fletcher was able to confirm that Rigione did indeed try it on with Emma Duckmanton, and having informed her husband of the incident he duly confronted Rigione only to get a bloody nose. 'Emma was then asked to leave Azzurri Furnishings and was given a financial inducement.'

'Do we know how much?' inquired Clarke.

'Five grand,' replied Fletcher.

'And she took it, I assume?'

'She did – and quite readily apparently.'

'Was there anything else?'

'Although Emma and Gary appear to be indifferent to Mr. Rigione's disappearance, I'm convinced that neither of them are involved in any way. They just want to put everything behind them.'

Clarke nodded in appreciation and then suddenly referred back to the previous day's briefing. 'This other athlete we caught on CCTV...'

He was interrupted by a voice from the back of the room. 'That would be "Moonstruck", Sir.'

'What was that?' replied Clarke with a puzzled look on his face.

Fletcher leaned across. 'I think that's Sergeant Meakin, Sir.' She wasn't wrong.

'The man caught on CCTV?' shouted Meakin. 'He's known locally as "Moonstruck", Sir.'

'Would you care to enlarge upon that, Sergeant?' said Clarke, as yet ignorant of the connection between Meakin and the two farmers from Tapley.

And so Meakin went on to tell Clarke and those assembled about Billy Finch, and that "Moonstruck" was one of the names given to him by locals because of his impairment or disorder. 'He lives with his mum on Pit Lane, down by the *Lyttelton Arms*,' recounted Meakin. 'He's in his early sixties, but he's got the mind of a child.'

'Nevertheless,' said Clarke in a serious tone, 'I think someone should go and talk to him and his mother.'

'I can do that, Sir,' shouted Meakin. 'I know the family very well.'

'Fair enough – you do that,' replied Clarke approvingly. He then turned to Webster. 'And what have you managed to uncover, Detective Constable?'

There was a brief pause as Webster frowned and seemed a little troubled by Clarke's decision to allow Meakin to interview the

Finches. 'Oh, yes,' he began somewhat absent-mindedly. 'I went to see the couple who live across the road from the Rigione's, Sir.'

'That would be the Bacon's?'

'That's right, Sir. Well, it's pretty obvious that Mrs. Bacon wears the trousers and...'

'Yes, yes, yes, but get to the point!' said Clarke with a degree of impatience.

'Right...well...apparently Mrs. Bacon complained about parties and wild orgies...' continued Webster, at which there were audible sounds of laughter from some of those assembled.

'Alright, alright,' growled Clarke. 'Settle down and let the man go on.'

'Thank you, Sir,' replied an appreciative Webster before proceeding further. 'Apparently Mrs. Bacon's complaints were met with an abusive and foul-mouthed response from Mr. Rigione.'

'Basically he told them where to shove it?'

'That's right, Sir. However, both Mr. and Mrs. Bacon are adamant that Mr. Rigione poisoned their dog.'

'And what do you think, Webster?'

'I believe that the Bacon's inadvertently and yet foolishly poisoned the dog by giving it tea tree oil, Sir.'

'They did what!' exclaimed a suitably astonished Clarke, accompanied by gasps from those assembled.

Webster went on to describe how the Bacon's were keen adherents of the Green cause and that their kitchen and cupboards were awash with herbal products. 'I've taken away the offending bottle of tea tree oil for analysis, Sir,' continued Webster. 'And if I am right in believing that they did indeed poison their dog with the stuff, then I shall be paying them another visit, Sir.'

'Good,' replied Clarke.

'What's more, I shall give them a right bolloc...' Webster stopped and then corrected himself. 'I mean...I shall seriously admonish them and then have the dog exhumed from their garden for an autopsy.'

Clarke was duly pleased with Webster's work. 'Excellent. Well done!'

But Webster hadn't finished. 'Mrs. Bacon has also been handing out posters around the village with regard to the Rigione's poisoning their dog, and I've told her to get rid of them.'

'And quite right too,' replied Clarke firmly. 'Was there anything else?'

'Mrs. Bacon did suggest that both Mr. *and* Mrs. Rigione were having affairs, Sir.'

'Were any names mentioned?'

'No, Sir.'

'Mmm, interesting,' was Clarke's rather reserved response. There was a brief pause before he went on to tell the audience about his activities the day before. 'Well, I paid a visit to the first Mrs. Rigione and then her son, Marco.'

'Did they divulge anything of significance, Sir?' interjected Fletcher.

'Nothing at all, Sergeant,' replied Clarke, conveniently omitting to tell Fletcher about Phil Whittaker or that he had sent Webster to interview the man. 'And I am fairly certain that neither were involved in Luciano Rigione's disappearance.'

With that he wound up the briefing, but as he sent everyone on their way Fletcher had one more question for him.

'And what will you be doing, Sir?'

'I'm going to see the second Mrs. Rigione again,' he replied pensively. 'You know, I'm sure that woman is hiding something.'

Although she found Clarke's reference to the second Mrs. Rigione as "that woman" a tad too offensive for her liking, Fletcher declined to say as much on this occasion, but she had to admit that he did have a point. 'I tend to agree with you on that score, Sir,' she acknowledged grudgingly.

'Right, I'd like you to continue co-ordinating the searches, Sergeant, if you would, please.'

For someone who always harboured the desire to be engaged in the thick of the action, Clarke's words had a rather deflating effect upon the Deputy Senior Investigating Officer, but her hackles most decidedly began to rise when Clarke called Webster over and asked him to remain momentarily.

'You wanted to know if this Brendan Molloy had a record, Sir?' began Webster.

'I did indeed,' replied Clarke excitedly.

'In 2005 Molloy was arrested for his part in a criminal enterprise that supplied fraudulent passports to organised gangs, including former IRA terrorists.'

'Yes!' exclaimed Clarke as he almost punched the air.

'He was sentenced to four years imprisonment later that year,' whispered Webster with almost equal excitement.

'I bloody well knew it!' shouted Clarke, who was now in a state of what can only be described as euphoria.

This had not gone unnoticed by Fletcher, who stormed across the room in the direction of her two colleagues just as Webster was informing Clarke of his interview with Phil Whittaker.

'Is there something that *I* should know, Sir?' she snapped angrily. 'Something that you're keeping from me – again?'

Clarke was visibly taken aback by this outburst from his second-in-command. 'I beg your pardon?'

'As your Deputy SIO, don't you think that *I* should be kept up-to-date with *all* developments?'

'Quite right, Detective Sergeant – I couldn't agree more. However, whilst you were otherwise engaged yesterday – namely interviewing the Duckmanton's – another potential suspect came onto our radar, and I had no alternative but to ask Webster here to undertake the task of questioning him.'

'Well – who is this potential suspect?' demanded Fletcher tetchily.

And so Clarke referred back to his interview with Yvonne Rigione and to the appointment of her then husband as regional head of the GMB Union. 'Apparently he had a rival for this post.'

'And who might that have been?'

Webster decided to intervene. 'A man by the name of Phil Whittaker,' he replied calmly. 'May I continue?'

'Please do, Detective Constable,' replied Clarke with a degree of firmness.

'Mr. Whittaker confirmed that there was indeed bitterness and rivalry between him and Mr. Rigione before, during and after the election of the latter to the afore-mentioned post, and that blows had been exchanged.'

'Is there more?' asked Clarke.

'Yes there is, Sir. Mr. Whittaker also confirmed that Mr. Rigione quit as regional union leader when it was established that he had indeed been bribing members to win that post. Mr. Whittaker was then elected regional leader unopposed.'

'And do we know anything about his movements at the time of Rigione's disappearance?'

'I'm afraid that Mr. Whittaker has a cast iron alibi, Sir.'

'Well, that rules him out then!'

Fletcher was about to chime in and give her opinion as to the management of the case when Webster cut her short.

'Sir, there's something else that I think you should know.'

'And what would that be, Webster?'

And so Webster recounted the conversation that he had overheard in the station toilets the previous day. 'I wasn't able to hear the entire conversation, Sir, but I rather had the impression that whoever was behind the cubicle was disclosing details of the case to someone.'

'Oh, yes,' replied Clarke abruptly. 'And do you know who this person was, Webster?'

'I am fairly certain that it was Sergeant Meakin, Sir.'

The response from Clarke was immediate. 'Right, Webster, you go and catch up with Meakin and tell him that he is to continue with door-to-door enquiries.' As Webster duly set off in pursuit of Sergeant Meakin, Clarke turned to Fletcher. 'And you can go and interview the Finches, Sergeant.'

'Thank you, Sir,' replied Fletcher gratefully and excitedly before heading off to Pit Lane and the Finches. At least she was getting involved again and Clarke had now brought her up-to-date with the case – or so she thought. Had she known that Clarke had kept from her the fact that Brendan Molloy had a criminal record then she might not have been so upbeat – or forgiving!

Chapter 23

Thursday, 26 October 2017 (a.m.)

It was still drizzling with rain when Fletcher pulled up outside the terraced house on Pit Lane to question Shirley Finch and her son, Billy. She knew nothing about the family other than what Sergeant Meakin had related earlier, but at least she was doing *something* – or so she thought. And what could it be that Meakin was up to? No doubt all would be revealed sooner or later.

The Finches lived in the middle of the three terraced houses that stood opposite the site of what was once the Tapley Colliery. There was a shared entry either side of the building that led to the rear of the house and an enclosed garden area (of sorts), and a brick wall at the front together with a wrought iron gate. The wall was about chest height and it was separated from the front door by a couple of feet. Above the door was a large bracket, from which a hanging basket had probably hung during the summer months. To the right of the door was a large window (curtains drawn), beneath which was an empty wall trough planter.

Opening the gate, Fletcher literally winced as it made a terrible screeching sound, and she was loathe to close it again until she departed. She knocked on the door and within seconds it was opened by a small, unassuming woman with grey hair and glasses, and she was wearing slippers and a lime-green cardigan over a floral-patterned dress.

'Mrs. Finch – Mrs. Shirley Finch?' began Fletcher.

'I hope you're not selling anything, luv?' replied Shirley with a slight frown.

Fletcher broke into a smile and shook her head in response. 'No, no – nothing like that. I'm Detective Sergeant Jacqui Fletcher from Leverton CID,' she said as she proffered her identity card.

'Oh, I see.'

'We're investigating the disappearance of one of the residents of Tapley, a Mr. Luciano Rigione...'

'Who did you say?' shouted Shirley with yet another puzzled look on her face.

'A Mr. Luciano Rigione,' shouted Fletcher in return.

'I've never heard of him.'

'I understand that your son lives with you?'

'That's right.'

'He may have been a witness to Mr. Rigione's disappearance – may I come in?'

'Yes, but I doubt if he'll be of much help, luv.'

'Thank you.'

With that Shirley beckoned Fletcher into the house, and closed the front door behind them. As Fletcher stepped inside she was confronted by another door which led into the hallway. On her left several coats hung from the coat hangers. Up ahead was a staircase which apparently led to two double bedrooms and a bathroom with toilet. On her immediate right was a door leading to the living room, and at the foot of the stairs another door on the right led to the dining room and kitchen. There was also a ground floor toilet beyond this.

'We'd be better off in the dining room,' said Shirley with a weak smile. 'Come this way.'

'That's fine by me, Mrs. Finch,' replied Fletcher.

'Please call me Shirley, luv – Mrs. Finch sounds so formal.'

'Okay, Shirley it is.'

'Sit yourself down then, luv – would you like a cuppa?'

'No, I'm fine, thank you,' replied Fletcher, who by now was becoming frustrated and irritated by what she deemed to be the lack of progress. 'As I said, it's your son I've come to speak to.'

'He hasn't done anything wrong, has he?'

'No, it's just that he was seen on CCTV cameras near *The Lyttelton Arms* on the morning Mr. Rigione went missing, and he may have witnessed something that could be vital to the development of the case.'

'Like what?'

'We don't know as yet.'

'Well he was out running up and down the lane as he does most days just lately, but he came back when it started to rain.'

'Nevertheless, I'd like to speak to him if I may?'

'He's upstairs in his room, but as I say I don't think you'll get much out of him.' She then made her way to the foot of the stairs and called out to her son. 'Billy? Can you come down here, luv – there's somebody wants to talk to you.'

Shirley returned to the living room and gave yet another weak smile to Fletcher, who heard movement up above followed by what sounded to her like quick steps coming down the staircase. Seconds later the dining room door opened and Fletcher sat mouth agape as she was confronted by a middle-aged man in vest and shorts who proceeded to jog on the spot before her very eyes.

'Well...I...would...' began a clearly flustered Fletcher.

'Stop that now, Billy,' whispered Shirley in a gentle but firm manner. 'This lady is from the police and she'd like to ask you some questions.' At which her son immediately stopped jogging on the spot and stood ramrod to attention.

Fletcher pulled herself together and tried again. 'I understand that you were out running on Tuesday morning, Billy. Is that right?'

Still at attention, Billy turned to look at his mother as if seeking her permission to reply. She nodded her head, at which Billy barked out in military fashion 'Yes, Miss!'

Feeling slightly more confident, Fletcher continued. 'Did you see anyone else out running on Tuesday morning, Billy?'

Billy looked at his mother once more and upon receiving her approval he shouted 'Training for the Olympics, Miss!'

Before Fletcher had any chance to reply Billy suddenly bent down and started touching his toes. His mother stepped in and admonished him once more. 'Billy, stop doing that,' she said with a little more firmness.

As he stood to attention again, Fletcher continued. 'Yes, so I understand from your mother.' She then produced a photograph and showed it to Billy. 'Did you see this man at all while you were out running?'

Billy glanced at the photograph briefly and then looked straight ahead again. 'Training for the Olympics, Miss,' he repeated, almost as if he were on a drill square.

Shirley could see that Fletcher was showing signs of frustration. 'I did say that you would have difficulty getting anything out of him, Sergeant,' she said with yet another weak smile.

Realising that she wasn't going to get anywhere, Fletcher agreed to halt the questioning. As she thanked Billy, a look of indignation appeared upon his face together with a deep frown, but as he looked down at his mother once more she merely nodded her approval.

Clearly vexed at the reactions of the policewoman *and* his mother, he started jogging on the spot again – and with more vigour.

As Shirley led Fletcher to the door she apologised for her son's behaviour and for the fact that she was unable to be more helpful.

'I'm sorry, but I did tell you,' she said ruefully.

'That's alright, Mrs. Finch,' replied Fletcher with a weak smile of her own and one that hid her immense frustration. 'Waste of bloody time that was,' she heard herself say as she closed the screeching gate behind her.

She had almost reached her car when she suddenly heard a noise behind her, and looking back over her shoulder she saw Billy Finch standing at the front door of the house behind his mother and shouting 'Training for the Olympics!'

Chapter 24

Thursday, 26 October 2017 (a.m.)

'That bloody copper,' said Linda Rigione under her breath. And she wasn't talking about DCI Clarke either!

As Family Liaison Officer, DC Laura Preston had stuck rigidly to her orders so far, and she had barely let Linda out of her sight. It was beginning to get to Linda big time, but somehow she managed to bite her lip. She was curled up on the sofa in the lounge sipping yet another brandy and coke on this particular morning, whilst Preston sat opposite her on one of the easy chairs flicking through a magazine somewhat disinterestedly.

'I don't suppose you'll join me in having a drink?' snapped Linda suddenly in a rather snarky manner.

'Sorry, but not while I'm on duty,' replied Preston rather meekly.

'Shit!' grunted Linda looking down at the table beside her. 'Looks like I'll have to get some more coke from the kitchen – is that alright with you?' she said whilst waving an empty bottle in the air. Preston merely shrugged in approval, and with that Linda rose from the sofa and headed for the kitchen – followed by Preston!

Linda was about to turn on Preston when through the kitchen window she saw Clarke climbing out of his silver Ford Focus outside. She looked up to the ceiling, shook her head and gave a heavy sigh.

Unable to follow Linda's gaze, Preston sensed that they were about to receive a visitor. 'Who is it?' she asked as she attempted to strain her neck.

'Hercules bloody Poirot is here again I see!'

Preston didn't have to ask who she meant by that rather caustic remark, and as the doorbell rang she turned on her toes to open the front door for her superior.

'Hello, Sir.'

'Morning, Preston,' replied Clarke as he stepped inside. 'How's Mrs. Rigione?'

'Still not giving much away I'm afraid, Sir.'

'No, I don't suppose she is.'

'I'm in here,' shouted Linda from the lounge, and as the two detectives entered the room she raised her freshly replenished glass of brandy and coke in the air.

As Clarke looked at her, Linda's high cheekbones seemed to be tinged with red, and the thin, piercing blue eyes had taken on a glazed grey colour, but he put it all down to the effects of alcohol. 'Hello again, Linda,' he said in what can only be described as a rather doleful voice – and expression.

'Ah, Inspector Clarke, how nice to see you again,' she said sarcastically once more. 'Do take a seat, please.'

'Thanks, but I'd rather stand,' he replied firmly.

'Please yourself,' she answered in a rather devil-may-care manner. 'Have you found my husband yet?' she then asked rather brusquely.

'Well, I can tell you that we...'

She cut him short and leaned forward on the sofa. '*Have you found my bloody husband yet?*' she snarled aggressively.

Clarke paused briefly before replying and then looked her straight in the eyes. 'No, Linda, we haven't.' She sank back onto the sofa as he continued. 'It's my belief that some of those questioned so far are withholding evidence or simply not telling us the truth.'

She shot him a quick glance. 'Are you including *me* in that statement?'

'I'll come to that in a moment,' he said brushing aside her question. 'But what I *can* tell you is that all of our searches have as yet failed to reveal anything – and that goes for our door-to-door inquiries too.'

'And is that it?'

He changed tack. 'I find it odd that none of your neighbours or other members of the community have come forward to help in the search for your husband?'

'We haven't been here long,' she replied with a shrug of the shoulders.

'Or could it be that your husband wasn't very popular with the locals?'

'Absolute nonsense!' she protested vigorously.

'He certainly wasn't popular with the Meakin's up at the farm, was he?'

'I thought we'd discussed that?'

He ignored her and moved on to the Bacon's. 'We have spoken to your neighbours across the road...'

'What – that pair of bloody idiots?' she scoffed.

'We believe that they inadvertently poisoned their dog...'

'I could have told *you* that,' she said scornfully as she turned her head away from him.

'We are looking into that probability as we speak. If that is the case, then they will be cautioned and they could face a term of imprisonment.'

'What about those bloody posters?'

'You won't be seeing them again.'

'Thank God!' she exclaimed with some relief.

'We've also spoken to Emma and Gary Duckmanton. Emma was able to confirm that your husband tried it on with her, and both she and her husband confirmed the...shall we say...altercation between him and your husband.'

'So what?' she shrugged.

'Well, far from leaving Azzurri Furnishings under a cloud, you gave Emma a financial inducement and sent her packing – five grand it was said.'

'She could hardly stay there, could she?'

'You never thought of admonishing your husband for his little indiscretion, which – I hasten to add – was witnessed by most of the workforce?'

'What was the point?'

'Or could it be that you too were having an affair and one which your husband was aware of?'

There was a long pause before Linda gave her reply. 'It was nothing,' she said with yet another shrug of the shoulders.

'Would you care to go into more detail?'

'Okay, so I had a brief fling with someone,' she admitted grudgingly. 'It was a case of anything he could do...'

'And you ended the affair?'

'Yes, I did,' she replied.

But Clarke detected a brief and yet noticeable pause in her reply. It was a split second maybe, but it was sufficient to for him to be unconvinced by her answer. 'I wonder,' he said laconically.

Linda turned on him immediately. 'And what's *that* supposed to mean?' she snapped angrily.

Clarke ignored her momentarily. 'Mr. Molloy – the works foreman?'

'What about him?'

'He came across as being somewhat defensive and protective towards you when I interviewed him on Tuesday afternoon – that is with regard to your husband's little infidelities, shall we say?'

Linda seemed noticeably ruffled by Clarke's question. 'Well, he's known my husband – Luciano – a long time,' she said with a degree of apprehension. 'He knows what he can be like.'

Clarke considered taking Linda's mobile phone away for examination at that particular moment, but he decided to give her the benefit of the doubt for the time being and brought the conversation to a close. 'Well, I think that's all for now, Linda,' he said with a slightly smug smile.

'Thank Christ for that,' she replied sardonically. She literally felt exhausted and that she had been interrogated yet again; which she was to some degree. But Clarke had one last parting shot to make.

'Oh, I almost forgot,' he said a trifle absent-mindedly. I've also spoken to the first Mrs. Rigione and her son.'

'And what did they have to say?'

'They were very helpful of course, but I'm confident that neither of them has played a part in your husband's disappearance.'

'I'm pleased to hear it,' she replied with a sense of relief.

'But I shall be speaking to Mr. Molloy again soon,' he said as he turned and headed for the front door. As Linda rose from the sofa he shouted over his shoulder. 'Thanks, but I can see myself out!'

There had been outbreaks of chronic copper poisoning amongst some of the cattle at a number of farms in the area recently, so the Meakin's of Upper Grange Farm deemed it wise to call out the veterinary surgeon to carry out an inspection of their herd. Mercifully for them he had given them the all clear, and he was just emerging from the cowshed with Kath Meakin when Clarke pulled into the yard in his Ford Focus five minutes after leaving Linda Rigione. Parting company with the vet, Kath Meakin made her way over to Clarke as he climbed out of his car.

'Thought we might be seein' you again,' she said with the semblance of a smile.

'I take it that was the vet?' replied Clarke ignoring her remark.

'Just a precautionary measure, Inspector - we dunna want copper poisonin' amongst our 'erd.

'I should hope not,'

Preliminaries over, Kath decided to establish the reason for Clarke's visit. 'So, what brings you 'ere again?'

'Your husband's younger brother?' replied Clarke inquisitively.

'Which one are you referrin' to?'

'Peter.'

'What about 'im?'

'Are he and your husband close?'

'Why do you ask?'

It's going to be one of those days, thought Clarke to himself. 'It's just that we believe that Peter has been tipping you off about the progress of the case.'

'Nowt wrong with that is there?' replied Kath with a shrug.

Clarke paused as if to gather his thoughts before proceeding with his next question. 'Well, it might be construed that you and your husband have something to hide,' he said eventually. 'Especially as he and Mr. Rigione were hardly on friendly terms.'

'We got nowt to 'ide,' she said adamantly.

'Are you sure about that, Mrs. Meakin?'

'I told you, the name's Kath!' she snapped. 'And what's that supposed to mean?'

Clarke made no attempt to answer her question; he'd made his point. 'I'll be leaving now, Mrs. Meakin,' he said deliberately ignoring her entreaty. 'But I think it highly likely that I shall be returning before long.'

As he turned and headed for his car, a young woman came out of the house attired in a black short-sleeve shirt and matching trousers. What's more, there was a name badge above her left breast that bore the name Rachel. It was the girl that he had seen with Marco Rigione at the golf club on the previous day. Clarke would be the first to admit that he had little confidence with the opposite sex, but on this occasion he decided to make a point of introducing himself.

'Hello,' he began somewhat gingerly. 'I believe that our paths crossed yesterday at the golf club.'

'Did they?' replied Rachel Meakin nervously.

'Yes, you were with the young gentleman that I came to interview.'

'I don't know what you mean.'

'Yes, you do. You were with Mr. Rigione before you headed off to the bar.'

Rachel glanced quickly at her mother who was still standing nearby, and this prompted Clarke to turn his head in the same direction. He may have been wrong of course, but unless he was very much mistaken the look on Kath Meakin's face said it all – if looks could kill!

Chapter 25

Thursday, 26 October 2017 (p.m.)

Although he was still no nearer to finding out what had happened to Luciano Rigione, DCI Clarke was in a somewhat upbeat mood when he arrived back at Leverton police station. He had left Linda Rigione and Kath Meakin in absolutely no doubt whatsoever that he knew that they were either lying through their teeth or keeping something from him, and he had discovered that *his* prime suspect, Brendan Molloy, did indeed have a criminal record. So yes, it wasn't all doom and gloom!

He had barely set foot in his office when Sergeant Fletcher knocked on the door and stepped in to inform him of her visit to the Finches.

'How did you get on?' he asked in the hope that she had something positive to report.

'Waste of time, Sir,' she replied, barely able to disguise her frustration. 'The man – or should I say boy, as he clearly has the mental age of a juvenile – just kept repeating himself and letting it be known that he was "training for the Olympics" or something like that!'

'This would be Billy Finch, I take it?'

'It would indeed.'

'And his mother wasn't able to add anything?'

'Only that her son had been running up and down the lane on the morning of Rigione's disappearance.'

'Well at least you tried,' said Clarke forlornly. Fletcher was again about to give her opinion as to the management of the case when he spoke out again. 'Get Webster in here will you – but I want you to stay too, Sergeant.'

Ah well, better luck next time, thought Fletcher as she went to fetch Webster. Several minutes later Webster followed Fletcher into the office, and he stood before the boss with a smile like a Cheshire Cat. 'You wanted me, Sir?'

The look on Clarke's face was one of disdain intermingled with resignation, and shaking his head he casually asked the young detective to take a seat. 'Pull up a chair, Webster – and you too Sergeant.' Webster and Fletcher did as requested – the former more eagerly than the latter. 'I don't suppose they've found anything that might lead us to find out what has become of Rigione?' said Clarke as he gave Webster a decidedly dejected look.

'As I said, Sir, these things take time.'

'Nevertheless,' he snapped. 'I remain convinced that there is fraudulent activity going on at Azzurri Furnishings and that it is linked to his disappearance.'

Fletcher glanced at Webster and the two detectives raised their eyebrows in unison. 'What have you in mind, Sir?' asked Fletcher with discernable trepidation.

'Have either of you heard of "Authorised Push Payments", otherwise known as APP scams?'

'Isn't that where money is transferred into a fraudulent account, Sir?' replied Fletcher with a frown.

'That's right, Sergeant. To achieve this criminals mostly resort to identity theft, passing themselves off as a supplier, an employee or a manager.'

'And you think that this may have happened at Azzurri Furnishings?' she asked somewhat warily.

'Let's just say that I have a sneaking suspicion that someone may have committed invoice fraud, Sergeant,' he said with a wry grin.

'Go on, Sir.'

'It's like this, Sergeant,' he began rather cockily. 'The perpetrator draws up fraudulent invoices and processes them in the supplier system...'

'And they can also make transfers for personal use through business bank accounts, can they not?' she said interrupting him.

'Well done, Sergeant, you'll go far,' he said somewhat drily. His remarks brought a smile to her face, but then he suddenly slapped the desk with his left hand and turned to Webster, who seemed to jump a mile in response. 'We've got possession of the laptops, have we not?'

'That's right, Sir,' replied a suddenly re-invigorated Webster.

'Here's what I want you to do, Webster.' The excitement in Clarke's voice was tangible. 'Get yourself down to forensics or wherever they're holding the buggers and get me a list of *all* the suppliers for Azzurri Furnishings.'

'You're not interested in employees then, Sir?'

'Not at the moment, Webster – just suppliers.'

'Right you are, Sir.' And with that Webster set off on his assignment like a born again gun dog, sent to retrieve the game!

Clarke sat back in his swivel chair with a look of smug contentment on his face, but Fletcher still had her doubts. 'You really do think that we're on the right track, don't you?' she suggested with a hint of pessimism in her voice.

'Yes I do,' he snapped. 'What's more, I think that I know where that track will lead!'

It didn't take Webster long to achieve the task of obtaining a list of suppliers, as Clarke had requested, and it was with a triumphant look on his face that he subsequently re-entered the latter's office bearing a number of print-outs.

'Well done, Webster,' said Clarke excitedly. 'Did you have any trouble getting hold of them?'

'They were a bit peeved at first, Sir,' replied Webster grinning all over his face once more, 'but when I told them that you wanted them pronto they were only too happy to oblige.'

The three detectives then proceeded to comb through the print-outs, looking for anything that might be construed as suspicious or out of the ordinary, but after only twenty minutes or so Fletcher's frustration got the better of her. 'Oh, this is ridiculous,' she suddenly said with undisguised irritation. 'How the hell are we supposed to know what we're looking for?'

'Just keep looking, Sergeant,' replied Clarke through gritted teeth, 'if it's not too much trouble.'

Duly chastened, Fletcher continued to trawl through the print-outs, albeit reluctantly. A couple of minutes later Webster suddenly began chortling to himself.

'Something amusing you, Webster?' said Clarke with a vexed look on his face.

'There's one here that says *John J. Lydon & Son*,' replied Webster, who by now was almost beside himself with laughter. 'I didn't know Johnny Rotten was involved in the upholstery trade,' he sniggered.

Clarke suddenly sat bolt upright. 'Give that here,' he snapped, and then suddenly snatched the print-out from Webster, who *still* chuckled away at what he thought was a rather amusing quip. But it was no joke; at least it wasn't to Clarke. Indeed, as he looked down at the print-out and the name *John J. Lydon & Son* his heart began to pound. Beads of sweat appeared on his frown and at that precise moment his phone suddenly burst into life. He picked it up immediately. 'What!' he bellowed; at which both Fletcher and Webster quite literally jumped out of their skins.

And then suddenly there came the softly spoken voice of Joel Bishop of the Leverton Gazette on the other end of the line. 'Hello Allan,' he began calmly. 'I can see you're in a good mood as usual. Shall I call back when it's more convenient?'

The look of embarrassment on Clarke's face said it all. 'I'm so sorry, Joel. I didn't mean to snap your head off like that.' The look of amusement on Fletcher and Webster's faces was equally perceptible as they took great pleasure in the discomfort of their boss.

'That's alright, Allan. I've become used to it in recent years!'

Clarke continued to squirm in his swivel chair, but sought to overcome his present malaise by getting the conversation moving along. 'What can I do for you, Joel?' he said as if nothing had happened.

'Well, I was just wondering how the case was going, that's all.'

'Not to put too fine a point on it, I'd have to say that we're struggling, Joel.'

Bishop picked up on Clarke's frustration. 'That bad, is it?' he replied earnestly. 'So, there are no suspects as yet?'

Clarke gestured to Fletcher and Webster to leave the office. 'And close the door behind you,' he barked. The two detectives did as requested and Clarke resumed his conversation with Bishop. 'I shouldn't be telling you this, Joel, but there *is* someone who I believe may be implicated in Rigione's disappearance.'

'Are you prepared to give me a name?' replied Bishop hopefully.

'This is just between you and me, Joel, and it mustn't go no further.'

'You have my word.'

'Brendan Molloy,' whispered Clarke. 'He's the foreman at Azzurri Furnishings and a former schoolmate of the missing man.'

'What makes you think that he's implicated?'

'I don't bloody like him for starters!' snapped Clarke.

'Oh well, if *you* don't like him then he's got to be guilty, hasn't he?' replied Bishop mockingly and yet with a sense of frustration. Then he suddenly paused for several moments before continuing. 'Wait a minute,' he said pensively. 'Now you come to mention it that name does ring bells.'

'How do you mean?'

'Can I come back to you on that one, Allan, old boy?'

'If you must,' replied Clarke with a touch of resignation.
'I'd like to trawl through our files – I may have something for you.'
'Bye for now, Joel.'
'Bye,'

Clarke put the phone down and sat back again for a few moments. He contemplated going through the print-outs on his own, but then decided against it. Boy, what he'd give for a glass of Laphroaig right now! Trouble was, he was running low on stock if he remembered rightly. He was just about to call it a day when the phone rang yet again.

'What!' he roared as he picked up the receiver.

He recognised the voice on the other end of the phone immediately. 'Clarke?' It was Superintendent Annable.

'Sorry, Sir,' he replied almost dejectedly. 'It's been one of those days.'

'I've just come back from a meeting with the ACC,' said Annable somewhat gravely. 'She's not happy with the progress of this case and nor for that matter am I. What have you got to tell me about today's events?'

'Not a lot really, Sir,' replied Clarke sheepishly. 'But I get the sense that we're getting closer to establishing what became of Mr. Rigione, and for that reason I'd like a little more time to...'

But Annable cut him short. 'I want you *and* DS Fletcher in my office at eight o'clock in the morning – sharp!' he grunted before slamming the phone down.

'Shit!' exclaimed Clarke with due vehemence. There was only one thing for it as he saw things. Grabbing his coat, he stormed out of his office and the building before climbing into his car to head for home. However, he did have one more task to fulfil before reaching his destination. He paid a visit to the Tesco supermarket. Not that he had any shopping to do. No, there was only one item on his receipt – and it showed twenty-five quid!

At the same time that Clarke was purchasing his bottle of *Laphroaig* whisky from the Tesco supermarket, Rachel Meakin had just arrived home from work.

'There you are,' snapped her mother. 'I want a word with you, young lady.'

'Is that right,' replied Rachel dismissively.

'And don't come that bugger with me, madam – you know very well what I'm talkin' about!'

'What if I do?'

'What the bloody 'ell do you think you're playin' at?' shouted Kath aggressively. 'Gettin' involved with the offspring of that bastard, Rigione?'

'What's it got to do with you?' snapped Rachel.

'Your dad will go up t'bloody wall if 'e finds out!'

'We love each other.'

'Love each other, my arse! You're both barely out o' school!'

'Stay out of my life,' screamed Rachel, before storming off upstairs to her bedroom.

'You 'aven't 'eard the last o' this, young lady!' shouted her mother after her. 'I can promise you that!'

Rachel had been expecting this from the moment that copper turned up at the farm. She had tried to keep the affair from her parents from the outset, but that *bloody* copper had to open his *bloody* mouth, didn't he? Dropped her right in it, he did! What was she going to do now? There was nothing else for it. She took out her mobile phone and sent off a text message that read "We need to talk"!

Chapter 26

Friday, 27 October 2017 (a.m.)

Clarke was crashed out on top of the bed in t-shirt and underpants when the alarm clock went off at 7.00 a.m. that Friday morning. 'Jesus H. Christ,' he shouted as he woke with a start. He really shouldn't have shouted.

Not for the first time – and probably not the last – he had a truly horrendous hangover complete with an almighty headache. The offending bottle of *Laphroaig* whisky (and glass) stood beside him on the bedside table and it was half empty (or half full, depending on how one looks at these things). What was that about 'never again' he'd said a few weeks previously? Oh God, why did he do these things, he asked himself for the umpteenth time. And then it hit him. Meeting with Annable at 8.00 a.m. – sharp!

Deeming it wise not to move quickly, he slowly but surely inched himself out of bed until he stood a trifle unsteadily on his feet, and then he glared at the offending bottle of *Laphroaig* with eyes narrowed, almost as if to say 'I'll deal with you later!' He then sluggishly left the bedroom for the loo; the noise as he pulled the chain didn't help to ease his throbbing head. Making his way to the fridge in the saloon was by no means an easy task, but he did remember to snatch a couple of paracetamol caplets from the cupboard above. Bugger what the so-called "experts" had to say about these things and alcohol!

There was a large bottle of Buxton water in the fridge – sparkling of course – and he downed most of that in one go! He then climbed the two steps to the rear doors of the narrow boat and upon opening these he stepped onto the deck. The fresh air hit him immediately and he swayed slightly as a result. Thankfully it wasn't raining this morning and although it was still dark at that moment it would soon be getting light. Enough of this, he said to himself – it was time for a shower.

Minutes later and he had divested himself of the t-shirt and underpants, and was standing in the shower, absorbing the effects of the hot water. He still wasn't entirely convinced that a morning shower could act as a positive influence upon his mood or that it might increase his productivity level, but it sure as hell allowed space for some quiet time alone with his thoughts.

And what were his thoughts as the water cascaded down upon his head and body? At that particular moment he would have welcomed the prospect of Diana Marshall climbing into the shower to join him, but this and other slightly lascivious thoughts were tempered by the fact that he had to be in DCS Annable's office within the half hour, and by the time he climbed out of the shower his mood was far from being positive!

Indeed, what *had* Annable got in store for him? What's the betting it wouldn't be pleasant or to his betterment, he thought as he quickly dried himself with a fresh towel. His mood had not improved by the time he got dressed. Shirt, tie, trousers and socks were all selected and donned with a premonition of doom and gloom, and by the time he had given his shoes a good polish and grabbed at the nearby jacket he was again wondering why the bloody hell he had taken on the case in the first place. No, something was coming his way this morning, and he just knew that he wasn't going to like it!

Snatching at his car keys, he climbed the steps to the deck once more, locked up and headed for the Ford Focus. For a moment he sat before the steering wheel and pondered as to whether he should insert a CD. He decided against it. Besides, what was the point? There was only one song that was appropriate for his mood and state of mind on this particular morning, and as he turned the key in the ignition to start the car up he suddenly found himself belting out the words from *The Pirates of Penzance*:

> *When constabulary duty's to be done, to be done,*
> *A policeman's lot is not a happy one, happy one.*

As Clarke pulled into the car park at Leverton Police Station, Detective Sergeant Fletcher was just climbing out of her Mini Cooper convertible, having also been told to attend the meeting in Superintendent Annable's office that morning. She locked her car doors and then waited for Clarke in the middle of the car park.

'I wonder what DCS Annable has in store for us, Sir?' she shouted above the noise of the nearby traffic.

Clarke appeared to wince as he made his reply. 'We shall have to see, Sergeant, won't we?'

Fletcher caught him by the arm as he approached – he didn't look at all well. 'Are you okay, Sir?' she asked in a deeply concerned manner.

He was obviously still feeling the effects of his hangover. 'There's nothing wrong with me – alright?' he snapped. He wasn't entirely sure, but he could have sworn that Fletcher's eyebrows were raised in response to his last comment!

They both entered the building together, but not another word was said as they made their way to Annable's office. Entering the foyer outside Annable's office, they were met by his secretary, WPC Prentiss. She knocked on Annable's door as the clock struck eight.

'Entaaah,' came the loud and penetrating voice from within.

'DCI Clarke and DS Fletcher to see you, Sir,' said WPC Prentiss diligently as she opened the door and directed them into Annable's office.

He was evidently busy adding his signature to a number of documents. 'Take a seat both of you,' he barked without looking up, and the two detectives did as requested.

Even when seated he cut an imposing figure, and although he was only slightly taller than Clarke he seemed to tower over Fletcher. There wasn't a grey hair in sight either – proof that the *Men Only, H-45 Dark Brown* hair shampoo was working in his eyes. The desk was neat and tidy, and as always the two family photographs stood before him; one of wife, Julie, and the other of the two of them with their three children.

At last he stopped writing and sat back in his swivel chair, glaring at the two detectives with that almost permanent frown of his. Bringing his shovel-like hands together, he suddenly made his feelings known.

'As I pointed out to you last night, Clarke, neither I nor the ACC are at all happy with the progress of this case,' he boomed. 'Indeed, we seem to have got absolutely nowhere; no body – nothing. And as we all know, nothing can come of nothing!'

Clarke groaned inwardly at yet another of Annable's Shakespearean quotes before replying. 'It is still my belief that foul play has occurred, Sir, and that we are getting closer to establishing the truth of what happened to...'

Annable interrupted him. 'Where is your evidence for this?' he snapped in a very brusque manner. 'The searches have yielded nothing to suggest that Rigione has been done away with. Indeed, we have almost exhausted *all* lines of enquiry in that respect.'

Clarke attempted to put together a coherent answer. 'I beg your pardon, Sir, but whoever is behind the disappearance of...'

But Annable cut him short again and turned to Fletcher. 'What are your thoughts on this, Sergeant?'

She had been waiting for this moment almost from the outset, and she wasn't going to pull any punches. 'It is my belief that Mr. Rigione has staged his own disappearance, Sir,' she began calmly and succinctly. 'Furthermore, I also believe that he has fled the scene and may even be out of the country by now.'

'I am inclined to agree with you, Sergeant,' said Annable pensively. 'Indeed, to that end...'

But Clarke was having none of it. 'Absolute rubbish!' he scoffed. 'For crying out loud, the man was seen on CCTV cameras at both *The Lyttelton Arms* and at Sibley Lake...'

Fletcher turned to face him with a look of undisguised contempt. 'With *all* due respect, Sir,' she snapped angrily. 'He could have come off the Peacock Pathway at *any* time thereafter, using alternative routes or footpaths.'

'When you've been in this game as long as I have, young lady...'

'Who the hell do you think you are talking to...'

Annable realised that it was time he stepped in. 'When you have *both* quite finished,' he stood and bellowed, causing one of the two photographs on his desk to topple over. The two detectives turned to face him. 'I will *not* have my senior officers at each other's throats – do I make myself clear?'

The ploy worked. 'Yes, Sir,' replied Clarke and Fletcher in unison.

Annable took his seat once more. 'Thank you,' he shouted with some relief before continuing. 'As you are now both aware, I had a meeting with the ACC yesterday, and it transpires that there is an ongoing parallel investigation into the disappearance of Mr. Rigione.'

Whereas Fletcher's face and body language betrayed a sense of excitement and triumph at Annable's remarks, Clarke looked positively aghast. 'What parallel investigation?' he queried anxiously.

Annable pressed the buzzer on his desk. 'Has the officer from the National Crime Agency arrived yet, Prentiss?' he asked.

'Yes, Sir,' she replied.

'Send him in will you, please.'

'I'll do that right away, Sir.'

It was clear that Clarke *still* hadn't quite grasped what was happening before his eyes. 'National Crime Agency?' he said with a look of complete bewilderment.

It was only when the door opened and Annable made the introductions that the look on Clarke's face turned from one of bewilderment to that of sheer horror and utter demoralisation.

'Ah, do come in.' said Annable positively beaming with delight. 'I understand that you know Detective Chief Inspector Clarke,' he continued as Detective Sergeant Donal Cullinan of the National Crime Agency held out his hand!

Chapter 27

Friday, 27 October 2017 (a.m.)

It was one of those déjà vu moments; and one which revived some rather unpleasant memories for Clarke. He was a Detective Sergeant with the Drugs Squad on the Derby City Police Force. The year was 2009 and the team were joined by an arrogant and yet hard-working new Detective Constable by the name of Donal Cullinan.

Then aged thirty, Cullinan was six feet and two inches in height, with a shaven head and brown eyes. His dark, bushy eyebrows always reminded Clarke of former Labour Party Chancellor, Denis Healey, and of course the large, fleshy nose, big ears and thick lips were still prominent, so little had changed on that score. To give him his due, he always came into work smartly attired in a two-piece suit and tie, but now he appeared before Clarke in a black cotton nylon shacket, with a white t-shirt, dark blue jeans and trainer's. It was a wonder Annable didn't give him a right bollocking!

The son of an Irish bricklayer from Donegal, he was born in Derby and always wanted to join the police (against his father's wishes). Having done exceptionally well at school (6 GCSE's), he enrolled on the Police Constable Degree Apprenticeship with Derbyshire Constabulary in 1995. This led to the University of Derby three years later and a BA with Honours in Professional Policing. He then returned to the Derbyshire Constabulary. Having successfully applied to become a detective in 2009, he was assigned to Derby CID as a Detective Constable later that year; which is when he came into contact with Clarke.

Of course 2009 was the year in which Clarke was suspended from duty by his boss, DCI Maxine Greenhough, for allegedly stealing confiscated drugs and supplying them back to criminal gangs. He always suspected that Cullinan had played a part in his suspension, purely in order to ingratiate himself with his superiors, but he was never able to prove it. Then it transpired that it was actually Greenhough who had committed the crime as part of her involvement in a major drug supply conspiracy, and he was allowed to return to duty. In spite of the fact that he was completely innocent of any wrongdoing, Cullinan gave him the cold shoulder thereafter until he was posted back to Leverton following the establishment of the East Midlands Regional Police in 2011.

Cullinan evidently remained with the Drugs Squad in Derby. Promoted to Detective Sergeant in 2014, he was seconded to the National Crime Agency (NCA) a year later. Having never married, he continued to live in the Derby area.

Coming from humble beginnings, he seemed to possess a remarkable ability that set him apart from others, but Clarke would say that he liked to give the impression that he had always been aware of this ability. It was as if he was constantly trying to battle a powerful foe for a righteous purpose, but then as Clarke remembered all too well he did have a tendency to become a workaholic, which was undoubtedly his way of responding to stress.

Unbeknown to Clarke, however, Cullinan was leading an unbalanced life, because the battle he fought on the surface coincided with an internal battle – a struggle with identity. Nevertheless, the guy was always determined to show that he was courageous, but as Clarke soon discovered he was arrogant, impulsive and at times reckless, because if there was one thing that Cullinan feared above all else it was incompetence. Indeed, it was common knowledge throughout the force in Derby that Cullinan once arrested his own father for being drunk and disorderly one night when a PC!

Clarke also had Cullinan down as being something of a dreamer, and yet he would be the first to acknowledge that the guy was at times innovative and original. Not one for conformity, stagnation and mediocrity, Cullinan was always a deeply driven idealist who tirelessly pursued his vision of creating a better future through change; needless to say, this did not sit well with Clarke.

Neither detective could ever be accused of being afraid to go against the grain, for both prided themselves on their originality or out-of-the-box ideas, but although Cullinan's inherent originality can be the source of his innovative ideas, he always had a tendency to be less receptive to the ideas of others, and this frequently led to clashes with Clarke. Indeed, the latter regarded him as being something of a perfectionist, clearly caused by a desire for the ideal, and this led to him becoming inconsolable when the results of his work were disappointing (Clarke referred to him as a "mardarse" on a number of occasions).

Furthermore, Cullinan also had a tendency to become unhappy when the fruit of his expression was not met with the anticipated ecstatic response. He may not have an opinion on everything, but he tended to hold strong convictions that he was passionate about, and this too led to clashes with Clarke, who accused him of having his "head in the clouds" in front of colleagues on one occasion.

Not to put too fine a point on it, Clarke regarded him as a know-all. He simply refused to listen because he considered himself five steps ahead of all the participants in any conversation. As Clarke remembered all too well, if the guy did engage, then he infrequently ended up paying more attention to his own thoughts than the thoughts of others, no matter how relevant. Indeed, if there was one thing that this know-all feared, then it was being wrong!

And now here he was in the flesh once more, and Clarke's contempt for the guy was palpable when he grudgingly shook him by the hand. Fletcher on the other hand was clearly smitten with the tall, shaven-headed officer, and Clarke was prepared to swear that the woman actually curtseyed as she and Cullinan were introduced. As for Annable, he was in his element and welcomed Cullinan with open arms.

'We're all delighted that you could join us, Sergeant,' he chirruped. 'Do take a seat.' Cullinan gave a weak smile in response and it was of some relief to Clarke that his former colleague from Derby chose to park his derrière on the other side of Fletcher. 'Now then,' continued Annable. 'Perhaps you'd care to inform us of your investigation into Mr. Rigione.'

Cullinan gave a slight cough before proceeding. 'For some time now we believe that there has been a drugs ring operating between here in Leverton and Spain,' he began in a deep voice with little trace of an accent. 'We also believe that the mastermind behind this ring is your Mr. Rigione.'

'Tosh,' scoffed Clarke audibly and disparagingly. Annable glared at him angrily.

Ignoring Clarke, Cullinan continued. 'It is our belief that Mr. Rigione has fled to Spain...'

At this Clarke cocked his head back and gave another derisive response. 'Ha!'

'Clarke – show some courtesy!' snapped Annable.

Cullinan tried again. 'Mr. Rigione seems to have got wind that we were on to him – someone has obviously tipped him off – and now he has quite literally done a runner.'

'Oh, I can't listen to any more of this crap,' shouted Clarke impatiently as he shook his head.

'Clarke...!' bellowed Annable; but Clarke wasn't listening.

'You always were full of yourself and your fancy ideas...'

Fletcher was forced to lean back as Cullinan lunged across her and jabbed his left forefinger at Clarke. 'And you never could accept it when you were proved wrong!'

'Hark who's bloody talking!' shouted Clarke with flared nostrils and eyes ablaze.

Cullinan hit back. 'That's the trouble with traditionalists like you...!'

'You always did like the sound of your own voice, didn't you?' said Clarke, taunting the younger detective.

Fletcher now found herself literally cowering and squirming in the middle of this slanging match – and it showed. That was enough for Annable. Leaping to his feet, he slammed his fist on the desk and confronted the two combatants with an ear-splitting roar that caused the entire office to shake, almost as if it had been hit by an earthquake of magnitude 3 on the Richter scale. 'Will you *sit* down the pair of you and *stop* behaving like bloody football hooligans!'

It did the trick.

It also prompted Annable's secretary to burst into the room. 'Is everything alright, Sir?' she asked anxiously as Clarke and Cullinan returned to their seats following their little spat.

'It's quite alright, Prentiss,' replied Annable almost casually, but with little beads of sweat forming on his forehead. 'I have everything under control, thank you.' Suitably reassured, Prentiss closed the door behind her as she left the office and Annable took his seat once more. Dabbing his forehead with his handkerchief, he returned it to his trouser pocket before turning to Clarke. 'One more peep out of you, Inspector, and I shall have no alternative but to suspend you from duty,' he growled. 'Do I make myself perfectly clear?'

Clarke bit his lip before replying. 'Yes, Sir,' he hissed through gritted teeth.

Annable then turned to Cullinan. 'I expected better from you, Sergeant.'

With head bowed, Cullinan was forced to make a grovelling apology. 'I'm sorry, Sir,' he replied. 'It won't happen again, I can assure you.'

'I think you should both save your apologies for Sergeant Fletcher here,' suggested Annable nodding in the direction of the only female officer in the room. The two male detectives were the embodiment of contrition as they duly made their apologies to Fletcher, and then Annable turned to Cullinan once more. 'Perhaps you would now care to pick up where you left off, Sergeant?'

Assured that there would be no more interruptions, Cullinan continued with his résumé of the National Crime Agency's investigation into the possibilities of a drugs ring. 'Although we believe Rigione to be the mastermind behind the affair, it is thought that the *actual* hub of the drugs ring is here in Leverton – at *The Navigation Inn*, close to the Woodend Estate.'

Clarke's eyes literally popped out of his head at the mention of *The Navigation*, but Annable put his hand up as if to prevent any outburst. '*The Navigation* you say?' he said somewhat benignly and ignorant of Clarke's connection with the place, including the landlady of the pub.

'That's right, Sir,' continued Cullinan. 'We believe that drugs to the value of several million are being smuggled in from Spain on a fairly regular basis – heroin, amphetamines, but chiefly cocaine.'

The bloody golfing weekends, thought Clarke to himself. That's it! Diana's partner is going back and forth to Spain several times a year ostensibly to play a few rounds of golf in the sun, but in reality he's bringing bloody drugs into the country! But surely Diana herself can't be involved? Such was his concern for her that Clarke had briefly forgotten all about Rigione. Annable's reaction to Cullinan's last statement caused him to snap out of his reverie.

'So you think that Rigione is now in Spain and that we will find evidence of drug smuggling at *The Navigation*?'

'Yes, Sir,' replied Cullinan excitedly. 'Spanish police have assured us that they will take care of Rigione.'

'So what are your intentions now, Sergeant?'

'We'd like to commence a raid on *The Navigation* immediately, Sir,' replied Cullinan as he got to his feet. 'All my men are in place and we're just waiting for you to give the go-ahead.'

'Then what are we waiting for?' beamed Annable.

Clarke still hadn't quite come to terms with the enormity of what was happening, but as Annable and the other two detectives headed for the door he swiftly rose from his chair and shouted after them. 'I'd like to come too,' he pleaded nervously.

The curtains were still drawn at *The Navigation* as the clock turned 9.30 a.m. Although it wasn't raining, there was a noticeable nip in the air as an elderly man in a green anorak shuffled along the canal towpath opposite the pub with his border terrier. Furthermore, most of the women from the nearby estate had returned home having taken their children to the primary school just up the road. Other than that there was very little to suggest that a police raid was imminent.

But then it began.

As if from nowhere, a convoy of police vehicles suddenly flew into the car park of *The Navigation* and pulled up before the pub doors in a swirl of dust. Armed police officers burst out of the first couple of vehicles and surrounded the pub. The last vehicle to arrive was a dark grey Audi A4 Avant Estate, and it contained Cullinan, his driver, Annable, Clarke and Fletcher. As they climbed out of the vehicle, two or three uniformed officers approached the door and awaited Cullinan's orders.

'Go, go, go,' he shouted, and the uniformed officers began banging loudly on the door of the pub.

Within seconds the door was opened by a bewildered-looking, middle-aged woman with blue eyes in her dressing gown and smoking a More Red 120 long brown paper cigarette. Her shoulder-length, wavy auburn hair had been taken up on top of her head and unusually for her there was little sign of any make-up, other than the very long, burgundy-coloured nails. There were no earrings this morning, but there were rings on most of her fingers. As the uniformed policemen burst past her and into the pub, the look of bewilderment on her face turned to one of terror.

'Where is he?' shouted the first policeman. Diana Marshall was still half asleep and struggling to comprehend what was happening. 'Where is he?' demanded the policeman once more.

Diana finally managed to find her voice. 'If you mean my partner, then he is upstairs and still in bed,' she snapped. The uniformed officers looked for access to the upstairs bedroom, she pointed to the door beside the toilets on the right-hand side of the building. 'Look, what the bloody hell is going on here?' she shouted indignantly as they headed upstairs and other plain clothes officers entered the pub.

One of these was over six feet in height, she surmised, and he was wearing a black cotton nylon shacket, with a white t-shirt, dark blue jeans and trainer's. 'Diana Marshall?' said Cullinan gravely. 'I'm arresting you on suspicion of involvement in drug trafficking offences.'

'What the...' she protested angrily.

'You do not have to say anything,' continued Cullinan. 'But it may harm your defence if you do not mention when questioned something which you later rely on in court. Anything you do say may be given in evidence.'

'But...I...don't...'

Cullinan wasn't prepared to listen. 'Take her outside to the car,' he barked to one of the uniformed officers.

Tears began to stream down her face as she was led to the waiting car. It was then that she saw him. He was standing back from the pub, alongside a female colleague and what looked like a senior officer in uniform. Their eyes met as they were busy bundling her into the car, and she was almost certain that there was a look of sadness and disappointment on his face. She wanted to shout out to him, but the car sped off before she could do or say anything.

Clarke wasn't sure what he felt at that particular moment – it was all like a bad dream. But as they bundled her into the car her dressing gown slipped to reveal the partially hidden tattoo of Marilyn Monroe on her left breast, and at that moment he could have sworn that Marilyn was crying too.

Chapter 28

Friday, 27 October 2017 (a.m.)

As Diana Marshall was being driven away in one of the police cars for questioning, her partner, Graham Chambers, was being dragged out of his bed kicking and cussing at the uniformed officers. He had calmed down sufficiently by the time he was cautioned by Cullinan, and it was with a smug grin that he was bundled into one of the other waiting cars. Both he and Diana were taken to Derby for questioning, which just made matters worse as far as Clarke was concerned.

Naturally the pub was cordoned off and searched from top to bottom by forensic officers, who didn't take long to find what they were looking for. Hidden away in compartments inside Chambers golf bags were numerous packages, mostly containing cocaine, but also amphetamines. It was quite a haul.

Meanwhile Clarke had returned to Leverton Police Station alongside Annable, Fletcher and Cullinan. Annable was all over Cullinan like a rash, and it hadn't escaped Clarke's notice that Fletcher was still gazing starry-eyed at the detective from Derby. And then Cullinan went on to describe that they had been watching both Rigione and Chambers for some time. As Clarke had already surmised, Chambers would collect the drugs on his golfing weekends and clearly use his bags as a means of smuggling them back to Britain. But what part did Diana play, if at all, thought Clarke?

And then Cullinan's phone rang. He stepped out of Annable's office briefly only to return moments later with a cocky swagger. 'I've just been informed that Spanish police have arrested Rigione at his villa near Marbella, on the Costa del Sol,' he announced triumphantly to those present.

Well, that's that then, thought Clarke to himself. The Rigione's had a villa in Spain. Funny how Linda had never mentioned this to him? But then he'd always suspected that she was holding something back. She'd better be told about Luciano's arrest and that she would almost certainly be brought in for questioning. He was just about to slip out of

Annable's office and head for her house on Tapley Lane when Cullinan came over to him.

'No hard feelings, Clarke,' he said holding out his hand.

Clarke accepted the offer – albeit grudgingly. 'Congratulations – you've obviously done your homework,' he replied.

'It pays to be thorough in my experience.'

There was a wry grin on Clarke's face as Cullinan returned to the celebrations with Annable and Fletcher. If truth be told he could have decked the arrogant bastard there and then, but he didn't want to be seen as a sore loser. Besides, he had to go and see Linda before the smartarse and his team descended upon her like a ton of bricks, and so he turned around and left the office without being noticed.

He was still deep in thought as he passed Scattergood at the reception desk without saying a word, but just as he was about to leave the building Webster came running after him.

'Sir,' shouted Webster a trifle breathlessly.

Clarke stopped in his tracks and turned to face the young detective. 'What!' he snapped irritably.

'I thought you should know that the Bacon's dog has been exhumed and I've ordered an autopsy to be carried out on the beast.'

Clarke gave full vent to his frustration. 'What the bloody hell does that matter now!' he roared angrily.

Webster scuttled off with his tail between his legs, and it should be said visibly hurt by the Inspector's response. He was clearly no longer flavour of the month. As a matter of fact Clarke began to regret his outburst almost immediately, and as he turned to leave the building his conscience was pricked all the more, as he noticed Scattergood shaking his head and with a look that told him he was bang out of order.

Clarke wasn't the only one who began the morning with a significant hangover. It was gone 11.00 a.m. when Linda Rigione woke with a start and immediately felt the full effects of the previous day's bout of excess drinking. Aside from the headache and the almost inevitable feelings of nausea, she had a raging thirst that required her immediate attention.

As she attempted to roll out of bed, she felt the sweat clinging to her nightdress. 'Shit,' she said to herself somewhat awkwardly. But even this exclamation of embarrassment and – one might say – regret only seemed to make matters worse, as she felt her head throbbing as if it were being pounded by the legendary *Led Zeppelin* drummer, the late John Bonham!

She made her way unsteadily to the bathroom, and after relieving herself she took two paracetamol tablets with several glasses of water. Stepping into the shower, the flow of warm water had an almost relieving effect upon her entire body, but she was conscious of the fact that this feeling would only be temporary. One thing was for sure, she told herself. She was going to lay off the sauce – for now!

Shower completed, she returned to the bedroom where she selected a pair of jeans and a light grey t-shirt. As expected the headache was still giving her grief, and as she made her way down the stairs it was compounded by the sound of a kettle boiling and a radio in the background. 'That bloody copper,' she said to herself once more. As she reached the foot of the stairs she was able to make out the song on the radio. How bloody appropriate, she thought to herself – it was The Smith's and *Heaven Knows I'm Miserable Now*!

'Cup of coffee?' shouted DC Laura Preston, who had heard the movement up above and was now aware that Linda was coming down the stairs.

'No I don't!' snapped Linda as she entered the kitchen. 'I'll get myself some fresh orange juice.'

'You ought to leave that stuff alone,' said Preston nodding to an empty bottle of brandy on the kitchen worktop.

'This I know!' replied Linda irritably. 'And can you turn that bloody thing off?' she said pointing to the offending radio.

Preston duly obliged and watched as Linda made her way into the lounge, where she slumped exhaustedly onto the sofa. Perhaps it was a good job that Preston did turn off the radio, for it's doubtful that she would have heard the knock on the front door a couple of minutes later otherwise.

'I'll get it,' shouted Preston as Linda lay almost comatose once more on the sofa. Opening the door, she was confronted by a rather severe-looking DCI Clarke.

'Morning, Preston,' he said unsmiling. 'Is the lady of the house up and about yet?'

'She's in the lounge, Sir, and she's only just got up.'

'Hangover?' suggested Clarke as if he had some authority on the subject.

Preston nodded. 'Like a bear with a sore head this morning.'

Clarke made his way to the lounge followed by Preston. 'Morning, Linda,' he said delicately.

'Do you have to shout?' replied Linda groggily.

'I wasn't aware that I *was* shouting.'

'Well, what have you got to tell me this morning?'

Clarke seated himself in the easy chair opposite the sofa. There was a long pause before he felt himself able to give a reply. 'We've found Luciano,' he said somewhat apprehensively as he fiddled with his fingers.

Linda sat bolt upright at Clarke's words and her headache seemed to disappear at a stroke. Staring at him open-mouthed for several seconds, she suddenly found the will to make a reply. 'Oh my God,' she exclaimed with a sense of disbelief. 'Where did you find him?' she continued. 'Is he okay?'

Clarke looked down at the floor. 'He's been arrested...'

'Arrested?' interrupted Linda with a look of bewilderment on her face.

'That's right,' continued Clarke as he raised his head to look her in the eye. 'He's been arrested at your villa in Spain.'

The look on Linda's face turned from one of bewilderment to astonishment. 'Our villa in Spain?' she repeated.

'Yes, he is being held in custody in Marbella and...'

Linda suddenly threw her head back and positively cackled with laughter at Clarke's last remarks. 'Ha,' she scoffed. 'Can't you lot ever get *anything* right?'

'What are you saying, Linda?'

'We've never had a villa – let alone a bloody villa in Spain!'

It was now Clarke's turn to look bewildered and extremely puzzled. 'Are you saying that they've arrested the wrong man?'

'You catch on quickly, Inspector!' she said thrusting her head forward as if to make her point. 'The man with the villa near Marbella is Luigi Rigione, Luciano's brother!'

And then he remembered. Of course, there *was* a younger brother, and in spite of the fact that their father had fled from the Camorra, this younger brother grew up idolising the Italian mafia and associated groups. For crying out loud, he was always bragging about having seen *The Godfather* countless times as a teenager, and when a girl in his class spurned his advances, he killed her cat, chopped its head off and put its remains inside her desk!

'I'd forgotten all about him, Linda,' said Clarke pensively. 'If my memory is correct, the two brothers weren't very close. Am I right?'

'They were like chalk and cheese,' replied Linda. 'Luciano always used the word *stronzo* when referring to Luigi.'

'*Stronzo?*' repeated Clarke. 'I'm sorry, but Italian isn't one of my strong points.'

'It means *asshole* – believe me, there was no love lost between the pair of them.'

'Is there anything else that you can you tell me about Luigi?'

'He did well at school,' Linda replied with a nod of her head. 'But then it was rumoured that he had cheated at his exams.'

'Go on,' insisted Clarke.

Linda sighed heavily. 'He was involved with petty crime from an early age – shoplifting mostly, and theft from pockets. He felt it unnecessary to look for work, so he continued with robbery and then resorted to extortion – but on a small scale at first. Things got too hot for him eventually, so he moved to Nottingham and then to London, where he first became involved with organised crime – chiefly the trafficking of drugs and firearms. We heard that he had fled to Italy, where he made contact with the Mafia, who sent him to Spain to set up a drug trafficking enterprise with small scale money laundering.'

'And you're sure that Luciano wasn't involved with the Mafia at any time?'

'Do me a favour,' scoffed Linda. 'He may have been a bully, but he was *never* involved with organised crime.'

The fact that Linda had referred to her husband as a bully caused Clarke to raise his eyebrows somewhat, but then he stood and looked up to the ceiling. 'So we *still* don't know what has happened to Luciano?' he said with a deep sigh.

'It looks that way, doesn't it?' she replied sarcastically.

'I'd better get back to the Station and fill them in with what you've told me,' he said as if deep in thought. 'I strongly suspect that you will be getting a visit from the National Crime Agency unless I can persuade them otherwise. If they do, then tell them *exactly* what you've told me – got that?'

'But of course,' she replied with a shrug of her shoulders. As Clarke turned to go she shouted after him. 'Inspector, I need to get out and do some shopping this weekend. Is that okay with you?'

'Of course – but only if Detective Constable Preston accompanies you!' replied Clarke with the vestiges of a smile.

The look of annoyance on Linda's face as he left the room said it all, but he wasn't too bothered about that. Even the fact that Diana was still in police custody didn't seem to trouble him at that specific moment. Indeed, as he headed for the Ford Focus his pace seemed to increase considerably, and he left the Rigione's and Tapley Lane in a far happier mood than when he arrived!

Chapter 29

Friday, October 27, 2017 (p.m.)

Bob Scattergood was having a crafty fag outside the entrance to Leverton Police Station when the silver Ford Focus came screeching into the car park at about 1.00 p.m. that Friday afternoon. Quickly stubbing it out, he had a sneaking suspicion that DCI Clarke had either won the lottery or he was on the warpath – and it was very probably the latter. He therefore deemed it wise to return to his desk before all hell broke loose.

He had barely sat down behind the desk when Clarke burst through the outer door of the building in an agitated state.

'Is Annable in?' Clarke asked breathlessly.

Scattergood jumped out of his seat. 'He's upstairs in his office, Sir...'

Clarke cut him short. 'What about Fletcher and that dimwit from Derby?'

'You mean Detective Sergeant Cullinan, Sir?'

'Who else would I be referring to?'

'They went out for lunch together about...'

Clarke was no longer listening. 'I've got to see Annable now!' he shouted as he headed for the staircase that led to Annable's office.

'But, Sir...!' shouted Scattergood after him.

'*What*!' bellowed Clarke as he stopped in his tracks and turned to face the Desk Sergeant.

'You've had a call from Mr. Bishop at the Leverton Gazette,' said Scattergood calmly.

'He'll have to wait,' replied Clarke as he attempted to ascend the staircase once more.

'He says it's very urgent – wants you to call him back, ASAP.'

Clarke stopped in his tracks again. Sighing heavily, he then turned and headed outside once more to make the call to Joel Bishop on his mobile. The call was answered almost immediately. 'Joel?' said Clarke with a marked degree of impatience.

'Ah, Allan,' replied Bishop excitedly. 'I think I've got something for you.'

'It had better be good, Joel.'

'I've been trawling through our records and found this from 2005. I'll read it out to you: Leverton-born man sentenced to four years for supplying fraudulent passports to organised gangs, including former IRA terrorists. Brendan Molloy, 38, from Belfast...'

But Clarke cut him short and quite literally exploded. 'For crying out loud, Joel,' he screamed. 'I bloody well know all about this...'

'Ah, but wait a minute – there's more,' replied Bishop, ignoring Clarke's angry outburst. 'The police were unable to find *all* of the passports!'

Clarke was suddenly all ears. 'What did you just say?'

'I said that the police were unable to find all of the passports.'

The change in Clarke's manner was instant – it was one of those eureka moments. 'But that's it!' he shouted triumphantly.

'That's what?' replied Bishop, who was now in a state of bewilderment.

'Joel, you're a bloody star!'

'What *are* you talking about?'

'I'll see you right for this!'

'See me right for *what*?'

But it was too late – the phone had gone dead. Clarke had switched off his mobile and was bursting through the door again. 'I bloody knew it!' he shouted as he literally skipped past Scattergood, who had an utterly mystified look on his face. He then began to head for the staircase once more, but he stopped, paused for several seconds and then turned and ran down the corridor to his office.

Once inside he began searching for the list of suppliers from Azzurri Furnishings. It didn't take him long to find it. Running his finger down the list he came to the name *John J. Lydon & Son* – but he continued. 'Yes!' he shouted as he came to another name. Moving on, he came to yet another name. 'Yes!' he shouted again; and again when he came to a fourth name. Snatching the list, he shot out of his office and headed for the staircase once more. As he passed Scattergood he waved the list at him. 'Charles Calthrop,' he shouted to a still bewildered Desk Sergeant.

'What's the daft bugger on about now?' said Scattergood to himself.

Just as Clarke had reached the foot of the staircase the imposing figure of Superintendent Annable was briskly making his way down.

'Sir,' shouted a jubilant-looking Clarke.

'What is it, Clarke?' replied a bemused-looking Annable.

'Cullinan and his band of merry men have made a monumental cock-up!'

'What *are* you suggesting?'

At that moment Fletcher and Cullinan entered the building through the main doors, laughing and joking with each other. Clarke wiped the smiles from their faces.

'Ah, here they come – Tweedledee and Tweedledum,' he shouted derisively. Annable tried to step in and prevent another bust-up between the two detectives, but Clarke was having none of it. 'What was that you said about being thorough?' he said sarcastically to Cullinan.

'What are you talking about?' replied Cullinan with a puzzled look on his face. 'Have you been hitting the bottle again?'

Clarke bit his lip and ignored the remark, and instead turned to Fletcher. 'I expected better of you, Sergeant,' he said with a grimace before turning once more to Cullinan. 'As for this narcissistic nincompoop...'

Annable decided that enough was enough. 'Will you *get* to the point, Inspector?' he bellowed angrily, as his voice echoed around the entire building.

'I've just been to see Mrs. Rigione,' he said through gritted teeth. 'And she has reliably informed me that the man arrested by the Spanish police is most definitely *not* her husband, Luciano Rigione. The man arrested is his brother, Luigi!'

The others stood with mouths agape and it was several seconds before Cullinan responded. 'Are you sure of this?' he said with a stunned look on his face.

'Get in touch with the Spanish police if you don't believe me,' replied Clarke. 'And then you can go back to school and do your bloody homework – thoroughly!'

Still unable to grasp what Clarke had just said, Annable chimed in. 'Are you saying that Luciano Rigione is still missing?' he said quietly.

'I am indeed,' replied Clarke before waving the list of suppliers at the others. 'And I know who is responsible for his disappearance. As my old mate Sherlock used to say, the game is still afoot!'

After Clarke's timely revelation, he suggested that they should all congregate in Annable's office. There was still a sense of disbelief from the others, but he insisted that they should all hear him out, and so they all gathered around Annable's desk as he proceeded to expound upon his theory.

'This is a list of the suppliers to Rigione's business, Azzurri Furnishings,' he said as he placed the print-outs on Annable's desk. He then turned to Fletcher. 'Remember what we were talking about yesterday, Sergeant?'

'Yes, of course, Sir,' she replied.

'Here is the name *John J. Lydon & Son*,' he said pointing to it with his right forefinger. He then moved down the list until he came to another name. 'Here we have *Stephen P. Jones*,' he continued, 'and here is *Paul T. Cook*. Finally we have a fourth name, that of *John S. Ritchie & Co.*'

'So what?' replied Cullinan, considerably lacking in enthusiasm.

'I don't get it,' said a puzzled-looking Annable.

Clarke persevered. 'Don't you see?' he said with a sense of frustration. 'I understand why the name *John S. Ritchie* wouldn't mean anything to some of you, but that was the real name of Sid Vicious, and together with the other three they made up The Sex Pistols!'

'What are you suggesting?' said Annable still looking slightly perplexed.

'Rigione's foreman at Azzurri Furnishings, Brendan Molloy, was a *huge* fan of The Sex Pistols.'

'How do you know that?' scoffed Cullinan.

'Because we were at school together!' snapped Clarke.

'So, you were at school with both Rigione *and* Molloy?' queried Annable.

'Yes, Sir, but Molloy has a criminal record!'

Annable's eyes suddenly lit up. 'Does he now?' he replied excitedly.

'Indeed he does,' replied Clarke. 'He was given a four-year sentence for passport fraud in 2005, but our colleagues in Northern Ireland were unable to find all of the passports.'

'And you believe that he hid those passports at the time, only to come back to them and use them at a later date?' interjected Fletcher.

'Exactly!' said Clarke excitedly. 'Those four suppliers are undoubtedly fake suppliers in my view, and Molloy is using them to pass himself off as one or all of them.'

'But why would he do that?' asked Cullinan reservedly.

'I'll come to that in a minute,' replied Clarke, who was now in full flow. 'Can any of you remember the film *The Day of the Jackal*, starring Edward Fox?'

Fletcher and Cullinan shook their heads, but Annable spoke out. 'Yes, I remember it well,' he replied with a look of nostalgia. 'He portrayed a contract killer if I remember rightly?'

'That's right, Sir,' said Clarke. 'And he stole the identities of a number of different characters, forging passports so as to pass himself off as someone else.'

'I see what you're getting at now, Clarke,' said Annable, warming to the theme.

Clarke stood back from the desk and began to rub his chin as if in deep thought. 'He must have had access to the accounts at Azzurri Furnishings,' he said pensively. 'And then he created the four fake accounts, falsifying invoices in order to process them through the supplier system.'

'But you still haven't explained *why* he's doing this?' said Cullinan with a sense of frustration.

Clarke nodded his head and turned to his last conversation with Linda Rigione. 'She readily admitted to having had an extra-marital affair,' he began. 'But she told me that it was over,'

'And you don't believe her?' said Fletcher.

'No I don't,' replied Clarke. 'Indeed, it is my belief that she has been conducting an affair with Brendan Molloy. What's more, I believe that affair to be still ongoing.'

Annable chimed in once more. 'Are you saying that *they* have done away with Rigione?'

'I believe that Molloy has done away with him – with or without Mrs. Rigione's knowledge.'

'And that he has transferred money to these false accounts in the hope that he and Mrs. Rigione can start a new life together?' hinted Fletcher.

'Yes, I believe so,' replied Clarke. 'I believe that I'm not far from the truth.'

But Cullinan *still* wasn't prepared to go along with Clarke's theory. 'It's all a bit fanciful if you ask me,' he said rather sulkily.

'It's a damn sight more plausible than your cack-handed approach to justice!' retorted Clarke angrily.

'Bring him in,' snapped Annable, as he gave Cullinan a look of undisguised contempt.

But Clarke put his hand up. 'Wait a moment,' he objected momentarily. 'Mrs. Rigione hinted that she wanted to go shopping this weekend, and I told her that she could only do so if accompanied by the Family Liaison Officer.'

'What are you getting at?' enquired Annable.

Clarke thumped the table. 'I believe that she and Molloy will attempt to meet up somewhere this weekend to discuss their next moves,' he said confidently and vigorously.

'I think you're right, Sir,' said Fletcher, who now seemed to be coming around to Clarke's way of thinking.

'I had thought of confiscating their mobile phones earlier, but I'm glad that I didn't do so now,' said Clarke smiling in appreciation at Fletcher's sudden loyalty.

'What are your plans, Inspector?' snapped Annable once more.

'I want Molloy watched 24/7 over the weekend,' he began. 'I'll get Webster to supervise that – we can rely on the Family Liaison Officer to keep an eye on Mrs. Rigione.'

'Splendid!' shouted Annable, who was clearly no longer in thrall to the detective from the National Crime Agency.

Clarke gathered up the print-outs. 'And we mustn't forget to find out what bank or banks Molloy is using for his little scam.'

'I'll look into that, Sir,' said Fletcher diligently.

And that was it; Clarke had won the day. But as the four of them proceeded to go their separate ways, Clarke's confidence and elation were tempered by the fact that Diana was still in custody. True, her partner was as guilty as sin of trafficking in drugs, but what part had she played in this sorry saga – if at all. And that was his dilemma; he had no way of knowing – as yet. It was then that the song came back to haunt him.

When constabulary duty's to be done, to be done,
A policeman's lot is not a happy one, happy one.

Chapter 30

Saturday, 28 October 2017

The tall figure of Ricky Meakin climbed into the family Land Rover at Upper Grange Farm with "Ned", his beloved Border collie. It was approaching 6.00 a.m. on this dark Saturday morning. He didn't mind getting up early; he was used to it. Farming was in his blood – and it showed. Only he had been asked (told more like!) to help out his Uncle Derek down at nearby Lower Grange Farm. He'd done it before when his Uncle Derek and his Aunt Nicola went to the caravan up in the Peak District, but apparently Aunt Nicola had left Uncle Derek – again!

The eldest of two children of Richard and Kath Meakin, he was born at Tapley in 1993, but it was common knowledge that he and his younger sister weren't that particularly close. He didn't excel himself at school and gained few qualifications, but unlike his sister he was born and bred for the farm and loved every minute of it.

Forced to learn independence at a young age, he has stamina and loads of energy, but then he is physically strong; that would undoubtedly stand him in good stead for what Uncle Derek had in store for him. But it wasn't the work that he would have to do that was troubling him as he pulled up in the yard to the farmhouse at Lower Grange Farm. Climbing out of the Land Rover and followed by "Ned", he knocked on the farmhouse door and walked straight in.

'Anyone at 'ome?' he shouted.

'Am in t'dining room,' was the equally loud response from Derek Meakin.

Ricky made his way through to the dining room with "Ned" and they were greeted by a sombre-looking uncle and *his* Border collie, "Max". 'Ey up, Derek,' said Ricky. 'I thought you might be in 'ere 'avin' a cuppa before we start.'

Derek looked up to see his tall nephew with the short, light brown curly hair and blue eyes wearing his usual attire of anorak, jeans and boots, but looking resplendent in a sheepskin trapper that he liked to wear in the autumn and winter months. 'Nearly done lad,' replied Derek as he made a fuss of "Ned" and then watched as the two dogs frolicked around.

'What's this I've 'eard about Aunt Nicola – 'as she scarpered again?'

Derek ignored the question, but noticed the nervous twitch that Ricky had in his right eye, almost as if he was winking. 'You ought to get that thing sorted, lad.'

'Allus 'ad it,' he replied before returning to his previous question. 'Anyway, what's happened to Aunt Nicola?'

Derek went over to the sink and rinsed his mug out. 'Never you mind about your Aunt Nicola – I 'aven't asked you to come 'ere and talk about 'er.'

'Well, it's not t'first time she's upped and gone, is it?' said Ricky with the vestiges of a suggestive smirk upon his face.

Derek knew all too well that his nephew had a tendency to put a lot of energy towards gaining the reciprocal love of another, but surely not *his* wife? 'I 'ope you 'aven't been sayin' or doin' summat you shouldn't 'ave?' he said jabbing his finger in Ricky's direction.

Ricky wasn't about to let on that his own aunt had been the object of his affection and that he had been pursuing her relentlessly, even though he was younger than her by a few years. For crying out loud, he had been trying it on with her in *The Lyttelton Arms* that night back in March when that bastard Rigione stepped in and head-butted him in the face. It seemed that everyone else knew about the incident, but not Uncle Derek! 'What 'ave I gone and done now?' he said in all innocence.

'I know what you can be like. Remember what 'appened in Torquay?'

He remembered alright. It was the night of the Young Farmer's Annual General Meeting back in 2015, when he got plastered and tried to chat up the girlfriend of a young farmer from Gloucestershire. A fight ensued and it had to be broken up by others who attended the meeting. Oh yes, he remembered, but he didn't like to talk about it. 'Well 'ave said and done nowt!'

'Suppose you'll be 'avin' a skinful up at *Cross Keys* tonight too?' hinted Derek, knowing that his nephew was most fulfilled when in a group – and that usually meant the lads.

'What if I am?' replied Ricky in a somewhat surly manner.

Derek glared at his nephew for a few seconds and then moved the conversation along. 'I want you to give me a 'and milkin' t'cows first,' he began. 'Then whilst am lookin' after t'farm shop I want you to set about repairin' that wall in t'bottom field. Is that alright?'

Ricky merely nodded. He'd be glad to get shut of his uncle for most of the day, and especially as it involved rebuilding a dry stone wall. Come rain or shine he was as happy as a pig in the proverbial when he was walling. And how he would have liked to have built a wall around his uncle at that moment!

Detective Chief Inspector Allan Clarke, on the other hand was not at all keen on waking up in the early hours of the morning and not being able to get back to sleep again. At 6.00 a.m. he had already been awake for over an hour, and he was willing to bet a pint or a penny that he wasn't going to get another wink of sleep on this particular morning.

He had gone easy on the *Laphroaig* the night before, so there was no hangover – thank Christ. The trouble was that he simply couldn't stop thinking about Diana and what she must be going through. Worse still, he was becoming increasingly fearful that she may have been involved in this drugs ring after all. No, not Diana, he kept trying to tell himself. But it was no good; the image of her behind bars was lodged in his mind and it wouldn't go away. He threw the sheets back and decided to get up.

He had to do something with himself otherwise the whole scenario was going to keep gnawing away at him and drive him mad. The afternoon was covered – the Leverton Lions Rugby Football Club were playing at home today, so he would go and watch them demolish the opposition. Getting through the morning was going to be a different matter. He was beginning to wish that he'd opted to do a stint watching Brendan Molloy's movements for a few hours, but Webster and other members of the team had jumped at the chance for some overtime, and so that had been dealt with.

A spot of breakfast was called for accompanied by a glass of fresh orange juice. That should give him time to consider how he was going to get through the morning. Indeed, he was halfway through his corn flakes when he came up with a plan. He would do some ironing to begin with, followed by some shopping and then prepare his evening meal in the slow cooker. On the menu tonight would be a pot roast – simple. Naturally all bar the shopping would be accompanied by some music, and he opted for The Who and their *Quadrophenia* album.

He had barely started the ironing when the track *The Punk and the Godfather* came on, and he started to chuckle to himself. One might think that this moment of mirth could be attributed to Luigi Rigione and his connection with the Mafia, but far from it. No, Clarke was feeling rather pleased with himself – and a trifle smug if truth were told – for he saw Donal Cullinan as the "Punk" in this instance, whereas *he* was the "Godfather" and *di capo di tutti capi*!

It was approaching 4.00 p.m. and starting to get dark. Ricky Meakin still hadn't completed the stretch of wall in the bottom field, but he'd decided to call it a day; he would come back and finish it at a later date. Uncle Derek would no doubt be clearing up back at the Farm Shop and it was almost time to milk the cows again; he had every hope that he'd be released from that particular chore and sent home. Collecting his walling hammer and other accoutrements, he, "Ned" and "Max" slowly made their way up the hill and back to the main farm buildings.

The Farm Shop was actually one of the outbuildings at Lower Grange Farm. It wasn't a grand affair, but it was quite popular with the locals. Entering the building at the side, there was top quality fresh fruit and vegetables over to the left. Directly opposite the door was the refrigerator, containing local farm eggs, fresh milk, pork pies, scotch eggs, a variety of different cheeses and a range of other products. Over to the right was the small counter, inside which were various cuts of meat, chicken products and sausages. Behind this was a small back room which acted as the cutting area, and contained a number of freezers.

The Farm Shop was devoid of customers when Ricky entered the building, but as expected Uncle Derek was in the back room chopping something up; he hadn't heard his nephew enter.

'Been busy Uncle Derek?' he shouted at the top of his voice.

Derek Meakin jumped a mile. 'Bloody 'ell,' was his equally loud response. 'You frit me to death lad – do you 'ave to creep up on folks like that?'

'I didn't mean to startle you.'

Derek stopped chopping and made his way towards the counter, closing the door to the cutting room behind him. 'I've saved these for you,' he said producing a carrier bag from behind the counter.

Ricky peeked inside the bag. 'Sausages!' he exclaimed. 'Shit 'ot!'

'You can 'ave some for your snap tonight, but don't eat all the buggers – save some for your mum, dad and Rachel.'

'You don't want any 'elp with t'milkin' then?'

'No, get off 'ome.'

'Cheers Uncle Derek.'

'Be seeing you.'

And with that Ricky turned on his toes and headed out of the shop. He was completely unaware that his uncle was watching him through the shop window, or that he only returned to the cutting room *after* the Land Rover had disappeared up the lane. 'He's not that bad, our Uncle Derek,' said a smiling Ricky to the faithful dog sitting beside him.

Clarke returned home from the rugby that afternoon in quite an upbeat mood. He had been joined at the ground as usual by the police surgeon, Dr. Alexander Fraser, and together they had watched the Leverton Lions defeat the opposition 29-6, with three quite scintillating tries. This was followed by a quick drink (supposedly) in the nearby *Nag's Head* public house, where they happily relived the entire occasion.

However, he was now back at the narrow boat and looking forward to tucking into his pot roast. He had done enough for at least four servings, but the way he felt he could have devoured the lot. He hadn't finished listening to the album *Quadrophenia* earlier, so he picked up where he had left off and this was playing in the background when his mobile phone suddenly burst into life. It was Webster.

'I assume that you've been watching our friend, Molloy, Detective Constable?' said Clarke in an uncharacteristically good-humoured tone as he paused the music.

'Yes, Sir,' replied Webster cautiously. 'I've just finished my stint.'

'And what can you tell me about his movements today?'

So Webster began by telling Clarke that Molloy had gone to the races in Nottingham, following which he returned to Leverton, where he sank a Guinness or two in one of the local hostelries before going home to Woodcock Drive. 'I left him with DC Rice, but as far as I'm aware he's still there, Sir.'

'And he made no contact with anyone during the entire period?'

'He was alone all of the time and I never saw him use his phone for any reason.'

'Oh well, let's see what tomorrow brings, shall we?'

The disappointment in Clarke's voice was palpable, but Webster deemed it best not to say as much on this occasion. 'I'll be off now then, Sir.'

'Thanks, Webster. Bye for now.'

And Clarke was disappointed, there was no denying it. He'd managed to put Diana's predicament on the back burner for most of the day and enjoyed the rugby too, but as he resumed listening to The Who and their *Quadrophenia* album, the song *I've Had Enough* came on, and the opening words seemed particularly appropriate:

You were under the impression
That when you were walking forwards
You'd end up further onward
But things ain't quite that simple.

Chapter 31

Sunday, 29 October 2017 (a.m.)

Kath Meakin was busy peeling the spuds when she briefly glanced up at the clock in the kitchen at Upper Grange Farm – it had just turned 11.30 a.m. on that Sunday morning. There had been rain during the night – not that she had slept much – and as she took her eyes away from the clock and gazed through the window it still continued to drizzle outside. Her husband and son would be getting ready to go to *The Cross Key's Inn* for their lunchtime session, whereas daughter Rachel had set off for work at the golf club earlier without saying a word. Indeed, it was Rachel and her involvement with Marco Rigione that was weighing heavily on Kath's mind, and the fact that she still hadn't discussed the matter with her husband.

As she finished peeling the spuds she heard footsteps coming down the stairs, and seconds later Richard Meakin entered the kitchen.

'I take it Rachel's gone to work?' he said looking casually around him.

'She left a while ago,' replied Kath without looking up. She suddenly downed tools (and spuds), wiped her hands and turned to face her husband. 'Look, there's summat you need to know.'

'Like what?' replied Richard as he donned his raincoat and cap.

'It's about our Rachel.'

'Well, spit it out then!'

'She's been seein' Rigione's son.'

Richard turned to face Kath with a puzzled look on his face. 'What do you mean?'

Kath's anger and frustration came to the fore. 'Do I 'ave to spell it out for you?' she snapped. 'Our Rachel and Marco Rigione are 'avin' an affair!'

Richard had only pulled the zip on his jacket halfway up when his face turned from puzzlement to rage. 'You what?' he bellowed.

'It's true I tell you.'

'Where did you get all this from then?'

'It wer' when that bloody copper came 'ere t'other day.'

Richard started striding towards the door. 'I'll put a stop to this bugger right now!' he snarled.

Kath went after him and took him by the arm. 'No, Richard. Don't do owt to show 'er up in front of 'er friends and colleagues.'

'Well, what do you expect me to do?'

'I told 'er you'd be angry, but she 'asna spoke to me since.'

'What are you tryin' to tell me?'

Tears began to well up in Kath's eyes. 'Am frightened she'll leave us and run off with 'im.'

'What do you suggest we do then?'

'I think we should talk it over with 'er 'ere.'

'And when do you think we should do that?'

'Tonight would be best, don't you think?'

Richard Meakin could see that it was pointless arguing with his wife; she was pleading with him now and he visibly relaxed before deciding to seat himself at the kitchen table. Kath went over to him and put her arms around him before resting her head on his shoulder.

Unbeknown to both Richard and Kath, their conversation had been overheard by their son, Ricky, who had been standing at the top of the stairs taking everything in. So, his sister had been seeing Rigione's son, had she? At first the twitch in his eye seemed to worsen and he bristled with anger as the conversation downstairs developed, but by the time it had finished a huge grin split his face from side to side. He knew what he had to do and he was going to do it come hell or high water! His thoughts were interrupted by a shout from downstairs.

'Are you comin' lad?' shouted a suitably becalmed Richard Meakin. 'Pub'll be open in five minutes.'

'Comin' dad,' shouted Ricky Meakin as he literally bounced down the stairs with a nonchalant air!

It wasn't very often that Clarke had a lie-in, but today was one of those days. Again, he tried to focus on the case and what might have happened to Luciano Rigione, but his thoughts always returned to Diana Marshall and her current predicament. Indeed, the longer he heard nothing from her, the more he convinced himself that she must have been involved in the drugs ring with her partner. Rising about 10.30 a.m., he looked out of one of the windows of the narrow boat and the wet, miserable weather seemed to match his mood, as he too contemplated preparing his Sunday lunch.

He'd called at the farm shop in the nearby village of Sapworth some days ago and treated himself to a piece of pork shoulder. He would be having that for lunch, together with some roast potatoes, greens (Brussels sprouts included) and stuffing. Raised by his grandparents, he recalled how his grandmother had admitted to him one day that she wasn't the world's greatest cook. This was in answer to his complaint that he didn't like the way she cooked the stuffing. 'Well, your granddad likes the stuffing done that way,' she had replied. But the food *always* had to be cooked the way granddad liked it done was his frequent reply, and one which *always* fell on deaf ears!

The vaguest of smiles came to his face as he harked back to his childhood. How glad he was that he had taken up cooking in his teens, because now he was going to do the stuffing the way that he liked it done!

Turning on the oven, he was about to place the pork shoulder into the tray when his mobile phone alerted him to the fact that he was receiving a text message. 'Who can that be?' he said to himself with a heavy sigh. Placing the tray and the pork shoulder onto the kitchen worktop, he went over to the phone which was lying on the table beside his laptop, and opened it. It was from Diana, and her message ran as follows: 'I was arrested as a suspect in connection with an ongoing investigation into a drugs ring, questioned at length by detectives and released from custody without charge, pending further investigation.'

Clarke suddenly felt his heart pounding and racing, and he tapped in his reply 'Where are you now?'

He waited several seconds before he received her next message. 'I'm back at the pub.'

That was all he needed. 'I'll be down there straightaway,' he typed.

'Please yourself,' was her curt reply. But he hadn't seen that – he was too busy rummaging around for some decent clothes to wear, and he settled for a navy blue t-shirt, jeans and training shoes. He rinsed his mouth out with mouthwash, brushed his hair and then told himself that it would have to suffice. He then grabbed his mobile, climbed the steps of the narrow boat and locked up, before jumping into his car and heading for the pub.

It didn't take him long to get there. The rain was still coming down steadily as he pulled up at *The Navigation*, and he was surprised to see just the one uniformed policeman standing at the door. Nervously producing his identity card, he stepped into the pub and there she stood behind the bar with one arm wrapped beneath her bust and smoking one of her More Red 120 brown paper cigarettes with her other hand. There was little evidence of make-up, although her very long nails were still painted a burgundy colour. She wore a tight-fitting black t-shirt, jeans and low-heeled, black slip-on shoes. Blowing the smoke out of the side of her mouth, she glared frostily at Clarke, who was clearly at a loss as to what to say.

'Are you...erm...are you okay?' he asked nervously.

'Thought you'd never ask,' she replied sarcastically as she stubbed out her cigarette.

'I...erm...came as soon as I could.'

She lit another cigarette. 'Is that a fact?'

'What do you expect me to say?'

'You could have warned me that there was going to be a raid,' she snapped.

'Don't be silly...'

'I'm not being silly – you're a copper, aren't you?'

'I only found out myself at the last minute...'

'I don't believe you...'

'It's true – I had no idea that the pub was being watched *or* your partner for that matter.'

'A likely story...'

'It isn't part of *my* investigation...'

'So what were *you* doing there when they forced me into the car?'

Clarke struggled to find an answer, but eventually spat one out. 'Because I was told that the pub was the centre of a drug's ring and that you might be implicated!'

'And you believed that – about me?'

'I...I...didn't know what to believe – it all happened so quickly.'

'How the bloody hell do you think I felt!' she screamed as the tears began to fall. 'Have you any idea what it was like being dragged away for interrogation and not knowing what for or why?'

Clarke moved as if to put his arms around her, but she shrugged him off. He then said something that he later came to regret. 'Surely you must have known what he – your partner – was up to?'

She paused before replying. 'You really do think that I was involved, don't you?' she whispered quizzically.

At that moment he wanted the ground to swallow him up. 'Like I said, I...I...didn't...'

'Yes, you think that I'm guilty, don't you?' she sneered.

'Look, Diana...'

'Get out,' she hissed at him without looking him in the face.

'What?'

'*I said get out!*' she screamed at the top of her voice. '*Get out and stay out!*'

There was no point in staying – not now. He turned on his heels and left the pub with his tail very decidedly between his legs.

As the door closed behind him Diana collapsed onto the bar in a veritable flood of tears. It had certainly not been the best of weekends for her, but she was sick to the back teeth of moments like this. However, was she going to regret bawling him out like that? Or was he just like all the others? Only time would tell.

Chapter 32

Sunday, 29 October 2017 (p.m.)

He was crushed. She wanted him out of her life and he was absolutely crushed. More importantly, he blamed himself entirely. He'd put his foot in it as per usual, and now he would have to face the consequences.

He was sitting on the edge of his bed back on board the *Emily* and he was really shaken up. There was a bottle of *Laphroaig* nearby and yet he couldn't bring himself to pour himself a glass, such was his anguish – and disbelief. When he and his wife, Lesley, split up he didn't feel as bad as this – or for that matter when his relationship with Carol Vaughan had come to an end.

Why hadn't he given Diana the benefit of the doubt on this occasion? But she was right; he *did* think that she might have been implicated in her partner's drugs ring. He buried his head in his hands and swore to himself. 'This bloody job,' he snarled. He was contemplating going to see Annable the following morning and telling him that he was quitting the force when his mobile phone sprang into life. 'Please, please, let it be Diana,' he said to himself. He picked up the phone – it was DC Laura Preston, the Family Liaison Officer.

'Laura, what have you got to tell me?' he sighed heavily as he answered the call.

'I've lost her, Sir,' she replied with a sense of anxiety in her voice.

'Lost who?'

'Linda Rigione, Sir.'

'How the hell did you manage to...'

Preston cut him short. 'We went shopping in Leverton, but she managed to evade me in one of the supermarkets – she told me that she was going to the toilets, but when I went in a few minutes later there was no sign of her.'

'I don't believe that I'm hearing this.'

'She must have sneaked out when I wasn't looking.'

'How long ago was this?'

'She's been gone twenty minutes now.'

Clarke paused only briefly before issuing his orders. 'Okay, if I'm right – and I believe that I am – then she has arranged to meet Molloy,' he said calmly. 'You keep looking for her – I'm going to get hold of Webster.'

And with that he switched off his mobile and searched his list of contacts for Webster's number. What was that about quitting the force?

It was still drizzling with rain as Detective Constable Matthew Webster sat in his Blue Toyota Aygo on one of the side streets close to Queen's Park in Leverton. He had been there for ten minutes, having followed Brendan Molloy from his home on Woodcock Drive. Molloy was sitting alone underneath the bandstand at the park, but he was completely unaware that Webster was watching him.

Molloy was constantly looking around, almost as if he was waiting for someone else to turn up, and Webster had a damn good idea who that someone might be. Just as he was trying to stifle yet another yawn, his mobile phone went off. It was the boss, DCI Clarke.

'Oh, hello, Sir,' said Webster unable to disguise the fact that he was rather sleepy.

'Falling asleep on the job again, Webster?' shouted Clarke with due sarcasm.

'Sorry, Sir – didn't get much sleep last night.'

'No, I'll bet you were at one of your bloody nightclubs again.' There was no response, so Clarke continued. 'Whereabouts are you, man?'

'I'm at Queen's Park, Sir – watching Molloy as you suggested.'

'Has he got anyone with him?'

'No, but it looks like he's waiting for someone.'

'Linda Rigione has managed to escape the attention of DC Preston, and I'm pretty certain that she...'

Webster interrupted him. 'Wait a minute, Sir – there's a blonde-haired lady with an umbrella making her way towards the bandstand and Mr. Molloy.'

'That's her, Webster.'

'Yes, Sir – she's now climbing the steps of the bandstand and Mr. Molloy appears to have recognised her. He's stood up to greet her.'

'Keep your eyes on them whilst I contact DC Preston and...'

'Hang on a minute, Sir.'

'What is it, Webster?'

'Another woman has appeared on the scene and seems to be remonstrating with the couple, especially Mrs. Rigione.'

'What the...'

'There's a lot of shouting going off between the two women now, Sir, and...' Webster paused for a few seconds and then continued. 'Well I never...'

'What is it now, Webster?'

'It looks like DC Preston has arrived, Sir.'

'Well at least it will save me having to call her now...'

'Oh boy!' shouted Webster incredulously.

'What now, Webster?' shouted an increasingly frustrated Clarke.

'The other woman has just slapped Mr. Molloy right in front of some of the locals and passers-by – people have obviously heard the commotion and come out to investigate.'

'Right, I'm going to get Fletcher to stop what she's doing and call her in,' shouted Clarke authoritatively. 'I want you to call for back-up. When they've arrived I want you *and* Preston to arrest Mrs. Rigione and Mr. Molloy, and bring them in to the station on suspicion of involvement in the murder of Mr. Rigione. I'll make my way there after I've called Fletcher.'

'What about this other woman?'

'Just do as I say and forget about her for the time being.'

'Okay, will do, Sir.'

And with that the line went dead. Webster called for back-up and they were there in minutes. Having climbed out of his Toyota he headed for the bandstand and duly arrested Linda Rigione and Brendan Molloy, who – it has to be said – seemed to be rather pleased to be out of the conflict that had erupted only minutes before. The two of them were bundled into the police car and driven off at speed.

However, the "other woman" was still on the scene and it was now that curiosity got the better of Webster. 'Excuse me, madam, but who are you and in what way are you connected with the two people who have just been arrested?'

The "other woman" was only too happy to step forward. 'My name is Wendy Price,' she replied earnestly. 'Brendan Molloy is my partner – and I'd like to talk to the Senior Investigating Officer about *his* part in the disappearance of Luciano Rigione!'

Detective Sergeant Fletcher was at her parent's house in Nottingham when she got the call from Clarke, and he had no problem persuading her to come in and interview Linda Rigione. He would be interviewing Molloy, but when he arrived at the station it didn't go unnoticed that he was attired in his bomber jacket and not the suit and tie. He was about to make his way to his office when Webster approached him and told him about Wendy Price.

'She said that her partner was involved in the disappearance of Mr. Rigione and that she wanted to speak to the Senior Investigating Officer,' said Webster excitedly.

'Did you bring her in?' replied Clarke.

'Yes, Sir – she's in Interview Room 3.'

'Good – you can do the interviewing. Tell her that I shall be busy questioning her partner.' And as Webster scuttled off, Clarke shouted after him. 'And make sure you get a statement from her.'

Whilst all this was going on both Molloy and Linda Rigione were divested of their mobile phones and their homes were to be searched for incriminating evidence. Several minutes later Sergeant Fletcher arrived and Clarke briefed her on what she had to do; she would be questioning Linda Rigione in Interview Room 2, whilst he would be doing likewise with Molloy in Interview Room 1. Indeed, all the interview rooms would be full – it was going to be a very busy evening at Leverton Police Station.

There hadn't been a Sunday evening like this at the Station for as long as anyone could remember – not even Peter Meakin, who was about to go off duty. 'What's all this about then, Bob?' he said to Scattergood as he approached the latter's reception desk.

'They've brought in Brendan Molloy and Linda Rigione,' replied Scattergood candidly.

'What have they been brought in for?'

'Involvement in the disappearance of *her* husband,' beamed Scattergood.

'But they still haven't got a body?'

'Aye, I know – but you know what Clarke's like when he's got a bee in his bonnet. Oh, and the suit and tie have seem to have vanished too.'

'He's in his bomber jacket again, is he? Didn't think that would last long – love life must taken a turn for the worse?'

'I never thought of that.'

'See you then, Bob.'

'Have one for me, Pete.'

No doubt Peter Meakin would be having a swift half before he retired for the evening. But as he left the building and headed for his car he pulled out his mobile phone; there was a call he had to make before he even considered calling at any of the local hostelries!

Chapter 33

Sunday, 29 October 2017 (p.m.)

If truth be told, Clarke was not in the best frame of mind for questioning his prime suspect in the case of the disappearance of Luciano Rigione. He was still smarting from his clash with Diana Marshall and the fact that he blamed himself entirely for losing her trust, amongst other things. At least he had Brendan Molloy where he wanted him now, however, and he was determined to get him for murder come what may.

Fletcher had already commenced her questioning of Linda Rigione and Webster had set about interviewing Wendy Price, so Clarke collected all the evidence that he had on Molloy and entered Interview Room 1.

Molloy was sitting back in his chair with his arms folded and his legs stretched out underneath the table. He wore a grey, button-down collar, washed Oxford check shirt, jeans and a pair of light brown Chelsea boots; he had an aura of quiet smugness around him. The Duty Solicitor, Christopher Aitchison, sat beside him; he was a tall, middle-aged man with wispy, receding hair. And it was common knowledge that the legal profession were *not* exactly the Chief Inspector's cup of tea!

Clarke removed his bomber jacket, loosened his tie and then undid the top button of his light blue shirt before switching on the tape. Introductions having been made, he began by referring to Molloy's criminal record. 'It says here that you found employment with the local social security office in Leverton after leaving school – that would be the DHSS,' he stated firmly. Molloy merely shrugged, so Clarke continued. 'During this period you met your wife and had two daughters. Then in 1999 you accepted a post with HM Passport Office in Belfast – that's when the trouble started, wasn't it?'

'No comment,' replied Molloy with a characteristic smirk on his face.

'And as we all know you were arrested and sentenced to four years imprisonment for your part in a criminal enterprise that supplied fraudulent passports to organised gangs – including former IRA terrorists. Is that right?'

'No comment.'

'But then you always did have a tendency to promote the Irish Nationalist or Sinn Fein cause whilst at school, didn't you?'

'No comment.'

'Not that anyone listened if I remember rightly,' said Clarke under his breath.

The Duty Solicitor tried to intervene. 'Chief Inspector, would you please...'

But Clarke put his hand up. 'Don't worry, Mr. Aitchison; I'm coming to the point,' he said abruptly before returning to Molloy's criminal record. 'If I read this correctly, at the time of your arrest and conviction the police didn't find all of the passports, did they?'

Molloy seemed to shift uneasily in his chair, but continued to give the same response. 'No comment.'

'But we did,' said Clarke leaning forward and with a huge smile across his face. He then threw a number of passports onto the table before him. 'Care to talk about these?' he said nonchalantly.

Molloy remained non-committal. 'No comment.'

Clarke was expecting just such a response. 'I've got to hand it to you – that was a very clever ploy on your part to set up fake accounts using the four members of The Sex Pistols.' Molloy said nothing, but Clarke continued. 'Although I never did share your taste in music, you were quite a fan as I recall.'

Molloy was suddenly communicative. 'What if I was?' he shrugged.

Clarke sat back again. 'I should add that we found six more unused passports from your previous scam.'

'Okay, I served my time – so what?'

Clarke ignored the comment. 'So, would you care to tell us about the fake accounts?'

Molloy returned to his previous stance. 'No comment.'

'No, I didn't think you would.' Clarke paused briefly before continuing. 'Shall I tell you what I think? I think that you decided to set up an Authorised Push Payment or APP scam, whereby money was to be transferred into fraudulent accounts – four in your case.'

'No comment.'

'You had access to the laptops at Azzurri Furnishings, and you then set up the fake accounts in the list of suppliers. That way, fake invoices could be processed in the supplier system, and the money would be duly transferred into these accounts.'

Molloy was *still* unwilling to play ball. 'No comment,' he replied casually.

'So what did you intend to do with the money from these fake accounts?'

'No comment.'

'You were having an affair with Luciano's wife; that much we do know.' Clarke leaned forward again and looked straight into Molloy's eyes. 'And I think that you got it into your head that if Luciano was out of the way, she would be yours and you could set up home with her, using the money from those accounts.'

Molloy threw his head back and quite literally scoffed at Clarke's suggestion. 'That's a ridiculous thing to say,' he replied and then laughed heartily.

At least he had opened up, thought Clarke, and so he continued to infer that Molloy had murdered Luciano. 'So, what have you done with the body?' he said confidently.

'I don't know what you're talking about,' scoffed Molloy once more.

Aitchison tried to step in again, reminding his client that he should remain silent. 'You don't have to say anything,' he said to Molloy with a modicum of alarm.

But Clarke clearly wanted to force the pace. 'Your house backs onto the Peacock Pathway,' he pointed out. 'Is that where you struck?'

Molloy again laughed at Clarke's suggestion, but this time Aitchison decided that enough was enough. 'Chief Inspector, you have absolutely *no* evidence whatsoever that my client has deliberately taken someone else's life or done away with them,' he shouted angrily. 'For crying out loud, where is your body? You haven't got one; and until you do then you cannot go around making outlandish assertions like this!'

Clarke gritted his teeth. 'I'll have him,' he snarled.

'You might – and I say *might* – have enough to charge my client with the setting up of fraudulent accounts,' replied Aitchison. 'But I repeat; you have no evidence whatsoever to charge him with murder. Now, if you don't mind?'

And with that, the Duty Solicitor and Molloy stood up and made their way out through the door. For a minute or so they briefly conferred with each other in the corridor, before Molloy was led away to be charged with fraud. All the time Clarke remained seated at the desk with clenched fists and a face like thunder. 'I'll get the bastard,' he said to himself. Once again it seemed that Diana's advice that he should be more objective had been consigned to oblivion – just like his suit and tie!

Chapter 34

Sunday, 29 October 2017 (p.m.)

Following his questioning of Brendan Molloy, Clarke remained in Interview Room 1 for several minutes; he had been thwarted in his attempt to get his prime suspect to confess to having done away with Luciano Rigione, and he was feeling angry and frustrated. Thumping the desk with his fist, he gathered up his paperwork and made his way out of Interview Room 1. It was then that he noticed the light above the door of Interview Room 2, indicating that the room was still occupied. He decided to intervene – probably against his better judgement.

Fletcher had almost concluded her interview with Linda Rigione when Clarke suddenly burst into the room, to the surprise of both women. What's more, he still had a face like thunder.

'Detective Chief Inspector Clarke has entered the room,' said Fletcher complete with frown.

'I'm sorry to butt in like this, Sergeant', he began. 'But there are a few questions that *I* would like to put to Mrs. Rigione, if I may?'

Linda Rigione was not at all happy. 'Oh, for crying out loud,' she snapped. 'I've told the officer here that I had nothing to do with the disappearance of my husband.'

Clarke wasn't going to be deterred. 'And yet you clearly lied to me about having ended your affair with Mr. Molloy?'

'So what if I did? That doesn't mean that I was involved in any way in the disappearance of my husband.'

Clarke paused briefly and then continued. 'How long have you and Mr. Molloy...'

Linda cut him short. 'It began a year ago,' she said whilst looking up at the ceiling.

'Would you care to tell us how it started?'

'Molloy was smitten from the moment he began working for us – Azzurri Furnishings. I rebuffed his advances at first...'

'But then what happened?'

'Well, Luciano couldn't keep his hands to himself, could he? And I thought okay, two can play at that game.'

'And so you finally succumbed to Molloy's advances?'

'Yes, that's right.'

'You must have been really angry with Luciano – I mean, what with his roving eye?'

'Of course I was!' she snapped.

'Did Luciano try it on with others besides Emma Duckmanton?'

'You could say he fancied his chances, yes.'

'Is that why you and Molloy plotted to do away with him?'

Linda exploded. 'Will you *stop* inferring that I had anything to do with Luciano's disappearance,' she screamed. 'For God's sake – it was me who reported him as missing!'

'So you were unaware of the fake accounts set up by Molloy?'

Linda was incredulous. 'What fake accounts?' she replied with a look of stunned amazement upon her face.

Clarke pulled out the list of suppliers and pointed to the four alleged accounts that they had uncovered earlier. 'See here, here, here and here. These are all fake accounts.'

'How do you know this?' she asked curiously.

Clarke referred to the Sex Pistols and then mentioned the fact that Molloy had a criminal record. 'Did you know of this when you took him on?'

'No, we bloody well didn't!' she snapped angrily.

'He was sentenced to four years imprisonment for his part in supplying fraudulent passports to organised gangs – including former IRA terrorists.'

'You're kidding me?'

'What's more, the police were unable to find all of the passports at the time.'

'What are you suggesting?'

'I'm saying that Molloy used forged passports to provide false documentation – for the fake accounts.'

'He must have gained access to all of our records, including our list of suppliers?'

'But of course.'

'The crafty bastard!' she hissed.

'So you're telling me that you had no knowledge of these accounts...'

'No I bloody well didn't!'

'Or that the money from those accounts was to be used to set you and Molloy up after Luciano had been done away with?'

'Are you bloody well listening to me – I had no knowledge of those accounts or what they were being used for!'

Clarke looked Linda in the eye for a few seconds and then turned to Fletcher. 'Do you have any further questions, Sergeant?' he asked somewhat forlornly.

'Not that I can think of, Sir,' replied Fletcher.

And so Clarke wound up the interview and told Linda that she could go. 'We may need to speak to you again though,' he added rather sternly.

And so they all rose from their seats and made their way to the door. As they stepped outside, Brendan Molloy was being led to his cell having just been charged with fraud. That was the cue for Linda Rigione to quite literally launch herself at her erstwhile lover. 'You fucking bastard!' she screamed. 'What have you done with my husband?'

It took Clarke and Fletcher all of their strength to restrain her as she tried to land blows upon the hapless former foreman of Azzurri Furnishings. Having succeeded to pull her away, Clarke ordered Scattergood to get hold of Detective Constable Preston. Minutes later the Family Liaison Officer appeared and took Linda home to Tapley Lane. There were to be no charges against her – yet.

Almost at the same time, Detective Constable Webster stepped out of Interview Room 3 and approached Clarke. 'Well, what did Ms. Price have to say?' grunted the Inspector.

'She's lying through her teeth, Sir,' replied Webster with a look of frustration upon his face. 'She has no evidence that her partner did away with Rigione – she just wants to spite him for cheating on her with Mrs. Rigione!'

'I've had my bellyful of these bloody charlatans for one day,' bellowed Clarke. 'Charge her with wasting police time!' He then stormed out of the building.

'What's the betting he'll be picking up a bottle of whisky on his way home,' suggested Webster to Scattergood as they watched Clarke drive away from the station.

'What's the betting he's drank the bloody lot before he goes to bed,' replied the Duty Sergeant with tongue in cheek!

Chapter 35

Monday, 30 October 2017 (a.m.)

There was to be no hangover for Detective Chief Inspector Clarke of Leverton CID on this dull but dry October morning. True, he did purchase a bottle of *Laphroaig* from the supermarket on his way home from the station the night before, but he had barely touched a drop before *he* had dropped off in the easy chair in the saloon of his narrow boat. Tiredness and exhaustion had overcome him, so at least he didn't spend the night lamenting on his love life – or lack of it!

And he didn't have much time to think about it when he woke that Monday morning either, for he had overslept somewhat and had given himself very little time to prepare for work. Being late on parade wouldn't go down well with Annable, and so he had a quick wash, selected his attire for the day and moments later he was setting off in the Ford Focus up Long Lane to the main Leverton to Grimley road.

As he entered the Station some ten minutes later, Scattergood had only just started his stint as Duty Sergeant for the day, and it didn't escape his notice once more that the DCI was wearing his bomber jacket again.

'Something troubling you, Scattergood?' said Clarke as he passed the reception desk.

'Not at all, Sir,' replied the Duty Sergeant in all honesty.

'Then kindly keep your opinions to yourself!'

'Never said a bloody word,' muttered a flabbergasted Scattergood under his breath.

Clarke failed to hear the last comment, but simply continued on and up the stairs to Annable's office, where he was greeted by the Superintendant's secretary. She knocked on Annable's door and received the usual response.

'Entaaah,' bellowed Annable.

'Chief Inspector Clarke to see you, Sir,' said the Secretary as she opened the door.

'Ah, just the man,' said Annable as Clarke entered the room. He then briefly turned to the Secretary. 'Thank you – that will be all for now.' And the secretary duly returned to her duties. 'Well, Clarke. I understand that there have been quite a few developments over the weekend?'

Unusually for Clarke, he chose to stand before the DCS and inform him of the events of the previous day. He went through the arrests of Brendan Molloy and Linda Rigione, and briefly touched on the suggestion by Molloy's partner, Wendy Price, that he had indeed been involved in the disappearance of Luciano Rigione. 'Unfortunately for Ms. Price, it would appear that she was merely cutting off her nose to spite her face in this instance.'

'What action have you taken against her – if any?' Annable asked with great interest.

'I've had her charged with wasting police time,' replied Clarke half-heartedly. 'Although whether or not the DPP will consent to proceedings is another matter,' he added under his breath.

'Wait a minute,' said Annable somewhat befuddled. 'Are you saying that Molloy is therefore innocent of Rigione's disappearance?'

'I'm not saying anything of the sort, Sir – I'm still confident that he is behind the disappearance of Rigione.'

'But you still haven't found a body?'

'Not as yet, Sir. But we will.'

'Don't you think you're being a trifle presumptuous?'

'That's as maybe, but...'

'I'm assuming that you have charged Molloy with *something*!' shouted Annable with a large degree of vexation.

'Of course I have!' replied Clarke somewhat affronted. 'He's been charged with fraud over the fake accounts.'

'And then there's Mrs. Rigione – what about her?'

'Well, she has been rather economical with the truth admittedly...'

'In what respect?' interjected Annable.

'With regard to her affair with Molloy – she had insisted that it was all over some time ago, but as we now know it was still ongoing up to her arrest.

'I see,' said Annable rubbing his chin.

'However, I believe her when she says that she had no idea about Molloy's little scam and therefore no involvement in her husband's disappearance.'

'Presumably you've let her go?'

'I have indeed, Sir. But she knows that we may need to talk to her again.'

'So what are you proposing?'

'We've got Molloy behind bars for the fraud charge, but I'd like an extension on the murder charge.'

'You're asking for a further ninety-six hours I take it?'

'Yes, Sir. That will give us time to question him further, and possibly seize and analyse any evidence that we may find.'

Annable bit his lip and nodded his head. 'I agree – on the condition that the search for Rigione is scaled down...'

'But, Sir...' Clarke protested.

'You know as well as I do that at the end of the day these things cost money, Clarke...'

'And yet the ACC is only too happy to throw money at her bloody ludicrous equality and diversity drivel...'

Clarke had clearly touched a nerve. 'I suggest that you concentrate on finding Luciano Rigione, Inspector,' bellowed Annable. 'It is *not* your place to take issue with the ACC!'

'Well...!' snapped Clarke with frustration.

'Stick to questioning Brendan Molloy and getting him to confess to having done away with Rigione!'

'Oh, I'll get it out of him,' said Clarke through gritted teeth. 'I did it before and I'll do it again!'

Annable was puzzled by Clarke's remarks. 'Did what before?'

Clarke ignored the question. 'Will that be all, Sir?'

Apparently it wasn't. 'It hasn't escaped my notice that you're back to wearing that bomber jacket, Clarke,' said Annable through what can only be described as squinty eyes. 'What happened to the suit?'

'Had to take it to the cleaners, Sir,' lied Clarke as he turned and left Annable looking somewhat unconvinced by his response!

Detective Constable Webster stood at the reception desk in conversation with the Duty Sergeant as Clarke made his way back downstairs after his meeting with Annable. Apparently Webster had some important information for the Inspector, but was loathe to pass it on in case he caught his boss in a bad mood again. Scattergood offered his encouragement.

'Go on – now's as good a time as any,' said the Duty Sergeant animatedly.

Webster visibly swallowed and decided to take the initiative. 'Sir,' he shouted across the reception area as Clarke reached the foot of the stairs. 'Could I have a moment of your time, please?'

Clarke had been in a world of his own from the moment he left Annable's office, but on hearing Webster calling to him he looked up and casually made his way over to the reception desk. 'What is it, Webster,' he said somewhat lackadaisically.

'I've got the results of the autopsy on the Bacon's dog,' said Webster guardedly and in expectation of having his head snapped off once more.

'And what does that tell us, Webster?' replied Clarke calmly and attentively.

Pleasantly surprised and relieved at Clarke's response, Webster continued. 'The dog was definitely poisoned by the Bacon's through the use of tea tree oil.'

'And what do you plan to do next?'

'I'm going to see them now, Sir, and inform them that the RSPCA will be involved.'

'Good work, Webster.' Clarke was about to turn and head for his office when out of the corner of his eye he saw Scattergood looking at him in a manner that suggested a little contrition would be welcome. 'By the way, Webster,' he continued. 'I owe you an apology.'

'What for, Sir?'

'My outburst the other day. It was totally uncalled for and I wish to offer you my profuse apologies.'

'We all have our off days, Sir.'

'Nevertheless, I shouldn't have taken my anger out on you, and I will endeavour to ensure that it doesn't happen again.'

'It's all water under the bridge, Sir,' replied Webster rather unconvincingly.

'Very well, Webster,' said Clarke with a rather benign smile. 'Get off and see to the Bacon's.'

As Webster left the building for Tapley Lane with a spring in his step, Clarke turned as if to make for his office, but at that moment he looked up out of the corner of his eye once more to see Scattergood nodding his head in approval.

Maybe life wasn't so bad after all; he tried to tell himself as he made his way to his office. Unfortunately it was then that he began to think of Diana Marshall, and he realised that he missed her more than he could have possibly imagined.

Chapter 36

Monday, 30 October 2017 (a.m.)

Clarke could have murdered a glass of whisky at that moment. However, he wasn't foolish enough to leave a bottle hidden in one of his drawers or cabinets, because someone was always bound to find it, and Annable would have sent him to hell for that. So he was going to have to wait till the evening, wasn't he?

Putting all thoughts of Diana to the back of his mind wasn't going to be an easy task under the circumstances, but he was a professional and he was fully aware that it was something that he simply had to do.

There were a number of reports on his desk awaiting his attention – and signature – as well as other forms of documentation that were of little or no importance to him as far as he was concerned. It just so happened that one of these was from the Assistant Chief Constable, giving the reasons why it was important to "proactively prioritise equality and diversity" in the East Midlands Regional Police. 'What a load of bollocks!' Clarke muttered under his breath. Needless to say, he read no further, but tore the document up and consigned it to the waste paper basket – where it belonged in his view!

With Webster absent and hopefully tearing a strip off the Bacon's, Clarke deemed it unnecessary to hold a full team briefing, so reports having been duly signed – and other documents disposed of one way or another – he popped his head out of the door and asked for Fletcher to join him in his office.

'Take a seat, Sergeant,' said Clarke as Fletcher closed the office door behind her. As was often the case, her long, dark hair had been tied into a ponytail and there was little evidence of make-up. Nevertheless, she still looked very attractive in a two piece navy blue suit with a collared blazer and in a shorter style that sat at the waist, and a pair of stretch trousers with a slightly flared hem. As she pulled up a chair, Clarke continued. 'I've been to see his nibs upstairs.'

'And what's he had to say, Sir?'

'Well, he has at least agreed to give us some time to question Molloy further on Rigione's disappearance.'

'He's granted us a further ninety-six hours then?'

'He has indeed.'

'So, what's the downside?'

'He wants the search to be scaled down.'

'I must admit that I was expecting as much, Sir.'

Clarke rose from his chair and went over to the window. 'Yes, I suppose that I should have seen that one coming,' he said more to himself than to Fletcher. 'Have the searches of Molloy's house or that of the Rigione's revealed *anything*?'

Fletcher leaned back in her chair and stretched her arms in the air whilst stifling a yawn. 'No incriminating evidence has been found at the Rigione's.'

'And other than the passports, nothing from Molloy's house I take it?'

'I'm afraid not, Sir.'

Clarke turned to face her once more. 'Just remind me how and where the passports *were* found again, will you?'

'Strangely enough, it didn't take long to find the passports at all.'

'Including the four that Molloy used for his scam?'

'Those *and* the six other empty passports were all found inside a large book entitled *The History of Ireland*.'

'I should have known it,' said Clarke somewhat ruefully.

'Some of the pages had been partly cut out and the passports placed inside,' continued Fletcher.

Clarke shook his head. 'And the mobiles proved that the relationship was still ongoing?'

'Yes, but there's no evidence that the two of them were planning to do away with Rigione or that Molloy was doing it all by himself.'

'Damn!' grunted Clarke.

'What's our next course of action then, Sir?'

'I'd like you to get everyone together and issue orders to continue the search for Rigione – albeit with reduced numbers. Think you can do that?'

'Shouldn't be a problem, Sir,' replied Fletcher enthusiastically as she rose from her chair. 'What will you be doing in the meantime.'

'I'm going down to the Peacock Pathway. I want to see for myself the route that we believe Rigione would have taken.'

As she left Clarke's office with her instructions, Fletcher muttered under her breath 'Needle in a haystack!'

Chapter 37

Monday, 30 October 2017 (p.m.)

As it approached noon on that Monday morning, the weather was holding nicely and Clarke decided to head back home to his narrow boat, where he made himself a couple of sandwiches before changing into appropriate walking gear. He had a pair of decent walking boots at hand and he finished off by donning a waterproof and breathable green cagoule.

He had decided to take the bus to Sibley Pond, which marked the start of the Peacock Pathway, and so leaving the Ford Focus parked beside the narrow boat he made his way on foot up Long Lane to the main road and the bus stop. He didn't have to wait long; the Grimley to Derby bus pulled up five minutes later.

It had been a long time since he had used a bus, and he was conscious of the fact that this one would be passing through the centre of Leverton. He was always glad when he came away from the town centre – too many people and too much concrete. No, it was always something of a relief to have put the town centre behind him, and this occasion was no different.

Alighting at the bus stop opposite Sibley Pond, he crossed the road to the Pathway and paused briefly to gaze at the wildfowl on the water and the nearby bank. Numerous Canada geese seemed to proliferate, together with several mute swans. Needless to say, coots and moorhens clashed here and there, whilst mallard's flitted to and fro, but the star attraction today had to be the two Great crested grebes in the centre of the pond, both of which took turns to dive for prey every so often.

Moving on, he passed the notice board and saw the first of many posters that had been put up around Leverton and surrounding communities with a picture of Rigione and asking locals "Have you seen this man?" He then made his way through the car park and on up the pathway. Other than the odd individual out walking their dogs, there were very few people following his example, and no cyclists to speak of. Perhaps it was the time of year, although it wasn't what he would have put down as a very cold day.

Once past the pond, all was wild scrubland over to his left, with blackthorn and hawthorn dominating. Over to his right the Leverton Golf Course stretched into the distance, and there was a footpath that led from the Pathway to the clubhouse. Of course, Rigione could have slipped through here, but CCTV cameras from the clubhouse didn't pick him up.

After a mile or so the golf course came to an end, and the Pathway suddenly took a sharp right-hand bend and then left again. He was now about to pass the Croxley Moor Estate on his right. Molloy's house backed on to the Pathway and when Clarke came to it he was confronted by a tall fence with a gate. Yes, he thought to himself; this must have been where the bastard struck. He waylaid him here, but what did he do with the bloody body? 'Wait a minute, wait a minute,' he said out loud. 'Too risky surely – the neighbours would have seen *everything*!' That put paid to that little brainwave! So how did he bloody well do it? Time to move on he decided.

As he reached the end of the Croxley Moor Estate, there was another footpath off to the right that ran alongside the estate and on up to the main Leverton to Grimley road. However, he continued along the Pathway, which suddenly veered off to the left and continued on to Croxley Lake.

On reaching the lake he stopped once more. The wildfowl was for the most part conspicuous by its absence compared to that which predominated at Sibley Pond, but at this moment his mind was focused on the work of the underwater search team, and their fruitless searches of this and the other lakes and ponds.

He then continued along the Pathway which then passed alongside the woods that stood behind the lake. Off to his right was a dirt track which led on to the narrow lane that passed the site of the old Croxley Colliery, before continuing on up to the main road and coming out opposite Long Lane. There was a large car park at the top of this narrow lane, complete with CCTV cameras, but yet again these had failed to provide any evidence as to what had happened to Rigione.

Shaking his head, he carried on until he came to Riley's Pond on the left and the end of the Pathway. So far it had taken him almost an hour and a half on foot. Did Rigione get this far, he wondered? Could Molloy have abducted the man here and disposed of his body elsewhere? Not for the first time he began to wish that he'd never taken on this case.

Turning left at the exit point, he then headed down Rosehip Lane in the direction of Croxley Country Park. It was quite densely wooded either side of the lane, but there appeared to be very little in the way of birdsong to his disappointment. After a quarter of a mile he came to another lane on the left which led all the way into Tapley village three miles distant. Choosing this route to begin with, he approached Croxley Wood on his left. Rather than continue on into Tapley, he decided to take the footpath that led through the Wood.

At most times of the year roe deer can be seen among the trees or in the various clearings, but today he was to be disappointed on that score too. As expected there was an abundance of grey squirrels, and he was pleasantly surprised to see birds such as the treecreeper, nuthatch and goldcrest as he made his way along the path. More importantly, he was aware that search parties had combed the Wood the previous week, but again there was nothing to suggest that Rigione had been attacked and disposed of there or thereabouts.

As he eventually came out of the Wood, the footpath took him down to Croxley Lake once more. From there it veered off right and there was a steady climb for a mile or so thereafter. At the top of the hill there was a sharp turn to the right and the path suddenly became a dirt track. This then merged into the lane that led into Tapley village straight ahead. As he made his way along this narrow lane, Pit Lane lay on his left and this came out beside *The Lyttelton Arms* at Great Sibley. At the top of Pit Lane stood Lower Grange Farm, and yet there seemed to be little in the way of activity as he passed by.

He had been walking for almost three hours now, and *The Cross Keys* was only five or ten minutes walk away; now seemed as good a time as any for a pint. When he arrived at the pub there were only three or four other customers and no sign of Derek Foster or Susan Addison. Instead it was a young girl who stood behind the bar as he approached.

'What can I get you, Sir?' she asked with a winsome smile.

'I rather like your *Chatsworth Gold*,' replied Clarke rather cheerfully. 'So I'll have a pint of that, please.'

A minute or so later she placed the glass of ale before him on the bar. 'Is there anything else I can get you?' she asked.

'No, that will be all, thanks.'

'That's £3.30 then, please.'

Handing over a five pound note, she gave him his change and he headed for a table directly opposite the bar. It was good to sit down after what for him was a long trek, but all the more so when he had a decent pint of beer beside him. He felt even more uplifted after knocking back the first few draughts.

He now had a few moments in which to mull over the afternoons walk and what he had gleaned from it. He was still convinced that Molloy had done the dirty deed, but whereabouts had he carried it out and what had he done with the body? He couldn't have done it at the rear of his home – the neighbours would have seen him. There were a number of exit routes from the Pathway by which Molloy could have lured Rigione away, but these were almost all covered by CCTV cameras. No, he had to have been lying in wait for him at the exit point from the Pathway, attacked the man there and then, bundled him into the boot of his car and then driven off to dispose of the body at his leisure. He would get forensics to go over Molloy's car with a fine toothcomb!

Finishing off his pint, he returned the glass to the bar and thanked the young girl before leaving. As he stepped outside the pub, he felt that the net was at last beginning to close in on Molloy. Not to put too fine a point on things, he felt more upbeat at that moment than he had done throughout the case. He pulled out his mobile – the clock was coming up to 4.30 p.m. He didn't particularly fancy returning home on foot, so he decided to call the station. Yes, it was all coming together very nicely thank you!

As Clarke was supping at the last dregs of his pint at *The Cross Key's*, Kath Meakin was busy preparing the evening meal just up the road at Upper Grange Farm when husband Richard walked in.

'Ricky not 'ere then?' he said with a sense of exasperation.

'Thought he wer' 'elpin you fetch t'cows in for milkin'?' she replied without looking up.

'The lazy bugger told me 'e wer' goin' to t'ouse to empty 'is bladder – and that wer' 'alf 'our ago.'

'Well I've been 'ere all afternoon and I 'avna seen 'im.'

'I'll bet the crafty bugger 'as sneaked off to t'pub for a swift 'alf.'

'I shouldn't be at all surprised, especially if that young lass is behind t'bar again tonight.'

'I don't know why I bloody bother!'

Bob Scattergood was just about to come off duty when he got the call from Clarke asking to be picked up from *The Cross Key's*.

'I'll get Webster to come and fetch you, Sir,' he replied in his usual jovial manner. Clarke thanked him and was about to hang up, but Scattergood apparently hadn't finished. 'Oh, there's a couple of things you might like to know before you go, Sir.'

'Go on, Scattergood,' said Clarke a trifle wearily.

'Well, Webster has been to see the Bacon's in the company of an officer from the RSPCA, Sir. The pair have been severely reprimanded and told that they will be appearing in court, with the likelihood that they will be facing a lifetime ban on keeping pets of any kind.'

'That's good to hear, Scattergood. What was the other thing that you wanted to tell me?'

'There's been a fracas down at the golf club, Sir.'

'What do you mean by "fracas", Scattergood?'

'Two young lads have been brought in after brawling outside the clubhouse.'

'Do we know who these two young lads are?'

'Ricky Meakin and Marco Rigione,' replied Scattergood.

'Bang them up overnight and inform their parents!' shouted Clarke angrily. 'I'll get Fletcher to deal with them in the morning!'

Chapter 38

Tuesday, 31 October 2017 (a.m.)

It looked like being another dry but blustery day for the inhabitants of Leverton and the surrounding communities. Clarke had arrived for work attired in his bomber jacket once more, and not in the least bit concerned as to what DCS Annable might say or do about it. He was in a relatively upbeat mood for a change, and hoping to pile even more pressure upon Brendan Molloy. For that reason he had ordered SOCO's to tear apart the latter's car with a view to finding incriminating evidence that would link him to the disappearance of Luciano Rigione.

Molloy was brought into Interview Room 1, and he was accompanied once more by Christopher Aitchison, the Duty Solicitor. Both gave the appearance of being supremely confident that they could handle *any* line of questioning, and that was the impression that Clarke had when he entered the room. It wasn't going to be easy.

Clarke threw his bomber jacket around the chair once more, and seated himself before Molloy and Aitchison without looking either of them in the face. The tape was switched on, preliminaries were dispensed with and only then did Clarke lift his head and gaze at Molloy. 'You've been charged with fraud,' he began. 'But as you are no doubt aware we have been given a further ninety-six hours to question you about the disappearance of Luciano Rigione. Do you have anything to say in that regard?'

The response from Molloy was as expected. 'No comment,' he said nonchalantly.

Clarke returned to the previous interview on Sunday evening. 'Well, there's one thing that we can be sure of,' he said with the vestiges of a smile. 'Your affair with Mrs. Rigione seems to have come to a rather ignominious end.'

'You win some, you lose some,' shrugged Molloy, before going on to taunt Clarke in regard to his school days. 'Funny, but I don't remember you having much success with women – if at all.'

Clarke refused to take the bait. 'What's more, it looks like she's come to the conclusion that you've done away with her husband too.' Molloy grimaced, but said nothing, and so Clarke continued. 'And you thought that with him out of the way she would come running – that right?'

Molloy was about to respond, but the Duty Solicitor grabbed him by the arm. 'My client does not wish to comment,' said Aitchison with an undisguised sneer. 'Now, unless you have any evidence...'

Clarke cut him short. 'You should know that we have impounded your car, and that Scene's of Crime Officer's are looking for *any* evidence that will link you to the disappearance of Mr. Rigione.'

Molloy and Aitchison stood and made as if to leave the room. 'Come along,' said the latter to his client. 'The Inspector is clutching at straws and hasn't got a shred of evidence to back his claims.'

'We'll find it – don't you worry!' shouted Clarke with growing confidence as the two men left the room.

Yes, he thought to himself as he switched off the tape. All that remained now was for SOCO's to find the evidence that Rigione was in that car, and the staff at the lab would confirm it. The wonders of technology were bound to ensnare this bloody weasel, and Clarke would have his man. No doubt Diana would have told him to be more objective and not let his feelings take over, but it was too late; Clarke had the bit between his teeth now and justice was going to be done come hell or high water – one way or another.

Ricky Meakin and Marco Rigione had spent an uncomfortable and rather sleepless night banged up in the cells at Leverton police station following their apparent confrontation. Kath Meakin and Yvonne Rigione were sat opposite each other in Interview Room 3, anxiously awaiting news of their respective offspring's fate, and one could have cut the air with a knife. It was somewhat fortuitous that a uniformed WPC was in the room with them, otherwise a monumental cat-fight would have probably ensued!

Detective Sergeant Fletcher had been assigned the task of questioning the two adversaries that particular morning, and naturally she did so separately. From what Fletcher was able to gather, it transpired that Marco had caught Ricky tampering with his bike at the golf club. When he began to remonstrate with Ricky, the latter began throwing punches; a fact that he strenuously denied.

Needless to say, Marco retaliated and a brawl ensued. At this point Rachel Meakin came running out of the clubhouse bar to intervene. She would subsequently corroborate Marco's assertion that Ricky threw the first punch. Others came over to separate the pair whilst a call was put through to the police. Both Marco *and* Ricky were subsequently arrested and brought to the station.

During her questioning of Ricky (who seemed to have damaged his nose during the brawl), Fletcher asked him why he went to the golf club and tampered with Marco's bike.

'I wanted to teach him a lesson,' grunted Ricky.

'But what had he done to you?' replied Fletcher with exasperation.

'He was seeing my sister, wasn't he?'

'What's that got to do with the price of fish?'

'You wouldn't understand.'

'Try me – I'm all ears.'

'I didn't want his kind trying it on with my sister.'

'His kind – what's that supposed to mean?'

'He's a Rigione, isn't he?' snapped Ricky. 'He's a fucking dago bastard, like his dad.'

'I think I've got the message,' replied Fletcher shaking her head. She paused briefly and then went on to comment about the damage done to Marco's bike. 'You do realise that he could have had a serious accident after what you did?'

'It was nothing – he would have broken down, that's all.'

Fletcher wasn't convinced, and following her questioning of Ricky it was decided to charge him with Common Assault; he was also told that he faced a fine. Marco, on the other hand, was released with just a few bruises and swelling around one eye. This did not go down well with Kath Meakin, who turned her fury and venom on Yvonne Rigione.

'That bloody son of yours is goin' to pay for this!' she screamed.

'Oh, piss off, you pathetic old hag!' replied Yvonne with a sneer.

'Who are you callin' a bloody 'ag?'

The WPC tasked with watching over the two women was forced to come between them, and she was subsequently joined by Marco, but the angry confrontation continued in the station car park, where Rachel Meakin had been sitting and waiting in Yvonne Rigione's car. The shouting attracted her attention, and she stormed out of the car and over to her mother.

'Stop it, stop it, stop it,' she screamed at her mother.

'See, even your own bloody daughter doesn't like you!' shouted Yvonne.

'If I catch your son anywhere near my daughter...' replied Kath as she jabbed her forefinger into Yvonne's face. She then turned to her daughter. 'Now get in t'vehicle!'

'No, I'm going back with Marco and Yvonne,' screamed Rachel. 'And nothing you can do will stop me!'

'You'll do as you're bloody well told, young lady.' But Rachel wasn't listening as her mother shouted after her. 'Come back 'ere!'

Rachel was as good as her word. She climbed into the car with Marco and Yvonne, and the three of them sped off out of the car park with the latter at the wheel. Kath was left standing red-faced beside her Land Rover – she was the very picture of rage. One of her kids had been charged with assault and now the other had quite literally shoved two fingers up to her. The morning had turned into a nightmare for her and her family. Surely it couldn't get any worse than this?

Chapter 39

Tuesday, 31 October 2017 (p.m.)

Clarke was sat in his office and feeling a trifle anxious – and bored if truth be told. Still not a peep from the SOCO's searching for evidence from Brendan Molloy's car, and the man himself was refusing to yield anything about the disappearance of Luciano Rigione when questioned. He looked up at the clock and couldn't make his mind up whether or not to go home and call it a day.

Then it occurred to him for the first time that particular day that it was Halloween, and the kids would be out trick or treating in a few hours time. God, how he hated that Americanised twaddle; why did we have to import the bugger, he thought to himself. At least he wouldn't be bothered down by the canal on his narrow boat. Diana would have been having a Halloween party at *The Navigation* under normal circumstances, but that was extremely unlikely and he wouldn't have been welcome anyway – not now. Would he?

Oh, for God's sake put your coat and get off home, he told himself. But at that precise moment the phone on his desk went off and he picked it up, thinking that it might be the SOCO's. It was Joel Bishop from The Leverton Gazette.

'Hello Joel – what can I do for you?' he said somewhat disappointedly.

'Hello Allan – how's tricks?' replied Bishop slightly more cheerfully.

'Oh, you know – fair to lousy!'

'That bad is it?'

'I've had better days,' said Clarke truthfully. 'Now what is it that you're after?'

'You've got me sussed, haven't you?' joked Bishop.

'I've known you long enough.'

'Well, I just wondered how the case was going, that's all.'

Clarke sighed heavily. 'We've charged Brendan Molloy with fraud, but as yet we can't get him to confess to having done away with Luciano Rigione.'

'I assume that you've been given more time to question him?'

'We've got until Friday.'

'And you're confident that he's your man?'

Clarke hesitated slightly. 'Yes, I am.'

'You don't sound too sure about that?'

'Don't I?' he said with slight indifference.

'Well, I'm beginning to wonder if...'

Clarke cut him short. 'If what?'

'It strikes me that you've got something of a grudge against Molloy.'

'What makes you say that?' replied Clarke, who was becoming just a tad irritated with the man on the other end of the phone. 'Has somebody been opening their mouth?'

'Nobody has said a word – it's just that you seem to have had it in for the man from the outset.'

'Joel, I happen to believe that the man has committed a serious crime, and I want to see him brought to justice for it. Now is that all?'

Bishop remained unconvinced, but chose not to say as much. 'I guess that's it for now,' he said rather lamely.

'Fine – you'll be kept informed of any developments.'

'Okay, thanks.'

'Bye for now.'

Bishop was about to reply, but the phone went dead before he could do so. He'd touched a nerve – there was no doubt about that, he thought to himself. What *had* Clarke got on Molloy? Was it something from the past? If that was the case, then he was letting his personal feelings get in the way of his judgement, and no good would come of that.

It had been an eventful day for Detective Sergeant Fletcher; what with having to interview Ricky Meakin and Marco Rigione following their brawl and the contretemps between their respective mothers afterwards. After lunch she had turned her attention to the scaled down search for Luciano Rigione once more, and now she was sat at her desk in the main office putting the final touches to her reports. Having completed that task, she sat back in her chair and ruminated on Clarke's approach to the case – not for the first time.

Not to put too fine a point on things, but she was becoming increasingly concerned that the case had got to Clarke. It had become personal for him – more like a vendetta really, or so she thought. Perhaps it was time for a new face at the helm; someone who could take a more objective approach to the case. Perhaps if Annable were to step in once more then he might just consider handing the case over to her; that is until someone with the appropriate rank assumed control of course? This and other rather fanciful notions were flowing through her mind when Detective Constable Webster entered the room.

'Ah, Webster, may I be so bold as to pick your brains?' she said in what might be construed as a slightly calculating manner.

Webster looked around him as if he wasn't quite sure that she was referring to him. 'Who, me?' he replied with noticeable trepidation.

'Yes, you, Webster,' she said with an alluring smile. 'How do you think the case is progressing – are we making any headway, do you think?'

He pondered the question for a moment. 'Well, that's hard to say really.'

'How do you mean?'

'Admittedly we seem to be no nearer to finding out what happened to Rigione...'

'Go on – you can tell me.'

'Well, the Inspector does seem to have a bee in his bonnet about this guy, Molloy...'

'And..?'

'And yet I'm sure we've got the right man...'

Fletcher's heart sank. 'Oh, I see.'

'It's just getting him to confess – that's the trouble.'

'You don't think that we'd be better with someone else taking over the case then?' she said with an ever decreasing sense of forlorn optimism.

'I hadn't thought of that,' he replied pensively, but then he suddenly realised the import of her statement. 'Are you suggesting that we go to the DSC and have Inspector Clarke removed?'

'Well it did cross my mind...'

'He'd never forgive you, Sarge.'

'No, I don't suppose he would,' she said somewhat laconically.

And that was the end of *that* conversation!

As Webster headed for the kitchen, Fletcher sighed deeply as she stood and donned her coat. She had hoped that Webster might be a trifle more supportive, but it was clear as daylight that he was just another loyal sidekick of DCI Clarke, and that if she was to reach the dizzy heights of Senior Investigating Officer then she would either have to wait for the right moment or go it alone. Neither option appealed to her, but if needs must...

Chapter 40

Wednesday, 1 November 2017

Wednesday morning dawned wet and miserable, and that was still the case as DCI Clarke arrived for work just before 8.30 a.m. More importantly, it seemed to match his mood. True, he hadn't been plagued by kids in their garish costumes plying their trick or treat nonsense the night before, but he hadn't slept well either, and now the rain was coming down in a steady, mist-like drizzle that had the effect of making him feel utterly despondent. Willie Nelson had a song for it – *Rainy Day Blues*.

Avoiding the puddles in the station car park, he burst through the doors of the building looking mean and moody, and Scattergood could have sworn that he was going to approach the reception desk with the words 'I've come for my boy' in a Deep South drawl! Instead he merely grunted 'morning' to the Desk Sergeant before striding off to his office, where he closed the door behind him as if to shut out the entire world.

He would be questioning Brendan Molloy again today, but how the bloody hell was he going to bring charges against the man when he had no bloody evidence and no bloody body! Where in God's name were those SOCO's? Surely they must have found something from Molloy's car by now? Tuesday's scaled down searches had revealed bugger all too, and time was running out.

Clarke was subsequently informed that Molloy and his solicitor were waiting in Interview Room 1, and this time he decided to take Fletcher in with him. He wasn't sure that it was the right decision, but perhaps she could succeed in getting the man to open up where he had failed. Unfortunately the interview descended into chaos, and Fletcher had very little opportunity to get a word in.

Once again Clarke put it to Molloy that he had done away with Luciano Rigione, and once again Molloy refused to play ball. And then Clarke went back to Molloy's previous conviction. 'You had a number of friends in the IRA at one time, didn't you?' he began. 'Did you turn to them for help in disposing of your erstwhile friend and boss?'

The Duty Solicitor intervened. 'Oh, this is getting ridiculous...' he snapped.

Molloy put his hand up as if to assure the Duty Solicitor that he could handle the questioning. 'You really are getting desperate, aren't you?' he sneered.

'I have to look at every possibility,' growled Clarke.

'I've tried to tell you that I had nothing to do with Rigione's disappearance, but you just refuse to listen, don't you? You're so obsessed with the idea that I'm the guilty party that you can't see beyond the end of your bloody nose, can you?'

'Like I said...'

Molloy had now got the bit between *his* teeth. 'I helped myself to some of Rigione's money, yes,' he said in a low voice. 'But I will *not* make an admission of guilt for something I didn't do or haven't done!'

Fletcher tried to get a word in. 'Perhaps we should take a break...' she shouted above Molloy, but it was to no avail.

'You're capable of anything, Molloy – as I know only too well!' snarled Clarke.

'And we knew how to deal with snivelling little shits like you, didn't we?'

Aitchison stepped in once more. 'My client will *not* be answering any more questions,' he boomed. 'This has descended into a farce, and I shall be speaking to your superiors, make no mistake.'

And with that the two men left the room once more. Clarke remained seated at the desk, but Fletcher stood up and made her views perfectly clear. 'I think that Molloy has a point, Sir,' she said with due conviction.

'What?' snapped Clarke, as if he had just come out of a trance.

'In my opinion you have turned the entire case into a personal vendetta.'

Clarke spat out his response in no uncertain terms. 'When I need your opinion, I will ask,' he said in an unpleasant tone. 'Until then, mind your own business, Sergeant!'

Clarke stormed out of the room and out of the building, leaving Fletcher lost for words. What was she to do? Under the circumstances she should have gone straight to DCS Annable and let him know what she thought, but in spite of Clarke's distasteful manner she didn't want to antagonise him any further. It was all turning into a shambles, and she headed for the canteen and a cup of coffee to contemplate her next move.

The village of Wendicott lay five or six miles to the south of Derby, in a pleasantly rustic setting. The only pub in the village was *The Royal Oak Inn*, and Clarke used to go there when things were getting on top of him during his time with Derby City Police and the Drugs Squad. Well, things were getting on top of him now, and it was no surprise that he should have ventured to *The Royal Oak* to let off a little steam following the events of that morning.

And so just after noon he sat alone at a table in the bar of *The Royal Oak* supping a pint of *Jaipur* ale from the Thornbridge brewery. The fact that it was 5.9% ABV did not deter him from selecting this particular ale, especially as he also declined the offer of something to eat from their classic pub food menu.

Things were not going at all well for him; both with regard to the case and to his private life. At that particular moment he could have packed it all in and set off in the *Emily* for who knows where; just as long as it was many, many miles away from Leverton. Not for the first time he began to regret taking on the case. For one thing it brought back many painful memories for him, but if truth be told the whole shebang was going bloody pear-shaped!

And then of course there was Diana. Should he call her or send her a text message? Or should he pop into *The Navigation* just to see how she was? He wanted to do all of these things, but the last time that they saw each other she had made it abundantly clear that he was very much *persona non grata*. Christ, what a bloody mess!

These and other dispiriting thoughts were passing through his mind when the new ringtone of *Jumping Jack Flash* by The Rolling Stones on his mobile phone informed him that he was wanted back at the station. It was Scattergood making the call, and that could only mean one thing – Annable wanted to see him.

Refusing to answer it, he continued supping at his ale until the phone stopped ringing. He knew of course that a text message would soon come up on his phone, and sure enough seconds later Scattergood sent a message informing him that Annable was on the warpath and wanted to see him *now*! 'Well he can bloody well wait,' muttered Clarke under his breath. But there was more. Scattergood's message went on to add that SOCO's had apparently failed to find *any* evidence whatsoever that Luciano Rigione had been in Molloy's car – dead or alive.

Well, that was that then – he would be off the case before you could say police harassment! Things just couldn't get any worse – could they? He slumped back into his chair and contemplated having a second pint. On second thoughts, perhaps it wasn't such a good idea after all, and so he took his empty glass back to the bar and bade farewell to the rather nubile young barmaid before heading for his car.

For several minutes he sat behind the steering wheel and convinced himself that Fletcher had gone over his head. If she thought that he had been unpleasant that morning, then one thing was for sure. 'She ain't seen nothing yet,' he said to himself as he turned on the ignition!

Chapter 41

Wednesday, 1 November 2017 (p.m.)

As Clarke headed back to the station in his car feeling utterly dejected, he suddenly had a change of mind. It would be one last throw of the dice before he himself was thrown off the case – and probably out of the force altogether. As he approached Little Sibley from Derby, he decided to turn off on the B7027 and head for Tapley Lane. He was going to see Linda Rigione one last time and see if she could reveal *anything* that might lead him to discovering what had happened to her husband. Annable would more than likely blow a gasket, but he was prepared to face that problem when he came to it.

Pulling up outside the Rigione's house on Tapley Lane that afternoon, he could have sworn that he saw the curtains twitch in the house across the road; the threat of a court appearance clearly hadn't stopped the Bacon's from being a pair of nosy bastards, he thought to himself. With a wry grin on his face, he shook his head as he climbed out of the car and made his way up the path to the house. The door was answered by the Family Liaison Officer, DC Laura Preston.

'Is she in?' asked Clarke quietly.

'She's in the living room, Sir,' replied Preston as she stood back to let Clarke pass. 'Go on through.'

Linda was sat on the sofa reading a magazine when Clarke entered the room. Not for the first time he was bedazzled by her appearance, and he readily appreciated why Luciano Rigione had fallen for the woman. He gave a little cough and she looked up from her magazine.

'I didn't think it would be long before we saw you again, Inspector,' she said in a droll monotone. 'Have you charged that bastard Molloy with murdering my husband yet?'

'He's been charged with fraud, but he claims to have had no involvement in the disappearance of Luciano,' replied Clarke with a shrug of the shoulders. 'In fact even I'm coming round to the idea that he's telling the truth on that score.'

'Then why in God's name was he stealing all that money from us and putting it all into fake accounts?'

'Merely to enrich himself at Luciano's expense.'

'But I thought that he and Luciano were great friends as well as colleagues?'

'He seems to have got a trifle envious of Luciano's lifestyle – at least that's the way I now see it.'

'So he wasn't hoping that I would leave Luciano in order to set up home with him somewhere in the sun?'

Clarke shook his head. 'It doesn't look like it.'

'The bastard,' she snarled as she looked out of the window.

Clarke paused for a few moments before continuing. 'Look, Linda, can you think of *anyone* else who Luciano might have been having an affair with?'

'Anyone in a skirt,' she replied sardonically.

'Please think long and hard, Linda...'

'I'm trying to bloody well think, but I can't...' And then she suddenly stopped and looked Clarke straight in the eye. 'That is unless he was having it off with Nicola Meakin?'

'Nicola Meakin?' repeated Clarke.

'Derek Meakin's wife – they live at Lower Grange Farm up the road here.'

'Would that be Richard Meakin's brother by any chance?'

'That's right – do you know the family?'

'I've met Kath Meakin, but I don't recall...'

She wasn't really listening, so she cut him short and simply carried on. 'We bumped into Nicola and Derek at *The Lyttelton Arms* back in February – Luciano and I.'

'Go on, Linda – you have my attention.'

'Well, they were hoping to go to their caravan in July, and Derek was looking for a new divan...'

'They have a caravan?'

'Yes, it's up in the Peak District – Derek stores it at the Collymore Caravan and Motorhome Club Site between March and November every year.'

'Please continue,' said Clarke apologetically.

'It's just that Nicola didn't seem interested in the divan *or* the caravan, but I rather had the impression that Luciano was interested in her.'

'What makes you say that?'

'I don't know,' she replied thoughtfully. 'But there just seemed to be some chemistry between the pair of them – at least that's how I saw it.'

'Did anything come of this?'

'Luciano suggested that Nicola and Derek make an appointment at Azzurri Furnishings – Derek agreed instantly, but I just sensed that Luciano was more interested in Nicola.'

'Did the appointment go ahead?'

'I made the booking,' replied Linda somewhat regretfully. 'And so the first week in March Nicola and Derek came to visit our showroom at Azzurri Furnishings.'

'To look at the divans...?'

'Ostensibly,' said Linda with a wry grin. 'If I remember right, Brendan – Molloy that is – showed Derek around whilst Luciano "entertained" Nicola.'

'You mean he tried it on with her right in front of you?'

'He was all over her like a rash!'

'And you said nothing to him about this at the time?'

'Well, I suppose that I could have done...'

'But?' said Clarke, urging her to continue.

'But I was involved with Molloy at the time, wasn't I?'

'And you think that Luciano and Nicola became involved at this time?'

'I wouldn't be at all surprised, knowing Luciano as I did.'

Clarke was almost exuberant. 'Thanks, Linda,' he said effusively. 'You've been really helpful.'

'And that's it?' she asked almost forlornly.

'If you can think of anything else that may lead you to believe Luciano and Nicola were having an affair or find something that may incriminate him, then you know where to find me.'

'There was *one* thing I wanted to ask you,' she said somewhat flirtatiously.

'And what's that?' he replied.

'Why do they call you "Sniffer"?'

'How did you know that?'

'Molloy happened to mention it one day.'

He looked down at the floor, almost as if he'd been found guilty of some slight misdemeanour, and then back up again. 'It's a long story, Linda.'

'Well I've got a lot of time on my hands,' she said seductively.

He sighed heavily before replying. 'Back in the seventies there was a well-known footballer by the name of Allan Clarke, who received the nickname "Sniffer" from his teammates.'

'And why was that – was he always sniffing?'

'No, it was because he was able to "sniff" out a goal from the unlikeliest of scoring opportunities.'

'That's weird,' replied Linda with a deep frown. 'And the kids at school called you "Sniffer" after this guy?'

Clarke nodded his head. 'My mum wouldn't have liked it.'

'Why was that?'

'Because she named me after Allan Clarke, the lead singer of The Hollies – you've heard of them I take it?'

'Yes, but didn't your mum know what they called you at school?'

Clarke looked down at the floor again. 'My mum and dad were killed in a car accident when I was quite young – I was raised by my grandparents.'

'I'm sorry to hear that,' she replied sympathetically.

Clarke gave a half-hearted smile and then departed. If he had a penny for every time that he'd had to explain why he was called "Sniffer" and what had happened to his parents, then he'd be a millionaire by now. That was soon forgotten as he climbed into his car and returned to the revelations that Linda had made earlier.

Of course it would have been better for all concerned had she told him about Nicola Meakin at the very outset, but at least he now had *something* concrete to go on and hopefully bring the case to a close. The stumbling block was Annable – and time, of course. He was running out of that with every passing minute.

Okay, the DCS would no doubt give him a bollocking for not returning to the station when told, but he knew how to handle the man. It was getting late now and he sure as hell didn't feel like receiving a dressing down at that precise moment, and so he decided to leave it until the morning. Besides, the DCS would have no option but to listen to him, and with any luck give him the chance to exonerate himself with this new evidence (if it was evidence). Yes, go home, Clarke – and don't forget to pick a bottle of *Laphroaig* up from the supermarket on the way!

Chapter 42

Thursday, 2 November 2017 (a.m.)

Not for the first time, Clarke woke with a thumping headache having hit the bottle the night before. He remembered to buy a bottle of *Laphroaig* from the supermarket alright; trouble was, when he eventually got up and staggered into the saloon, he noticed that most of it was gone!

It must have been quite a session – not that he could remember much about it. Oh, he'd washed and dried all the pots before putting them away, but the DVD player hadn't been switched off and an empty DVD cover lay on the table in front of it. It would appear that he'd been watching *The Eagles Farewell Tour 2005, Live From Melbourne*. Suddenly he remembered singing along to classics such as *Take It Easy, Lyin' Eyes* and of course *Hotel California*. Now he was paying the price for his exuberance; or was it his way of trying to get over Diana?

Copious amounts of water were called for, followed by a shower. Before he did any of these things he stepped outside to take in the fresh air and get an idea of what the weather was like. It was dry – much to his satisfaction – and the sun was trying to get through. What's more, it was a damn sight cooler than it had been in recent days. Things were looking good for bonfire night and the simultaneous display of pyrotechnics – not that he was in any way interested in either.

Having guzzled down almost an entire large bottle of Sparkling Buxton Water, he was standing under the shower head moments later as the water cascaded down upon him. It was bliss – and especially for someone whose head felt like it had been pounded by the late Keith Moon during the live performance by The Who at Woodstock in 1969. However, he tried to turn his thoughts to the day ahead and the almost certain reprimand from Annable. Stop worrying, he told himself – it was part and parcel of being a Senior Investigating Officer, and all would turn out well in the end.

He climbed out of the shower feeling like a new man. Within fifteen minutes he was washed and dressed (teeth had been cleaned *naturellement*) and he was ready to take on the world. Just a glass or two of water, and then he was locking up and climbing into his car. He wasn't feeling quite so buoyant when he slammed the car door shut and his head reverberated and shook as if it had been hit by an Exocet missile!

Bob Scattergood had not been long at work when he decided to steal a few moments for a crafty fag outside the main doors of the station. His thoughts on this particular morning were directed towards the weekend. He had arranged to take the grandkids to a bonfire and fireworks display at one of the local hostelries on Saturday night, and he was really looking forward to it. Needless to say, they would be putting on the requisite pub grub for such an occasion and some quality real ales, and he was determined not to miss out on either.

As he stubbed out his fag on the wall-mounted cigarette bin, he looked up to see Clarke's silver Ford Focus pull into the car park. He scurried back inside the station and stood behind the reception desk to await the arrival of the Chief Inspector. He wasn't looking forward to it.

A couple of minutes later the doors opened and in stepped Clarke somewhat gingerly and yet cheerfully. 'Morning Scattergood,' he said in a low voice before heading towards his office.

Scattergood made as if to stop him. 'Sir,' he shouted, much to Clarke's annoyance before repeating himself. 'Sir, you are to go up to Superintendent Annable's office immediately.'

'Would I be right in thinking that I'm in bad books, Scattergood?'

Scattergood nodded. 'He's after your blood, Sir.'

'I see,' replied Clarke as he turned and made his way slowly up the stairs.

At that moment Webster arrived for work, glanced up at Clarke and then approached the reception desk in his inimitable carefree manner. 'Trouble at t'mill?' he asked casually. Scattergood merely made a throat-slitting gesture with his right hand. Webster got the message.

As Clarke reached the top of the stairs and made his way to Annable's office, he was sure of one thing; there was going to be an awful lot of shouting. Having knocked on the outside door, Annable's secretary showed him into the Superintendent's office, and Clarke was surprised to see Fletcher sitting there. As she turned to look up at him,

Clarke returned the favour and his face was a picture of outright indignation. She merely shook her head as if to imply her innocence.

Clarke approached the desk as Annable continued to put his name to one or two documents without looking up. Clarke decided to speak first. 'Sir, I wish to apol...'

Annable was having none of it. 'Sit down, Chief Inspector,' he boomed. Clarke did as he was told and pulled up a chair, as Annable put down his pen and looked at him with a face like thunder. 'Been at the bottle again, have we?'

Clarke attempted a reply. 'I may have had...'

Annable cut him short. 'Not only did you disobey my order to return to the station yesterday, but you then made every attempt to avoid me.'

'Well, actually...'

'I'm not interested in your excuses, Chief Inspector,' he bellowed once more. 'To be quite frank, I'm sick and tired of your insubordination.'

If Clarke's head was throbbing earlier, it was nothing compared to what it was now. He tried to get a word in again. 'If you would only listen...'

'No!' roared Annable as he rose from his chair and began to pace around the room. 'You listen to me. This entire case has descended into a farce, and the Duty Solicitor has informed me that not only have you turned it into a personal vendetta against Mr. Molloy, but you haven't got a shred of evidence against him.'

Clarke shot a quick glance at Fletcher, but she shook her head once more. 'Well, that's what I'd like to talk about. You see, I've come around to thinking...'

But Annable interrupted him yet again. 'What is it that you've got against Molloy – is it something personal?'

There was silence for several seconds before Clarke made his reply. 'I was at school with both Rigione *and* Molloy, and for three years they made my life a living hell.'

Annable suddenly stood rooted to the spot and the shouting seemed to have dissipated. 'Are you telling me that you were bullied at school?' he asked quietly and with what seemed like keen interest.

'Oh, I wasn't the only one to be singled out for their mutual oppression and persecution, but at times it bloody well felt like it.'

'Well, in my day it was part and parcel of growing up...'

Both Clarke and Fletcher gave the Superintendent a look of utter astonishment that he could come out with such a statement, but it was

Clarke who reacted first. 'You clearly don't know what it's like to be on the bloody receiving end!' he snapped.

Annable realised that he'd made a monumental gaffe. 'I...I...I hope you don't think that I would ever condone such a thing, because...'

Clarke interrupted him. 'You see, it wasn't just the physical aspects of their bullying that affected me and the others – such as being impaled on a wrought iron fence or being kicked and punched during a game of rugby. Oh, no, it was the mental side too – like having all of your books emptied out of your rucksack and thrown into the canal, or the threats and the name-calling.'

Fletcher chimed in. 'Didn't you tell anyone what was going on?' she asked in a concerned manner.

'I told my games teacher,' replied Clarke without looking up.

'And what did he say?' inquired Annable.

Clarke suddenly looked up. 'The same as you – that it was all part of growing up.'

Annable began to look significantly embarrassed and he coughed before continuing. 'And how long did you say this went on for?'

'Three years – until I eventually snapped.'

'You turned against your oppressors?' inferred Annable.

'It was in my final year – the Christmas disco. I'd climbed up onto the stage to join in the dancing when Molloy pushed me off.'

'And what happened?' asked Fletcher.

'I saw red,' replied Clarke. 'I climbed back up onto the stage and smacked Molloy in the mouth. He fell to the floor and I suddenly pounced on him and began to pummel him repeatedly.'

'Good for you,' she said with an encouraging smile.

'I just couldn't stop hitting him. Three or four of the other lads tried to drag me off and one of them went to fetch the teacher, Mr. Carson...'

'Did it end there?' asked Annable.

'Yes, but I later received the cane from the headmaster – as did Molloy. *And* I was put on Special Report too.'

'And this was in spite of the fact that you were the one who had been bullied?' Fletcher remarked with a sense of amazement.

Clarke shrugged and gave a wry grin. 'Yes, but I had no trouble from either Rigione or Molloy after that!'

Annable now began to realise what Clarke had been implying during their conversation earlier that week, with regard to having tackled

Molloy before. 'Were there any further ramifications from this?' he asked politely.

Clarke paused again before replying. 'Yes, everybody suddenly wanted to be my friend – but I didn't want to be theirs.'

There was yet another pause before Annable spoke up again. 'And why did this all come about in the first place?'

'It was all because I wasn't one of them.'

'How do you mean?'

'I may have been Leverton-born, Sir, but I grew up in a rural community, and I was the only one who passed the Eleven-Plus exams at junior school. When I went to Leverton Grammar School I stood out like a sore thumb – I was easy prey.'

'Well I wish you had told me all about this at the outset, Clarke,' said Annable abruptly.

'It's not the kind of thing that you like to bring up – even after thirty years or so.'

'Nevertheless,' continued Annable. 'In spite of what happened to you at school, I don't think that it was a clever thing to take out your wrath on Molloy and go after him.'

'No, Sir,' replied Clarke almost apologetically.

'Indeed, I ought to take you off the case right now,' shouted Annable.

'But, Sir...' pleaded Clarke.

'And if it wasn't for Sergeant Fletcher here then I damn well would have done.'

Clarke sat there open-mouthed for a few seconds before attempting a response. 'But I thought that Sergeant Fletcher had...'

Annable stepped in once more. 'Following the complaint from Molloy's Duty Solicitor, I called Sergeant Fletcher in here this morning to give me *her* appraisal of the case so far, *and* to ask her if she would consider working under someone else with immediate effect.'

'So, it wasn't Sergeant Fletcher that...'

'However, Sergeant Fletcher reminded me that I gave you a further ninety-six hours in which to question Molloy, and at the end of that time you were to either charge the man with Rigione's murder or just stick with the charge of fraud.'

Clarke was almost lost for words. 'Well, I don't....'

'But I want to make this perfectly clear, Clarke,' shouted Annable as he jabbed his forefinger at him. 'If by noon tomorrow you have *not* established what has become of Luciano Rigione or you have failed to find *any* evidence that Molloy is behind his disappearance and murder, then I shall have no alternative but to take you off the case.'

'I understand perfectly, Sir,' replied a very contrite Detective Chief Inspector, who then paused briefly before continuing. 'Have you any idea who will be my replacement should I fail to...'

'Do *not* push your luck, Chief Inspector!' bawled Annable. 'Now get out of my office – and you too Sergeant.'

'Yes, Sir,' came the simultaneous response from Clarke and Fletcher.

As the pair made their way out of Annable's office and down the stairs, Clarke turned to Fletcher. 'It looks like I owe *you* an apology too, Fletcher.'

'You thought that I'd gone over your head, didn't you?' she replied with the vestiges of a smile.

'Was it that obvious?'

'I won't deny that it had crossed my mind.' Clarke stopped and gave her a look of slight disdain before she continued. 'But Webster talked me out of it.'

As they reached the foot of the stairs, Clarke stopped yet again. 'Look, there's something else I need to say, Fletcher.'

'I think you've said more than enough, Sir,' she replied somewhat disarmingly.

'What?' he said with a puzzled look on his face. 'No, I'm not referring to my past.'

'Then what *are* you referring to, Sir?'

'Molloy didn't do it,' he whispered with wide eyes and a look of cockiness about him.

'Come again, Sir?'

'Molloy is *not* responsible for Rigione's disappearance,' he whispered once more. 'But I think that I know who *is*!'

Chapter 43

Thursday, 2 November 2017 (p.m.)

It had been a very pleasant day for the beginning of November, and as the afternoon drew to a close it was becoming extremely likely that there would be a frost that evening at Lower Grange Farm. Consequently Derek Meakin decided to put this year's calves indoors before the temperature dropped too far. As he was doing so, a silver Ford Focus pulled up in the farmyard and a man wearing a bomber jacket and tie climbed out.

Careful as to where he put his feet, DCI Clarke stepped forward gingerly and introduced himself. 'Would I be addressing Derek Meakin?' he asked with a faint smile.

'Who wants to know?' asked Meakin impassively.

Clarke proffered his card. 'Detective Chief Inspector Allan Clarke of Leverton CID,' he replied firmly but calmly.

Derek glanced down at the card. 'I'm Derek Meakin – what is it that you want?'

'Well, actually I'd like to speak to your wife – Nicola – if I may?'

'She's not 'ere,' replied Meakin brusquely.

'Where can I find her?' asked Clarke as he glanced around the farmyard.

'Dunno – she left about a week or so ago.'

'How do you mean?'

Meakin stopped what he was doing and gave a heavy sigh. 'She just packed 'er bags and left me,' he said somewhat frustratedly.

'Oh, I'm sorry to hear that,' said Clarke with a lack of enthusiasm. 'And you don't know where she might have gone?'

'Not unless she's gone to 'er mum's in Mablethorpe. I can't be certain like – she just upped and left.'

Clarke pressed ahead. 'Has she done this sort of thing before?'

'What sort of thing?'

'Packed her bags and left you.'

'It's not t'first time, if that's what you mean.'

'Do you think she'll come back?'

'Ow the bloody 'ell should I know!'

You asked for that, Clarke, he said to himself. 'Did she have her own transport?' he continued.

'Yes, she did.'

'And what make or model was that?'

'Is it important?'

'I wouldn't be asking that question if it wasn't.'

'It was a Blue Hyundai.'

Now for the tricky bit, thought Clarke. 'I have to ask this question, Mr. Meakin, but has it ever crossed your mind that your wife might have been having an affair with someone?'

Meakin's temper was wearing very thin. 'Look, what's all this about?' he snapped.

'We're concerned that something may have happened to your wife.'

'Such as...?'

'That's what I'm here to find out – now would you answer the question, please, Mr. Meakin?'

Meakin sighed once again. 'Let's put it this way,' he began. 'She wasn't cut out for farmin' life, so she might 'ave met someone outside of t'farmin' community.'

'Someone like Luciano Rigione, perhaps?' hinted Clarke with all seriousness.

'What makes you say that?' replied Meakin somewhat guardedly.

Clarke referred to his meeting with Linda Rigione the day before. 'According to Mrs. Rigione, you were looking to buy a new divan for your caravan.'

'What if I was...?'

'She said that you made an appointment at Azzurri Furnishings and were shown around the showrooms by the foreman, Mr. Molloy. At the same time Mr. Rigione entertained your wife.'

'What are you driving at?' snapped Meakin once again.

'Did you and your wife go to your caravan up in the Peak District back in July?'

Meakin looked down at the ground. 'No, I went alone.'

'And why was that, Mr. Meakin?'

'My wife's mum was ill – she went to stay with 'er.'

'Were you happy about that?'

'What do you mean?'

'Well, the fact your wife having to pull out of a holiday at the last minute might have caused friction or triggered an argument.'

'Look, 'er mum was ill, so what could I do about it? Besides, I like my own company.'

'Do you miss your wife, Mr. Meakin?'

'What kind of question is that?' he growled. 'Of course I miss 'er. It's just that I don't think she'll come back – not this time.'

'Well we desperately need to talk to her, Mr. Meakin. Do you have a contact number for her – and the address and phone number of her mum in Mablethorpe?'

Meakin turned and stepped into the farmhouse. Moments later he came out again and handed Clarke a slip of paper. 'Will this do?' he asked with what Clarke thought was a degree of indifference.

Clarke looked at the paper and then put it into the inside pocket of his bomber jacket. 'Thank you, Mr. Meakin. We'll be in touch.' As he turned to make his way back to his car, he noticed a trailer full of hedge trimmings, wood and other debris in the field on the other side of the gate. 'Would that be for your brother's bonfire party on Saturday by any chance?' he shouted.

'Aye, it would,' replied Meakin before disappearing into the barn.

Unaware that her brother-in-law had received a visit from the police, Kath Meakin was busy preparing a light supper later that evening up the road at Upper Grange Farm. What with her daughter having left home (and left home to stay with Marco Rigione and his mother), her son had appeared before the magistrate's earlier that day and bailed until his trial could be fixed for the charge of Common Assault, so it would be something of an understatement to say that she was in a decidedly foul mood.

Her husband was down at the pub, but he would be back soon. As she chuntered away to herself at the kitchen sink, her mobile phone suddenly sprang to life and signified that she had an incoming text message. Somewhat irritably, she dried her hands on the nearby tea towel and made her way over to the table and the offending mobile. To her surprise and astonishment, the message was from her sister-in-law, Nicola. It was a short message, telling Kath that she was alright but that she wouldn't be coming back. There was no explanation as to why she left in the first place.

But it wasn't this that left Kath curious and with a puzzled look on her face. No, it was the fact that Nicola had even bothered to send *her* a message at all, because she had never done so before! So why now, thought Kath? There was only one thing for it; she decided to call her other brother-in-law, Peter Meakin. 'Is that you, Pete?' she asked a trifle breathlessly.

'Yes, what is it?' he replied anxiously.

'Sorry to call you so late in t'day, but I think you'd better get up to Derek's as soon as you can.'

'Well it won't be tonight, Kath. What's the problem?'

'I've just had a message from Nicola!'

Chapter 44

Friday, 3 November 2017 (a.m.)

Sure enough, the skies had been clear overnight in and around Leverton, and the sun eventually broke through that morning to reveal a light ground frost. Clarke was very fond of mornings like this and especially when he had a clear head, and on this particular morning it was clearer than it had been for some time.

Arriving for work in bomber jacket and tie, he virtually skipped through the doors of Leverton Police Station, and one wouldn't have thought that he faced being taken off the case later that day. Indeed, Scattergood was almost lost for words when the Inspector greeted him with a cheerful 'good morning' instead of the customary grumpy salutation.

As he passed through the main office, Clarke approached Fletcher's desk and handed her a slip of paper. 'That's the phone number for Nicola Meakin's mum in Mablethorpe,' he whispered. 'I want you to get in touch if possible and find out if Nicola is there.'

'And if she isn't?' replied Fletcher.

'Then ask her if she knows where her daughter is or might be.'

'What are you going to be doing in the meantime?'

'I'm going to give Nicola a call on this number,' he said pointing to another piece of paper. 'But I have a sneaking suspicion that she won't be answering.'

He wasn't wrong. He made several attempts to call Nicola on the number provided, but on each occasion there was simply no response. 'Damn,' he said to himself before eventually removing his jacket and wrapping it around the back of his chair. As he did so there was a knock on his door, and he looked up to see Webster standing in the doorway.

'Have you got a moment, Sir?' said Webster somewhat nervously.

'Is it important?' replied Clarke a trifle irritably.

'I think so, Sir.'

'Then go on, Webster – but make it quick.'

'We've just had a call from Mrs. Finch – you know, the lady from Pit Lane,'

'And what has she got to tell us?'

'It turns out that her son, Billy, *did* see Luciano Rigione on the day of his disappearance.'

'For crying out loud!' exclaimed Clarke as he held his head in his hands.

'What do you want us to do, Sir?' replied Webster, expecting an expletive-ridden response from his superior.

Clarke sighed heavily. 'Get yourself off down to Pit Lane and interview her,' he said calmly and yet authoritatively. 'And take Sergeant Meakin with you – I understand that he knows the family.'

Just at that moment Scattergood knocked on the door. 'It's about Sergeant Meakin, Sir,' he said gingerly.

Clarke was becoming exasperated. 'What about Sergeant Meakin!' he bawled.

Scattergood looked at Webster and then the Inspector. 'I'm afraid he hasn't come into work this morning.'

'Well get on the bloody phone and find out why he hasn't come into work for God's sake!'

'That's just it, Sir,' said Scattergood sheepishly.

'Get to the bloody point, Scattergood!'

'Sergeant Meakin isn't answering his phone.'

'Well, get someone down to his place and find out what the bloody hell has happened to him,' shouted Clarke.

'Yes, Sir,' replied Scattergood as he scuttled out of Clarke's office with his tail between his legs.

'And *you* might as well get off to the Finches by yourself, Webster.'

'Right you are, Sir,' replied Webster as he almost bumped into Sergeant Fletcher on his way out of Clarke's office.

'This had better be good, Fletcher.'

'I managed to get through to Nicola's mum, Sir.'

'And...?'

'I'm afraid she hasn't seen or heard from her daughter for weeks!'

Peter Meakin had risen earlier than usual that morning, having promised his sister-in-law that he would go and see his brother, Derek, before going in to work. He'd donned his Sergeant's uniform as a matter of course, but as he climbed into his car and set off for Lower Grange Farm he was deeply troubled by what his sister-in-law had said over the phone the night before. Something about a message from Derek's wife, Nicola, and that she wouldn't be coming back to him. 'Leave it me,' he'd said. 'I'll go and found out what's goin' on in the mornin'.'

And that was Peter; he could be relied upon to solve other people's problems, but he could never sort out his own. He wouldn't be long up at Derek's, he'd told himself, and so when he pulled up at the farm he wasn't at all surprised that nobody seemed to be about. Derek's Land Rover was parked outside the farmhouse as usual, but there was no sign of the man himself. He tried calling out two or three times, but there was no answer.

As he looked around the farmyard he noticed that the Farm Shop door was ajar; he must be in there, he told himself. Stepping inside, he looked around and there was *still* no sign of Derek. Again he called out several times, but as before there was no reply. The door to the butchery at the rear of the building was open, and so he decided to check in there. Derek wasn't there either, but there was something on the chopping board in front of him and he decided to investigate.

Drawing closer to the chopping board, he initially had the impression that it must be part of an animal carcass, but then he suddenly began to shake his head in disbelief at what *actually* lay before him. His mouth opened wide and his eyes almost popped out of his head. Oh my God, he thought to himself; what was he to do? Unfortunately for him he wasn't able to do anything, for the blow he received to the back of the head at that precise moment was fatal, and he fell to the floor dead.

Chapter 45

Friday, 3 November 2017 (a.m.)

Time was really running out for Clarke as it approached noon on that Friday morning, and everything that could go wrong seemed to be going – well, pear-shaped. He had no idea of the whereabouts of Nicola Meakin – as calls continued to be made to her phone without success; a member of his team had not turned up for work and wasn't answering his phone; and although Webster had gone to see the Finches in the hope of getting more information on the disappearance of Luciano Rigione, they were still no nearer to finding out what had actually happened to him.

Clarke sat in his office impatiently tapping his biro on his desk, as he awaited news of any kind that would lift his spirits or bring the case to a satisfying conclusion. Fletcher sat with him; the noise from Clarke's biro rapidly grating on her nerves. It was time to say something, no matter how innocuous.

'I was really sorry to hear about your time at school, Sir,' she began. 'You must have hated both Rigione and Molloy?'

'For your information, Sergeant, I hated every moment of my time at school,' he replied laconically as the tapping thankfully ceased.

'At least we got Molloy for *something* – even if it is only fraud.

Clarke glared at her briefly with narrowed eyes and then stood up. Well, I feel that Nicola is now the key to solving this case.'

At that moment there was a knock on the door and Scattergood popped his head through the gap. 'I thought that you might like to know that DI Wilton has arrived from Derby CID, Sir.'

'That can only mean one thing,' said Fletcher with a sense of impending gravity.

Clarke's reaction was immediate. Grabbing his coat, he literally flung himself towards the door. 'Let's get out of here, Sergeant,' he shouted. 'We don't want to be around when the curtain falls.'

'What do I tell Superintendent Annable?' shouted Scattergood helplessly as Fletcher ran after Clarke.

'Use your bloody initiative – but make sure you tell him that we can't be contacted,' shouted Clarke over his shoulder!

The Foundry Inn was situated on the outskirts of Leverton, not far from what was once the Welham Ironworks. Clarke had frequented the place in his youth, but it wasn't exactly the kind of pub that was to his taste. Nevertheless, as he pulled into the pub car park with Fletcher by his side he was pleased to see that it was a Free House, and they also boasted "good pub food," as she pointed out.

The pub seemed to be quite busy as they entered the bar, but Clarke noticed a free table near the door. 'Here, take this,' he said as he handed over his debit card. 'I'll have a pint of *Rutland Beast* and get whatever you want – I'll grab this table over here.'

Fletcher shot him a puzzled look. 'Are you sure that you should be drinking that stuff on an empty stomach?' she replied cautiously.

'Well, order some snap then.'

'Snap?' she repeated with a confused look on her face.

'Yes, food – order some food!'

Clarke sat at the table shaking his head whilst Fletcher went to the bar and ordered the food and drinks. Moments later and she had joined him at the table. 'Here's your pint, Sir,' she said as she carefully placed the glass onto the beer mat in front of her boss. 'And here's your card.'

'And what have you had?' he asked inquisitively.

'I've decided to have a small *Pinot Noir* – the food will be here shortly.'

And for the next five minutes it was like being back in his office as they barely said a word to each other. But Clarke was seldom talkative when he had a decent pint of ale in front of him, and he had to admit that his pint of *Rutland Beast* from the Grainstore Brewery at Oakham was top notch.

Then the girl came over with the food. 'Anyone for the Easy Pasta Salad?' she enquired.

'That's for me,' replied Fletcher.

'And the Bacon and Mushroom Pasta must be yours, Sir?' she said placing the second dish in front of Clarke before returning to the bar.

'What's this?' asked Clarke with a decidedly unpleasant look on his face.

'It's pasta with bacon and mushrooms – looks lovely.'

'I'm not eating that rubbish!' said Clarke as he disdainfully pushed the plate away.

'What's wrong with it?'

'I don't like pasta for starters!'

'But it's good for you – part of a healthy diet!'

'I don't care what it is – I'm not eating the bugger!'

'Oh, stop being such a bloody grouch and get it down you!' snapped Fletcher.

Clarke gave her a look of utter astonishment, clearly staggered and surprised that his Deputy SIO spoke to him in such a way, but then he grumbled and moaned under his breath as he started to pick out the bits of bacon and mushroom with his fork, whilst contemptuously shoving the pasta to one side. Fletcher merely shook her head before tucking into her meal with relish. Clarke momentarily took a few gulps of his ale to wash down what to him was the food from hell, as Fletcher then attempted to start a meaningful conversation.

'Will you be doing anything this weekend?' she asked somewhat tentatively.

Clarke took a few more gulps of ale before replying. 'I haven't really thought about it,' he said with uncertainty. 'What about you – have you made any plans?'

Fletcher took a sip of her wine and nodded her head. 'I'm going to a bonfire party with some friends on the outskirts of Nottingham...'

But Clarke suddenly dropped his fork and sat bolt upright. 'Oh my God...' he spluttered, as bits of bacon and mushroom flew out of his mouth.

'What's the matter?' enquired Fletcher anxiously.

'You blithering idiot...' he said as his eyes seemed to flash from side to side.

'I beg your pardon...' replied Fletcher, seemingly offended by Clarke's manner.

'It's been staring me in the face all the bloody time...'

'What *are* you talking about, for crying out loud?'

'The bonfire...' he shouted.

'What bonfire?'

'The one at Upper Grange Farm – the bastard has been dumping body parts on the bloody bonfire!'

'Who are you talking about?'

'Derek Meakin – he's killed his wife *and* her lover, dismembered them and now he's dumping their body parts on the bonfire up at Upper Grange Farm.'

'How do you know this?'

And so he told her all about his first visit to Upper Grange Farm and how Derek Meakin had appeared on the scene with a trailer full of debris. 'They're having a bonfire party at the farm tomorrow night,' he cried out. 'And I also saw the trailer again yesterday when I went to see the man.'

'And you think that the trailer contained body parts?' shouted Fletcher.

'You can bet your life on it, Sergeant!'

Fletcher's mouth suddenly gaped open. 'Oh my God,' she screamed. 'We'd better get up there!'

Before she could say anything else, Clarke had literally leapt from the table sending food, crockery and cutlery flying. 'Come on – let's go,' he shouted as he burst through the door and out into the car park. Fletcher attempted an embarrassing apology to the bar staff before following her boss outside.

As they climbed into the car, Clarke's phone went off. It was Webster.

'Make it quick, Webster,' snapped Clarke impatiently.

'I've just been talking to Mrs. Finch and her son, Billy,' shouted Webster excitedly down the phone.

'And what did they have to say?'

'It turns out that on the morning of Rigione's disappearance, Billy saw him enter Lower Grange Farm – he said that he was training for the Olympics too!'

Fletcher was listening in to the conversation and the words "training for the Olympics" caused her to bury her head in her hands. Clarke merely shook his head. 'Get yourself up to Upper Grange Farm, Webster – we'll meet you there.' He then switched off the phone and turned to Fletcher. 'We're gonna need armed back-up for this, Sergeant, and get SOCO's up there too.'

As Clarke turned on the ignition, Fletcher pulled out her phone. 'Christ knows what Superintendent Annable is going to say about this.' she shouted.

'Annable can go and do one!' replied Clarke scornfully as he drove away from the pub.

Chapter 46

Friday, 3 November 2017 (p.m.)

Although it had not been a good week for the Meakin's, they were still going ahead with their annual bonfire party and firework display on the Saturday night, and final preparations were being made that very afternoon at Upper Grange Farm. The weather forecast was good and all was boding well for a truly fabulous evening of entertainment and fun. Richard Meakin was ensuring that there would be ample seating for the display and making final arrangements for car parking along with his son, Ricky, whilst Kath Meakin had been busy preparing food and stocking up on drinks.

Indeed, Kath had just gone out to the dustbin when she looked up to see an unfamiliar unmarked car pull up just outside the farm, and a young man in a suit and tie climb out before making his way towards the farmhouse. Still coming to terms with the events surrounding her offspring, she was in no mood for what she construed as unwelcome visitors.

'Who the bloody 'ell are you?' she shouted to the young man as she stormed across the farmyard.

Somewhat taken aback by what appeared to be a particularly frosty welcome, the young man showed her is identity card. 'I'm Detective Constable Matthew Webster of Leverton CID,' he began somewhat shakily. 'Detective Chief Inspector Clarke will be here shortly and he'll provide you with an explanation as to why we're here today.'

At that moment the Silver Ford Focus pulled up, and both Clarke and Fletcher climbed out and made their way over to Kath Meakin and Webster.

Kath clearly recognised the vehicle. 'What the bloody 'ell is goin' on 'ere?' she bellowed fiercely at Clarke.

Clarke put his hand up as if to allay any bad-tempered outpourings from the woman. 'I'd like to speak to your husband if I may, Mrs. Meakin?' he said abruptly.

The conversation was then interrupted by Richard Meakin, who appeared from behind the farmhouse accompanied by his son. 'What's all this about?' he shouted angrily.

Clarke turned to face the two of them. 'We have reason to believe that a serious crime may have been committed involving your brother, Mr. Meakin.'

Meakin seemed a trifle flustered. 'What bloody crime – and who are you talkin' about?' he snapped.

'I'm referring to your brother, Derek,' replied Clarke in a grave voice. He then looked around the buildings and surrounding fields. 'I see you're still planning to go ahead with the bonfire party tomorrow night?'

'That's right,' replied Kath with a puzzled look on her face.

Clarke turned to face them all again. 'Then I'm sorry to have to tell you that the bonfire party will have to be cancelled.'

Kath looked like she was about to burst a blood vessel. 'What!' she screamed.

Before Clarke could give a reply, a stream of other vehicles began to arrive on the scene, some of which were marked and others unmarked. These contained uniformed police, SOCO's and the armed back-up that Clarke had demanded. Fletcher made her way over to them and began to give instructions, which included the sealing off of the farm and the diversion of traffic through the village.

Needless to say, the heavy police presence caught the attention of practically the entire community, but uniformed officers were detailed to keep the inquisitive and prying eyes from getting too near the farm. As Fletcher began to direct SOCO's towards the vicinity of the bonfire, Kath Meakin gave full vent to her fury.

'You 'ave no right to do this!' she screamed at Clarke.

Richard Meakin attempted to restrain her. 'Now, now, Kath,' he said in a patronising manner. 'Let them do what they 'ave to.'

Clarke appeared grateful for the farmer's actions towards his wife. 'Thank you, Mr. Meakin,' he said with sincerity. 'I shall be leaving Detective Constable Webster in charge here whilst I go down to your brother's farm – although I think it extremely unlikely if we'll find him at home right now,' he added almost as an aside.

'Perhaps you'd better take my son with you,' suggested Meakin. 'The lad knows 'is way around my brother's farm.'

Clarke briefly contemplated the suggestion and then nodded in agreement. 'That sounds like a good idea to me,' he said with a weak smile. 'In the meantime it would be appreciated if you and your wife went inside and remained there until we have completed our investigations.'

Clarke then spoke briefly to Webster before departing for Lower Grange Farm with Fletcher, Ricky Meakin, the armed back-up and several uniformed officers. Call it intuition, but something told him that the next half-hour or so wasn't going to be a pleasant experience for *any* of those involved – not by a long chalk.

The convoy of vehicles containing Clarke, Fletcher and Ricky Meakin amongst others arrived at Lower Grange Farm barely ten minutes after leaving Upper Grange Farm, and apart from one vehicle on the premises the place seemed absolutely deserted. However, the vehicle was a navy blue Audi Q5, and Fletcher was quick to point out that this belonged to Peter Meakin; Derek Meakin's Land Rover was nowhere to be seen.

Nevertheless, a couple of armed officers made their way stealthily over to the farmhouse, entered and then commenced a search of the building. A couple of minutes later one of them emerged to signify that the house was unoccupied, and at that moment Clarke gave Ricky Meakin the go-ahead to go inside, whilst he headed for the Farm Shop, followed by Fletcher, another armed officer and others.

On reaching the Farm Shop it was evident that the door was locked. As it was an interior door, minimum force was required to break it down, and the armed officer stepped forward to deliver a hefty kick just below the lock. The door flew back open and the armed officer went inside, with Clarke and Fletcher behind him.

Clarke stood rooted to the spot and cast his eyes around him, but as Fletcher moved forward she noticed the body of a uniformed policeman lying in the doorway of the butchery. 'Sir, you'd better come here,' she called out to Clarke before squatting beside the body.

Clarke came over promptly and gave a heavy sigh. 'Peter Meakin, I take it – is he dead?' he asked with a pained expression on his face.

Fletcher nodded. 'I'm afraid so, Sir.'

'Poor bugger was due to retire in a couple of months, wasn't he?'

'I believe so.'

'You'd better get Fraser here right away, Sergeant.'

Fletcher immediately put out a call for the police surgeon as Clarke attempted to take a closer look at the injuries sustained by Peter Meakin. He wasn't a squeamish copper by any standards, but it was clear from the wounds that Meakin had been struck from behind with significant force by a blunt weapon; the fact that there appeared to be no defence wounds also led Clarke to that conclusion. He was suddenly interrupted by Fletcher.

'Dr. Fraser will be here shortly,' she said before turning to look around the butchery. Almost immediately her eyes caught sight of something on the chopping board. Moving closer, she suddenly put her hand to her mouth. 'Oh my God...' she cried out.

Clarke looked up and then came over to join her. 'Jesus H bloody Christ!' he exclaimed in a low voice as he stood beside her.

On the chopping board before them was the headless torso of a male in the early stages of decomposition. The legs were missing, along with the right arm, but the left arm was still attached to the torso. Furthermore, there appeared to be a chest wound, which Clarke was fairly sure had to have been caused by a gun of some sort.

Fletcher was still reeling from the shock of seeing the torso, but she attempted to put together a coherent response. 'Would this be who I think it is?' she whimpered.

Clarke nodded. 'Yes, Sergeant – this is what remains of Luciano Rigione if I'm not mistaken.' He looked up once more and his eyes were caught by what appeared to be a large commercial chest freezer. 'I've got a feeling that we'll find more body parts in here,' he muttered as he slowly advanced towards it. Prising open the stainless steel lid, he suddenly let out a heavy sigh

'What is it, Sir?' asked Fletcher who was still standing by the chopping board.

'You'd better come and look for yourself,' replied Clarke as he shook his head.

Moving slowly over to the freezer, Fletcher looked down once more. 'Oh no,' she blurted out before turning her head away sharply and vomiting on the butchery floor.

'I take it that you've not seen anything like this before?' said Clarke, who continued to look down into freezer at what were the severed heads of one male and one female.

Fletcher attempted a reply. 'I'm so sorry, Sir,' she spluttered as the last remnants of her vomit spewed forth.

'No need to apologise to me, Sergeant – it's perfectly understandable under the circumstances.'

Fletcher had by now staggered over to the sink, where she attempted to clear herself up. Wiping her face and hands with a towel, she turned to face Clarke once more. 'Thank you, Sir,' she murmured. 'I...wouldn't...normally...'

Clarke interrupted her and turned to the contents of the freezer once more. 'He must have dumped the bodies in here, where the cooler temperature would slow down decomposition and the subsequent build-up of unpleasant smells,' he said with some authority. 'Then starting with Nicola, I'm assuming that he took the corpse out of the freezer, dismembered her and put the parts back inside again until it was time to take them to Upper Grange Farm on the trailer with the debris.'

'The heads, Sir – they do belong to Nicola Meakin and Luciano Rigione?' asked Fletcher with a slightly unsteady voice.

'I think that's almost certain, Sergeant.'

At that moment there was a commotion at the front of the Farm Shop as Ricky Meakin tried to step inside. 'There's a shotgun missin' from t'ouse...' he shouted before spotting the torso on the chopping board. 'What the 'ell is that?'

Clarke immediately went over to prevent him from seeing any more. 'You'll find out in due course,' he shouted in a firm voice. 'Sergeant – will you take him outside, please?'

As Fletcher took the stunned youngster by the arm and led him out of the Farm Shop, the tall, bearded figure of Dr. Alexander Fraser FRCPath appeared on the scene in a tweed suit and bottle green tie, his mousy-coloured wavy hair continuing to fade to grey. As he stepped inside the Farm Shop, he was giving his rendition of *Things Are Seldom What They Seem* from Gilbert and Sullivan's HMS Pinafore.

'Buttercup – Black sheep dwell in every fold; all that glitters is not gold...'

'Hello, Alex – I doubt very much that you'll be singing by the time you've finished here,' said Clarke with a touch of irony.

Fraser noticed the body on the floor. 'Help ma boab,' he said on seeing the uniform. 'Nae one of yer own?'

'I'm afraid so, Alex – and due to retire in a few months time.'

Fraser bent down to take a preliminary look at the body of Peter Meakin. 'Well, it's fairly obvious as to what's happened here,' he began. 'He's received a blow to the head, causing injuries to the skull, along with intercranial haemorrhaging and lesions – but I'm sure you already know this. Considerable force must have been used – probably a hammer.'

'Yes, we had reached that conclusion.'

'I'll be able to tell you more after the post mortem,' replied Fraser, who then looked up and saw the torso on the chopping board. 'Ye Gods, what have we got here...'

Before Clarke could reply his phone suddenly sprang to life. It was Webster – and he was in a very excited state.

'Sir, I've got something to tell you,' he shouted somewhat breathlessly.

'Calm down, Webster,' said Clarke sedately. 'You'll give yourself a heart attack.'

'It's just that SOCO's have found human remains on the bonfire site, Sir – and bloodstained clothing.'

Clarke punched the air. 'I bloody well knew it!' he shouted euphorically.

But Webster hadn't finished. 'Oh, and I thought you should know that DCS Annable has just arrived here at Upper Grange Farm.'

Clarke's initial euphoria suddenly subsided at the mention of Annable, and he gave an audible sigh. 'Okay, Webster – I'll be there shortly.'

At least they now knew what had happened to Luciano Rigione – and Nicola Meakin for that matter. It was just a question of finding the killer and bringing him to justice. Trouble was, this killer was armed with a shotgun, and Clarke was fully aware that he would have to be the man to prevent him from using it again.

Chapter 47

Friday, 3 November 2017 (p.m.)

Following the gruesome discoveries at Lower Grange Farm, Clarke instructed DS Fletcher to remain there with Dr. Fraser whilst he completed his preliminary examinations, and then to await the arrival of SOCO's. At the same time, uniformed officers were to seal off that farm too and ensure that members of the public couldn't gain access. He had been loath to leave Fletcher at the scene following her reaction to the sight of the remains of Luciano Rigione and Nicola Meakin, but she had assured him that she was up to the task of carrying out his instructions to the letter. In the meantime, he returned to Upper Grange Farm with Ricky Meakin and the armed response team.

It seemed to Clarke like the entire village had come out to line the route back to Upper Grange Farm, and he was almost tempted to wave to them in a style befitting of the monarch! However, decorum prevailed and he said and did nothing untoward for the brief journey from one farm to the other.

The vehicles eventually arrived at their destination, and as Ricky Meakin alighted he ran off to the farmhouse to inform his parents of the events at Uncle Derek's. As Clarke entered the farmyard, there stood the unmistakeable figure of Superintendent Annable, with hands on hips and legs apart engaged in conversation with DC Webster.

As Webster returned to the search of the bonfire, Annable looked up. 'Ah, Clarke – you kept this close to your chest,' he snorted. 'Perhaps you'd care to explain to us what in God's name has been going on here and hereabouts?'

'The eternal triangle, Sir,' said Clarke with tongue in cheek. 'Only nobody expected it to end so violently.'

'Yes, Webster has informed me about body parts and bloodstained clothing being found on the family bonfire,' shouted Annable. 'How on earth has all this come about?'

Clarke attempted to explain. 'It seems that our missing man – Mr. Rigione – had been having an affair with Nicola Meakin, wife of

Derek Meakin of Lower Grange Farm,' he began. 'Mr. Meakin evidently found out, and having done away with his wife *and* her lover, he dismembered their bodies with a view to destroying their remains and any incriminating evidence by means of his brother's bonfire.'

Annable screwed his face up to show his distaste at what he had just heard. 'And you're going to tell me that you've found more remains at the other farm, I take it?'

'That's correct, Sir,' replied Clarke. 'I've left Sergeant Fletcher down there with the police surgeon, and more SOCO's will be needed to carry out the necessary forensic work.'

'Any sign of Meakin?'

'It would appear that he's gone on the run, Sir.'

'Bugger!' exclaimed Annable loudly.

'That's not all, Sir.'

Annable looked up again. 'Oh my God – don't tell me there's more?'

Clarke nodded. 'I'm afraid we also found the body of Sergeant Meakin – Mr. Meakin's other brother.'

Annable put his hand to his forehead. 'This is going from bad to worse!' he boomed. 'How did he come to be there?'

'I suggest that we go into the farmhouse and put that very question to Sergeant Meakin's brother and sister-in-law!'

The pair strode across the farmyard towards the house, and as they approached the door was opened by Ricky Meakin. 'I've told my mum and dad what's 'appened,' he said almost breathlessly.

The two policemen brushed past him and entered the living room, where they found Richard Meakin slumped in an easy chair with his head buried in his hands. Kath Meakin sat on the arm of the chair attempting to console her husband.

'Is it true what our Ricky's been sayin'?' she whimpered with tear-stained eyes.

'It would appear that Derek has killed both his wife and her lover, Mr. Rigione,' said Clarke with a grave voice. He then swallowed before continuing. 'He then dismembered their bodies – their remains have been found on the bonfire and back at the Farm Shop at Lower Grange Farm.'

'It's like a bad dream...' said Richard Meakin as he shook his head.

'I have some more bad news I'm afraid,' replied Clarke.

Richard Meakin looked up. 'Surely it can't get any worse?' he gasped.

'We also found the body of your other brother, Peter, at Lower Grange Farm – it looks like he received a blow to the head.'

Richard Meakin let out a deafening scream as Kath flung her arms around him. 'This is my fault entirely,' she wailed.

Clarke tried to remain composed. 'The thing is Mrs. Meakin, what was Peter doing there in the first place?'

With a quivering voice, Kath Meakin referred to the message she had from Nicola the night before. 'She said that she wer' okay, but that she weren't coming back.'

Clarke turned to Annable and whispered. 'Nicola would have been dead already, so Derek must have sent the message.' Annable nodded in agreement and Clarke turned to Kath once more. 'I'm guessing that there was something about this message that troubled you, Mrs. Meakin – would I be right?' he suggested.

Kath nodded. 'It's just that Nicola never ever sent me any messages before, so why would she do so now.'

'And that's when you decided to get in touch with Peter?'

'I just knew that summat was wrong – and what with Pete bein' in t'force...'

Clarke shook his head whilst Annable decided to speak out. 'I'm sorry about your brother, Mr. Meakin,' he said candidly. 'I understand that he was due to retire soon. However, we obviously need to find your other brother, and as soon as possible. Have you any idea where he might have gone to?'

Both Richard and Kath Meakin were clearly still in a state of shock. 'I...'aven't...the...remotest...' replied Richard as his voice trailed off.

Clarke intervened once more. 'It doesn't matter,' he said in a reassuring voice. 'I think that I know where he'll be.'

The two policemen then thanked the Meakin's before stepping outside into the farmyard once more.

'So, you think that you know where Derek Meakin is hiding out, do you?' asked Annable in an unusually excited state.

Clarke replied in the affirmative. 'Yes, I do – but it will mean taking a little trip up into the Peak District!'

'A caravan site!' exclaimed Annable incredulously.

'A caravan site,' repeated Clarke, as the pair sat in Annable's car outside Upper Grange Farm. 'And in the heart of the Peak District – he wouldn't go on holiday anywhere else.'

'Well, what suits one...' replied Annable somewhat sneeringly.

'The man has taken his shotgun with him, so I'll need the armed response team with me too, of course,' said Clarke confidently.

'Now hang on a minute, Clarke...'

'Oh, I know what you're thinking, Sir – leave it to the Ashbourne boys...'

'Well, it's on their patch...'

'Yes, but they're part of the East Midlands Regional Police. More importantly, this is *my* baby and I should be the one to bring the man in – don't you think?' Clarke hinted hopefully.

'You should think yourself damn fortunate that you're still on this case at all, Clarke,' he said before pondering Clarke's remarks for a few seconds. 'Okay, I'll go along with it,' he said as he bit his bottom lip. 'I'll contact Ashbourne CID and tell them that you're already on the way with the armed back-up to – what was the name of the place?'

'It's the Collymore Lake Caravan and Motorhome Club Site, Sir.'

'I'll arrange for a senior officer to meet you there and get them to agree that you are to lead any negotiations as well as make the arrest if appropriate.'

'Thank you, Sir,' replied Clarke as he climbed out of Annable's car.

'And for God's sake don't go in there with all guns blazing,' shouted Annable after Clarke as the latter hurried off to brief the armed response team before departing.

'Sorry, Sir – didn't quite catch that,' shouted Clarke over his shoulder and with a broad smile on his face, suggesting that he had heard Annable's plea alright – loud and clear!

Chapter 48

Friday, 3 November 2017 (p.m.)

The Collymore Lake Caravan and Motorhome Club Site is situated in the heart of the Peak District, roughly twenty miles from Leverton. The lake is actually a man-made reservoir constructed in the nineteen eighties, and the site itself is set within twenty-five acres of woodland. There are a wide selection of pitch options within the woodland, where there is ample room for camping, caravans or motor homes.

The Visitor Centre lies at the entrance to the site, with a large car park nearby. Here one can hire equipment such as bikes, fishing tackle, small boats, kayaks, canoes and windsurfing apparatus. Alongside the Visitor Centre is a café and bar, and other nearby facilities include two independent toilet and shower blocks, a laundry room, a Jacuzzi, gym, children's play room, two play areas and a large sand-pit play area.

There is a horse riding track around the reservoir, along with a couple of bird hides, and there are several more of these within the woods. A nearby wildlife pond is available for the trout fishing season, which lasts from the beginning of March until the end of September.

DCI Graham Pounder of Ashbourne CID had been given the task of liaising with Clarke when he arrived at the site. A tall, fair-haired forty-two-year-old with a long face and blue eyes, he had already given orders for the site to be sealed off, and having established the location of Derek Meakin's caravan he now instructed his men to evacuate the remaining campers without making too much fuss. Thankfully they there few and far between on this late Friday afternoon in November, and as Pounder paced up and down the front of the Visitor Centre they started to gather behind the tape, looking bewildered and bemused.

Pounder was quite willing to accept that Clarke should be the one to lead any negotiations and make an arrest if necessary; Superintendent Annable had stressed that they were all part of the East Midlands Regional Police. But if Meakin were to commit another crime on the site then he was going to insist that he should take over. Moments later several vehicles pulled into the car park and Pounder realised that Clarke and the armed response team had arrived. Clarke climbed out of the silver Ford Focus as Pounder strode across the car park to greet him.

'I take it that you're DCI Clarke,' said Pounder in a deep voice as he held out his hand. 'I'm DCI Pounder of Ashbourne CID.'

'Pleased to meet you,' replied Clarke as he shook Pounder's hand. He then introduced the leader of the armed response team. 'This is Sergeant Rawlinson.'

Pounder and Rawlinson shook hands and then the three men retired to the Visitor Centre. Once inside, Pounder spoke first.

'We've isolated Meakin's caravan and evacuated all other campers from the site,' he said confidently and assuredly.

'Do we know if he's actually in the caravan?' replied Clarke.

'We've not been able to establish that, I'm afraid.'

Clarke grimaced. 'I assume that you'll be accompanying me?' he said with a slight swagger.

'I insist upon it,' replied Pounder with an equally smug expression.

Rawlinson chimed in for the first time. 'If that's the case then I insist that you both wear bulletproof vests,' he said firmly. 'I shall go down there with you, whilst my men will spread out through the woods.'

With that the three men returned to the van containing the armed response unit. Clarke and Pounder donned their bulletproof vests whilst Rawlinson issued orders and instructions to his men.

'I hate having to wear these,' said Clarke with a degree of irritation.

Pounder and Rawlinson gave him a disdainful look, and then the three of them set off for Derek Meakin's caravan. The tension was palpable as beads of sweat began to form on Clarke's forehead. Several minutes later they came upon the caravan *and* the Land Rover. Pounder made his way stealthily over to the latter and discovered that it was locked, whilst Clarke found that the caravan was locked too. As he peered through the window he almost jumped out of his skin as Meakin's Border collie appeared behind the glass and started barking at him aggressively.

'Jesus Christ,' he exclaimed abruptly.

'For God's sake keep your voice down,' muttered Rawlinson with understandable consternation. 'Any sign of Meakin?'

'He's not in the caravan,' replied a duly chastened Clarke.

Rawlinson ordered his men to fan out, and whilst Pounder headed for the woods with them, Clarke made his way down towards the lake alone. Quickly losing sight of the others, he followed the path through the trees and bushes until he came to an opening that revealed a secluded picnic area beside the lake. He paused briefly, but just as he was about to move on he suddenly heard the unmistakeable sound of a gun cocking behind him, and he knew that he had found his man.

Chapter 49

Friday, 3 November 2017 (p.m.)

'I've bin expectin' you,' said Derek Meakin quietly as he pointed the shotgun at Clarke's back. 'Turn around and don't make any sudden movements.'

Clarke did as requested until he came face to face with Meakin. The man was wearing a khaki anorak and hood, together with a pair of jeans and wellington boots. Moreover, the firearm appeared to be a 12-gauge over-under twin barrel shotgun, and probably with certain modifications. 'Hello Derek,' replied Clarke calmly. 'I thought that our paths would cross again sooner or later.'

'Kneel down,' ordered Meakin with the gun still pointing at Clarke.

Clarke did as was requested. 'I'm unharmed and alone,' he said unconvincingly.

'If you think I'm stupid enough to believe that...'

Clarke gave a weak smile before turning to Meakin's wife and her lover. 'So, how did you find out about Nicola and Rigione?' he asked somewhat tentatively.

'I went through 'er 'andbag a few weeks ago followin' an almighty row, didn't I?' he began. 'I came across a second mobile phone – a secret one – with messages from that bastard Rigione.'

'I see – was there more?'

'I'd 'ad my suspicions for some time, especially when she made out that she couldn't come with me to t'caravan in July because 'er mother was ill.'

'It never occurred to you that your wife might have been unhappy with the marriage and life at the farm?'

'Oh, I know everyone was always pointin' out the age difference between us, but she wer' *still* my wife – for richer, for poorer, as t'sayin' goes.' He paused briefly before continuing. 'But that philanderin' bastard tried to take 'er away from me, didn't 'e?'

'I assume that you confronted Nicola about the second phone?'

Meakin nodded. 'She came clean and made 'er feelin's known to me about Rigione.'

'And then what happened?'

'I just saw red and lashed out – I didn't mean to kill 'er.'

'No, I dare say that you didn't.

'But I must 'ave 'it 'er so 'ard that 'er 'ead 'it the corner of t'fireplace 'earth – I knew that she wer' dead immediately.'

'How did you react?'

'Well I thought of puttin' 'er body in the boot of 'er car and then dumpin' it to begin with...'

Clarke interrupted him. 'But then you hit upon the idea of dismembering her body in the Farm Shop and disposing of her remains on the bonfire, along with other debris from the farm?'

'I 'ad to get rid of 'er somehow, and I thought that nobody would ever find 'er that way?' replied Derek angrily.

'So what *did* you do with her car?' asked Clarke somewhat puzzled.

'I drove it up 'ere just after midnight and pushed it into t'lake. After that I got a taxi 'ome and then spent t'rest of t'night thinkin' 'ow to get rid of Rigione.'

Clarke seemed to be growing in confidence. 'You were determined that he should pay the ultimate price?'

'Like I said, 'e tried to take my wife away from me,' said Meakin with a snarl.

'So, what exactly happened with Rigione?'

'I knew that 'e went for a run every mornin' – I'd seen 'im pass t'farm many times, so I wer' aware of 'is route. All I 'ad to do wer' send 'im a text on Nicola's secret phone to lure 'im to t'farm...'

'Sorry to interrupt, but what did you do with this phone?'

'I took t'SIM card out, cut it into small pieces and then threw it on t'bonfire with everythin' else.'

Clarke nodded his head as if to acknowledge that Meakin was smarter than everyone had originally thought. 'Go on,' he said apologetically.

'I lay in wait for Rigione, confident that 'e would come runnin' and thinkin' that 'e wer' goin' to meet Nicola...'

'And that's when you struck?'

'The bastard came runnin' up to t'farmhouse door, and as I opened it I let 'im 'ave it with this 'ere shotgun of mine.'

'There must have been quite a mess?'

'Nothin' I couldn't 'andle,' boasted Meakin. 'But it wer' as I wer' draggin 'is body over to t'Farm Shop when that thicko from down t'lane appeared on t'scene.'

'You mean Billy Finch?'

'Yeah – 'e saw what wer' left of Rigione in 'is vest and shorts and asked if 'e wer trainin' for t'Olympics or summat like that!'

'He didn't realise that the man had been shot and was actually dead?'

'No, he wer' just joggin' on t'spot with that stupid grin on 'is face.'

'And presumably you just went along with him?'

'Of course I did – Rigione wer' trainin' for t'Olympics just like 'im, I said.'

'I suppose that he then ran off none the wiser?'

'Admittedly I felt relieved when 'e'd gone.'

Being forced to kneel was beginning to cause Clarke some discomfort, but he managed a wry smile at Meakin's previous statement. 'So, you now had two bodies to dismember?' he asked cautiously.

'I couldn't get them both into t'freezer without takin' their 'eads off, so that wer' my first task,' he replied almost nonchalantly as Clarke visibly winced. 'Then I set to work on Nicola and took some of 'er parts up to my brother's farm later that day – that would be when I saw you for t'first time. All I 'ad to do then wer' to tell Kath and my brother that Nicola 'ad left me again.'

'But you kept your wife's other phone and used it to tell Kath that she wasn't coming home?'

'That's right,' replied Meakin confidently.

Clarke's anger was rising. 'Surely you must have known that Kath would contact your other brother – Peter – and that he would come over and start asking questions?'

'Maybe so, but...'

'He was your own flesh and blood for Christ's sake – *and* he was about to retire!'

'I 'ad no option...'

Clarke suddenly decided that enough was enough and began struggling to his feet. 'I'm afraid that I've got to take you back with me, Derek,' he said through gritted teeth.

'I'm not goin' back...' replied Meakin as he stepped back nervously and attempted to keep his gun pointed at Clarke. At that precise moment a snapping noise came from behind him, as though someone had trodden on some twigs. 'What's that?' he cried anxiously.

DCI Pounder was still attempting to make his way through the woods around Collymore Lake when he heard the shot ring out. This time it was his turn to jump out of his skin, but almost immediately he turned and started running in the direction from which the shot came. Stumbling and fumbling his way through the trees and brushes, he eventually came upon the scene – as did Rawlinson and others from the armed response team. It wasn't a pretty sight.

The body of Derek Meakin lay sprawled before them, his face obliterated completely. Indeed, the head was a shattered and bloody mass of tissue, brain matter and bone fragment. One of the firearms team bent down to check on the shotgun and pointed out that only one chamber had been discharged. Several feet away from the body, the figure of DCI Clarke stood shaking with mouth agape and a look of sheer horror on his face.

'Are you okay, Clarke?' asked Pounder with genuine concern.

Clarke attempted to reply, but couldn't quite form a sentence. 'He...The man...he...'

'Never mind for now,' said Pounder. 'I think a glass of whisky wouldn't go amiss at this particular moment!'

Chapter 50

Friday, 3 November 2017 (p.m.)

It was beginning to get dark when the ambulance arrived to take away the body of Derek Meakin. Clarke was spattered with his blood and still visibly shaken by the events that had taken place a few minutes previously. Pounder suggested that the two of them return to the Visitor Centre as the bar was open, and Clarke was not about to protest.

On reaching the Visitor Centre he sat outside on one of the benches, whilst Pounder went inside to get the drinks. He reappeared several minutes later with a double *Glenlivet* for Clarke and a single one for himself. Handing the double to Clarke, Pounder then watched open-mouthed as his fellow DCI knocked the drink back in one go; it probably never even touched the sides. As Clarke sat holding the empty glass in his hands and shaking his head, Pounder felt the time was right to talk about what had occurred between Clarke and Meakin.

'So, what actually happened down by the lake?' he said as he took his seat beside Clarke.

Clarke stopped shaking his head and gave a deep sigh. 'The guy told me everything,' he began. 'The argument with his wife that led to her death – he claimed that it was accidental; the murder of Rigione and then the dismembering of their bodies.'

'But how did he meet his death?' implored Pounder.

Clarke gave Pounder a look of scorn. 'One of Rawlinson's men wasn't quite as adroit as he should have been!'

'How do you mean?'

'He must have come across the two of us, tried to get a little closer, but then gave himself away by treading on some of the bloody foliage.'

'And Meakin picked up on this?'

'I felt that I was on the verge of persuading him to give up – getting him to put down his weapon and throw in the towel, so to speak...'

'And then he heard the noise?'

'We both did, but then he briefly turned his back on me. I was just about to overpower him when he turned to face me once more, placed the gun under his chin and then pulled the trigger...'

'So he actually topped himself?'

'He told me that he wasn't going to come back – that he wouldn't let me take him in under any circumstances.'

This time it was Pounder who gave a heavy sigh. 'Well he sure as hell stuck to his guns, didn't he?' Clarke looked at him distastefully. 'I'm sorry – I didn't mean to...'

'It's okay,' replied Clarke with resignation. 'I just wish that it hadn't ended so bloody tragically.'

'It wasn't your fault.'

'Wasn't it? I'm not so sure...'

Pounder stood up. 'Don't be so hard on yourself,' he said in a consoling manner. 'Look, are you sure that you'll be okay to drive back to Leverton?'

Clarke merely nodded his head and then watched as Pounder walked away. There was no shaking of hands or slapping of backs; just a sense of unbelievable sadness and disappointment. It was at this point that Clarke rose and returned to his car. Christ knows what Annable was going to say about all of this, he thought to himself.

On his way back to Leverton, it suddenly dawned on Clarke that Linda Rigione would have to be informed of her husband's death and the factors that led to it. He would have to be the one to break the news to her; it just wouldn't be right coming from someone else. 'Damn,' he said to himself as he turned off the A52.

However, he couldn't present himself to *anyone* in his current state, so first things first he made his way back to the narrow boat, where he divested himself of his bloodstained attire and then had a hot shower. Selecting a suitable new outfit, he then set off for Tapley.

Ten minutes or so later he was knocking on the door of the house on Tapley Lane, and as always it was opened by DC Preston.

'You'd better come in, Sir,' she said with the traces of a smile.

'Thank you, Preston,' replied Clarke with a sigh. 'I take it that Mrs. Rigione is knocking about somewhere?'

Before Preston could answer, Linda Rigione shouted from the kitchen. 'I'm in here – and I thought that I'd told you before, it's Linda.'

Clarke entered the kitchen with a solemn look on his face. 'Hello, Linda,' he said with a rather morose voice.

'What the hell is going on around here?' she replied excitedly. 'This lane has been like a bloody racetrack throughout the day, and...'

Clarke interrupted her. 'I'm afraid that I've got some bad news for you, Linda,' he said looking down at the floor.

'Oh my God,' she cried. 'He's dead, isn't he?'

Clarke nodded. 'I'm so sorry, Linda.'

She leaned on the kitchen unit and looked out of the window as the tears began to fall. 'What happened to him?' she replied in a voice choking with emotion.

'I can't go into details just yet, but you were right about Luciano and Nicola Meakin.'

'They *were* having an affair then?'

'Derek Meakin found out and he killed both of them up at the farm.'

Linda swung around to face him. 'He killed Nicola as well?' she exclaimed.

'Like I said, I can't go into details at the moment.'

She made her way over to the kitchen table and seated herself on one of the chairs. 'I can't believe that this is happening...' she said shaking her head.

He knew full well that she would have to identify her husband's remains at some time, but how the hell they were going to do that was beyond him at that specific moment in time, so he just said the first thing that came into his head. 'You will be notified as to when you will be able to identify the body.'

Linda sank onto the table and buried her head in her hands. He desperately wanted to go over and put his arms around her, holding her close as if to console her, but deeming that improper he simply turned and left. He said a few words to Preston before departing and then headed back to his car. How he hated moments like this, but it had to be done and he was sure that he had handled it well under the circumstances.

As Clarke broke the news to Linda that her husband had been murdered along with his lover, the police and forensic services were continuing their work just up the road. Upper Grange Farm was still sealed off as SOCO's found more of the remains of Nicola Meakin at the bonfire site – and some of those that they believed belonged to Luciano Rigione. Word had clearly reached the police about the events up at the Collymore Lake Caravan and Motorhome Site, and Webster was given the unpleasant task of informing Richard and Kath Meakin that Derek was dead.

Down at Lower Grange Farm, Dr. Fraser was able to confirm that Peter Meakin was struck from behind by a blunt instrument, and from his examination of the torso of Luciano Rigione he verified that the man had been killed by a gunshot wound to the chest. He then departed the scene with the promise to Sergeant Fletcher that he would be able to say more after the subsequent post mortems.

Fletcher returned to Leverton shortly afterwards, leaving the farm sealed off and with two uniformed officers to guard the scene. She had been deeply traumatised by the gruesome discoveries at the farm, and the scenes would haunt her for years to come.

As darkness fell, most of the residents of Tapley who had come out to witness the comings and goings through the village that day had gone home, and only a few of the curious and inquisitive remained to stay the course. Others ventured to *The Cross Keys* to sink a few pints and deliberate over the events of the day. One thing was for sure; none of the residents of the small hamlet of Tapley would ever forget what happened on that particular day.

To Clarke's surprise and astonishment, everyone was pleased to see that he was unscathed when he arrived back at Leverton Police Station. Indeed, he was visibly touched by the welcome he received, and that was almost unprecedented for a man who rarely showed his emotions in public. Scattergood was about to end his shift, but even he came over hand shook Clarke by the hand.

And then out of the corner of his eye he saw the unmistakeable figure of Superintendent Annable standing at the top of the stairs, with legs apart and hands on hips. He motioned for Clarke to join him in his office.

'This way, Allan, if you please,' he said in an unusually calm and placid voice.

Allan? Allan? He's never called me Allan before, thought Clarke. But he made his way slowly up the stairs to Annable's little enclave without any protest.

'Take a seat,' said Annable as he closed the door behind them and then sat down behind his desk. 'I got a call from Pounder – he informed me as to what happened.'

'I thought he might,' mumbled Clarke barely audibly.

'I'm sorry that it all ended in such a way, but at least you came back safe and sound.'

'I blame myself entirely.'

'Why do you say that?'

'I just couldn't see the wood for the trees – including the wood on that bloody bonfire.'

'How do you mean?'

'I convinced myself that Molloy was the guilty party from the moment I confronted him in his office – I wanted *him* to be responsible for Rigione's disappearance and murder to such an extent that I was blinded to the fact that someone else could have done it.'

'At least you got Molloy for fraud – that was a marvellous piece of detective work on your part.'

'That's not the point,' snapped Clarke. 'I let myself down, I let you down and I let down my colleagues – and all because of my hatred for one of those who persecuted me at school!'

'There was nothing you could have done to stop the murders of Rigione and Nicola Meakin – what's done can't be undone.'

For once Clarke was oblivious to Annable's Shakespearean quote. 'But I could have prevented the death of Peter Meakin!' he barked.

There was a brief silence before Annable spoke out again. 'At the end of the day you found out what happened to Rigione and who was responsible for his death.'

'Yes, but I wasn't able to bring that man to justice!' snarled Clarke. 'And that's what pisses me off – big time!'

Annable looked at his watch. 'I've got to make an announcement to the press and media in five minutes – the man from the Leverton Gazette will be there no doubt.'

'You mean Joel Bishop?'

'That's him,' said Annable with a slight sneer. 'Look, you're owed a few days leave – I suggest that you take them now.'

'But there are things I have to do...' implored Clarke.

'That's an order, Clarke,' shouted Annable, who had clearly decided to dispense with the forename. 'Besides, Fletcher is more than capable of dealing with things for the time being.'

And so Clarke left Annable's office and the building to commence a period of leave. He was tired and quite frankly pooped, but sleep was the last thing on his mind at that precise moment. More to the point, he felt very lonely, but there was always one companion that he could rely on at times like this, and so he set off for the Tesco supermarket with every intention of purchasing it!

Chapter 51

Friday, 3 November 2017 (p.m.)

Clarke had just stepped aboard the narrow boat when he poured himself a large glass of whisky from the bottle of *Laphroaig* that he'd just purchased from the Tesco supermarket; as with the glass of *Glenlivet* at the Collymore Lake Caravan and Motorhome Visitor Centre earlier, this one also barely touched the sides. He quickly poured himself another glass and then decided that another shower was undoubtedly called for.

As he stood with his face pointed directly at the shower head, he closed his eyes and turned on the taps so as to get blasted with a shot of cold water before the temperature heated up. It was always an exhilarating and shocking experience for him at the same time, and that evening was no exception. He grabbed at the soap and began to work his way up the length of his body, and suddenly he thought of Diana; he would have given anything for her to have joined him in the shower at that precise moment – and just after having made love.

He tried to put all thoughts of her out of his mind, but what had happened between them kept coming back to haunt him. Should he go and see her at *The Navigation*? What would her reaction be if he were to walk through the door? Would she welcome him or would she turn him away again? For that matter, would she even be there? Forget about it, he told himself as he climbed out of the shower and began to dry himself with a towel.

The feeling of loneliness overtook him again as he donned a black dressing gown. He didn't mind being alone – he'd spent most of his life being alone, and he'd always liked his own company. But there was a vast difference between being alone and feeling lonely, when one desperately craves the company of others and at that moment he longed for the company of one particular woman.

He made his way back into the saloon and the bottle of *Laphroaig* stood on the table before him waiting to be consumed. He poured himself another large glass of the whisky and contemplated the evening ahead. He was feeling blue and some music from his favourite blues/rock band was called for, so he turned to his CD collection and *Led Zeppelin I*. But his glass was empty, so he poured himself another whisky, turned on the CD player and sat down in the armchair to listen to the opening track, *Good Times, Bad Times*; it seemed appropriate. He started to sing along:

> *Good times, bad times,*
> *You know I've had my share.*
> *When my woman left home for a brown-eyed man,*
> *Well I still don't seem to care.*

By now the whisky was taking hold, and for some reason he began to think of his wife. That was it, he thought to himself; she had left *him* for a brown-eyed man. At that moment he closed his eyes, and the music seemed to fade into the distance as he began to drop off. This brief reverie didn't last long. Before he knew it his mobile phone suddenly sprang to life and so did he. He stood up, swayed a little and then made for the offending apparatus. It might be Diana, he told himself.

It wasn't.

'Hello Allan,' shouted Joel Bishop. 'I hope that I'm not disturbing you?'

Clarke's heart sank. 'Just a minute, Joel,' he replied with a degree of irritation. 'Let me turn the music down.' He stepped over to the CD player and turned down the volume before returning to the conversation. 'What can I do for you, Joel?'

'I just wanted to say congratulations on discovering what happened to Rigione and how pleased I was that nothing untoward happened to you.'

Clarke began to slur his words a little. 'I take it that you attended the presh conference with Annable?'

Bishop picked up on Clarke's little slip of the tongue, but decided not to raise the matter at that moment. 'Yes, I was there,' he replied. 'Annable was full of praise for you and your team.'

'Was he really?'

'Yes, in particular he mentioned your dogged persistence in solving the case...'

'I dare shay he was,' slurred Clarke once more.

'Look, are you alright, old boy?'

'There's nothing wrong with me – okay?'

'I just thought that I'd ask...'

'Well if you would jusht get to the point...'

'It's just that – well, Annable told me personally that you'd been bullied at school and that Rigione and Molloy were among your persecutors...'

'Oh, did he now – he had no right to do that!'

'I was bullied at school too, so I know what it's like...'

'You know bugger all, Joel. Now if you don't mind I've got a hangover to arrange!' he snapped angrily as he switched off the phone. 'Bloody journalists!' he muttered to himself.

He quickly poured himself another drink, turned the volume up on the CD player and slumped back into the armchair to listen to *Babe I'm Gonna Leave You*, but before the track had even finished he had descended into the land of nod once more.

He began to dream that he was sitting in the armchair when there was a loud knock on the door of the narrow boat, and when he opened it there stood Diana in a long overcoat, but wearing high heels. It was raining outside, and so Clarke invited her inside. She pointed to the empty glass on the table.

'Had a bad day?' she purred.

'As bad as it can get,' he replied.

'Will this help?' she said before pulling another bottle of *Laphroaig* out from underneath her long overcoat. He nodded and smiled. 'It would be courteous to get your guest a glass too,' she hinted.

As he went to the cupboard to fetch another glass, she slipped off the long overcoat, and when he returned she was now standing before him in a basque that could barely contain her breasts and a suspender set. His jaw dropped and he almost dropped the glass too. He tried to say something, but nothing came out of his mouth, so she moved towards him, took him by the hand and led him to the bedroom. 'I think we've got some unfinished business,' she said oh so seductively.

Once in the bedroom she began to remove her basque, and he then turned his back on her and started to take off his clothes. As he slowly turned to face her once more and with the prospect of a night of unbridled passion before him, he found himself confronted instead by the figure of Superintendent Annable, who stood there alone in basque and suspender set, with legs apart and hands on hips.

'At the end of the day, Clarke, the course of true love never did run smooth,' boomed Annable in true Shakespearian fashion!

Printed in Great Britain
by Amazon